THE LAKE PAGODA

ANN BENNETT

For Dolly

PARIS, NOVEMBER 1946

A rielle pulled her shawl tightly around her shoulders and stepped out of the entrance to the apartment building and onto the broad pavement of Boulevard St Germain. An icy wind whipped around her, driving up from the River Seine, funnelled by the tall buildings. She shivered and gritted her teeth against the weather. It was so alien to her, this biting cold air that chilled you to the marrow of your bones. In her native Hanoi, the temperature, even in the cooler months, was always comfortable and she was so used to the sultry heat of that city that this Paris winter was a cruel shock.

Even so, she needed to get out. She couldn't stay inside the stuffy, cramped apartment a moment longer, and while her father was sleeping it was difficult to do anything in that tiny space without disturbing him. So, each morning she left the building to tramp the streets of this alien city, exploring the alleys of the Latin Quarter, the cobbled lanes and churches of the Ile de la Cité, the boulevards and gardens of the Eighth Arondissement. And as she walked, she watched the stylish Parisians going about their business, dashing to and fro in fashionable clothes, getting out of taxis, riding on trams, pouring down the steps of the metro. She was trying to understand her new home, to find her place in it, to find some meaningful connection with this great, intimidating city. And there was something else she was searching for too.

Now, as she braced herself against the wind and started walking along the boulevard away from the apartment, she glanced guiltily back up at the windows on the third floor. She always worried when she left Papa alone. What if he were to wake up and call out for her? What if he had one of his coughing fits? But he always encouraged her to go. 'Go on, explore while I'm resting. You need to get to know the place. You can't stay cooped up with a sick old man all day. I'll be fine on my own.' But still she worried.

She carried on down the road, making for the market in Rue Mouffetard. Cars and buses crawled past belting out fumes. Through the lines of slow-moving traffic wove bicycles and pony traps, army jeeps too. It felt so bleak here and so dull after the vibrant colours of Hanoi; the plane trees that lined the pavements had lost their leaves, their branches stark against the tall, pale buildings, and the sky between them was an ominous slate grey.

She walked past a couple of bus stops without pausing. She'd never yet got on a bus in Paris; she had no idea how they worked and was afraid of drawing attention to herself, even though she told herself it was perfectly safe here to do so. Years of having to keep a low profile in Hanoi had made her fearful of attention from anyone. Not that she need worry here in Paris, people barely noticed her. She could walk in the midst of a crowd as if she didn't exist. And if anyone's eyes did happen to light on her, seeing her dark skin and black hair they would quickly flick away, for she was half Vietnamese and it was as if she were invisible to them; a nobody.

She turned off the main road and walked towards the Jardin du Luxembourg. She loved these beautiful gardens with their wide-open lawns, broad sweeping paths and the elegant palace that dominated the centre. It reminded her of the gracious French colonial buildings of Hanoi; the Opera House, the Palais du Gouvernement, the Metropole Hotel. Despite the biting cold she would sometimes come here to sit on a bench and stare at the beautiful building; half-closing her eyes she could dream she was back home. But today there was no time. She needed to get to the market and back home before her father needed her.

Putting her head down against the biting wind, she hurried on and soon reached Rue Mouffetard where the market was in full swing, stalls piled high with fruit and vegetables. Despite the post-war rationing, stallholders at this market were adept at obtaining supplies; autumn fruits – apples and pears were piled up on one stall, potatoes and greens on another, yet another was selling whole, plucked chickens and another cheeses from the countryside, oozing and ripe. Arielle went from stall to stall buying what she and her father needed for the next couple of days. It reminded her a little of Hang Be market in the centre of Hanoi, where she used to buy food for the two of them until the war had swept that easy life away. But here there was no exotic fruit or plump, luscious seafood. There was no bartering either and she had to restrain herself from asking for a better price for a kilo of apples or a litre of unpasteurised milk. The stallholders dealt with her stiffly, unsmilingly and sometimes with suspicion, and as she turned away she could sense them whispering about her. It made her feel small, isolated, and a long way from home, but she knew there was nothing she could do about it.

It began to rain as she crossed the cobbles of a little square and carried on into the Rue Descartes. Her shopping bag was heavy now, loaded with produce. It dragged on her shoulder, but it was still quite a way back to the Boulevard St Germain. She wrapped her shawl more tightly around her, shivering in the chill winter air and looked around for somewhere to shelter until the shower had passed. A bar-brasserie loomed up ahead where the pavement widened out at a junction. It had a red-painted awning above the door. Perhaps she could stand under there for a few minutes? She was far too timid to even think about going inside.

When she reached the building, she sidled underneath the porch and glanced in through the steamed-up window, taking in the polished tables, the elaborate glass and marble bar, the rows of bottles stacked on the shelves behind it. It was just after noon and a rowdy lunchtime crowd was propping up the bar, laughing and joking, calling for more drinks. Arielle saw instantly that they were soldiers. She peered at their khaki uniforms, the dark caps they were wearing. Someone pushed open the door and left, walking quickly away from Arielle along Rue de Montagne, but before the door slammed shut, she caught a burst of conversation and her heart beat faster. The men were speaking English. They must be American GIs, still stationed in Paris after the end of the war, waiting for their transport home.

Her interest piqued, she leaned even closer to the window and stared inside, her hot breath clouding the glass. She was searching for something, someone. She scanned the faces, many contorted in exaggerated laughter, flushed with alcohol, but none were familiar. Then one man turned round and her heart leapt as she caught a flash of tawny hair. Could that be him? She looked closer, not even able to blink, but as he turned towards the window momentarily, she was quickly disappointed. The face was unfamiliar and the hair wasn't quite the shade of flaming red she was looking for. She shrunk back against the wall. The man she was looking for couldn't possibly be here in Paris, she reasoned. If he were here, he would surely have been in touch with her.

Suddenly she wanted to be away from the noisy bar. She was glad when the rain eased off after a few minutes. Leaving the shelter of the porch, she shouldered her bag and carried on, along Rue de la Montagne and Rue St Genevieve, eventually emerging onto the wide pavements of the Boulevard St Germain.

The concierge was standing in the doorway to her apartment, hands on hips as Arielle entered the hallway.

'Bonjour, madame,' Arielle said with a polite smile, but the woman just nodded curtly and turned away. With a sigh Arielle started the long walk up the steep stairs to the apartment.

Her father was sitting up in bed and as always she was shocked by how gaunt and pale he looked. His lined face was almost grey in the pale light.

'Are you alright, Papa?' She heaved the bag off her shoulder and went to his bedside to peck him on the cheek.

'Of course. How was your walk?'

'It was good,' she said brightly, not wanting to tell him how people shunned and ignored her. 'I bought fruit and cheese, some baguettes, oh and a chicken for supper.'

'You're a good girl,' he said, holding out a bony hand. 'I'm so lucky to have you.'

'Oh, Papa. Nonsense. I'm glad to be here.'

She went into the kitchenette to brew some tea. It was a tiny, windowless room, little more than a cupboard. The whole apartment was small, even though it was in a gracious building with high ceilings and floor-length windows. Her father's cousin had allowed them to stay there when they'd arrived, penniless from Hanoi a few months before. He'd only visited once, to give them a key and show them around, before retreating to his large house in Neuilly.

'The last tenants left it in a bit of a state...' It was true. They hadn't even washed up from their last meal and their dirty sheets were still on the beds, but even though she was dropping with exhaustion from the journey, Arielle had got to work straight away, washing and scrubbing, dusting the surfaces and cleaning the floors.

Now, she took the tea out to Papa and handed it to him, noticing how his hands shook nowadays. She forced herself to smile but inside she couldn't stop anxious thoughts from surfacing. He was fading before her very eyes. All those weeks on the ship from Haiphong, rolling around on the high seas had taken its toll, lying on a bunk in a cramped cabin, too sick to get out for fresh air. And the terrible months before that locked up in the Citadel. She shivered to think of them now. It was good to put them behind her, but they had left their mark on her father, for sure.

'Will you sit with me and have your tea, Arielle?' Papa asked with pleading eyes.

She shook her head. 'In a few minutes, Papa. I need to get the soup on for lunch first.'

She went back into the kitchenette and peeled onions, potatoes, garlic, leeks and carrots, sweated them in butter in a saucepan over the flickering gas flame. Then she added stock and water and left it to simmer. Wiping her hands, she slipped into her bedroom. It was hardly big enough to qualify as a room, just wide enough for a single bed. There, she felt in her top drawer for the picture. It was hidden under her under-wear. She wasn't sure why, but she didn't want Papa to look at it. Perhaps the memories it held for her were too precious to share? She drew it out and placed it on the end of the bed so she could look at it in the weak light from the window. It was a charcoal sketch of the Tran Quoc Pagoda on the West Lake, Hanoi, its many tiered roofs reaching to the sky. It stood proudly on its promontory, surrounded by palm trees, its reflection clear in the still waters of the lake. Just looking at it took her back there, to where so much had happened to her over the years. She could almost feel the sultry air of that city wrap itself around her as she stared at the sketch. And as she looked, the past became real and it was as if he was beside her again, his arms around her, and when she turned to smile at him he kissed her on the lips.

2

HANOI, 9TH MARCH 1945

Arielle was a little late to work that morning – that Friday morning in March 1945 when her world was suddenly torn apart. Her father had set off before her to the office in a cyclo, waving it down from the pavement outside their townhouse in the French Quarter. Normally they walked through the city to work in the Mairie together, but Papa had a meeting with Monsieur Decoux, the governor-general, at nine thirty, and had been a little preoccupied at breakfast time. Arielle had still been eating her breakfast of pho, noodle soup, when he had got up from the table, grabbed his linen jacket and given her an absentminded kiss on the top of her head.

'Goodbye, Ari chéri, I need to leave now,' he'd said and she'd beamed up at him, her mouth full of noodles.

'Good luck this morning, Papa. I'll see you later on.'

It was the last exchange they'd had for many long, painful months.

She'd finished her breakfast and cleared the table, stacking the dishes in the kitchen for Trang, their elderly but jovial housekeeper, to wash up when she came in later. Then she'd left the tall, yellow-painted house to walk the two or three kilometres through the elegant French Quarter to the Mairie. Usually, she and her father chatted as they walked, about the war, about the personalities at their work in the puppet French administration, about the Japanese occupation, so most mornings she didn't take much notice of the traffic or of what was going on around them. But this morning things felt a little different; there seemed to be more traffic on the road, more horns blaring, more people hurrying along the pavements. And a group of Japanese soldiers on the march down the Boulevard Felix-Faure, five abreast, holding up the traffic. Although not an unusual sight, there was something in their gait that looked strangely sinister. Her eyes lingered on the marching soldiers. Was it just because she was walking alone that things felt different today?

A feeling of dread stole over her. She could sense something new in the air but she didn't want anything to change. Her menial administrative job for the French government suited her very well, and living with her father, keeping her head down here in the French Quarter of Hanoi suited her too. It had done so since the death of her husband, Etienne, in 1935, when she'd wanted the earth to swallow her up and to be able to disappear for ever. She'd moved back home with her widowed father then, taken a quiet job in the same office as him and had basically gone to ground.

And nothing had changed since. Despite the Japanese invasion in September 1940, Jean Decoux, the French governor-general, had quickly reached an agreement with the new occupiers that the French could carry on administering the colony themselves, as long as they toed the Japanese line. The agreement permitted Japanese soldiers to be stationed in Indochina and the Japanese military to use all the important ports and airports. This agreement had made Indochina the most important staging post for the build-up of Japanese troops in South-East Asia. Arielle and her father, alongside all the others working for the French government in Hanoi, just carried on as if nothing had happened. Perhaps, she thought now, they'd simply been burying their heads in the sand for almost five years.

But there had been rumblings at the Mairie, the headquarters of the French administration, for a couple of weeks. The Japanese were tightening their grip on the shaky French administration, making more and more demands. Papa had been at various top-level meetings where the governor-general and his senior officials tried to decide what to do in response. He told her that they'd agreed to hold firm, not to give in to unreasonable Japanese requests, but Arielle could see in his face that the whole situation troubled him.

She reached the Mairie where, to her relief, everything appeared normal. The same old Annamese man sat behind the reception desk, barely looking up from his newspaper as Arielle swept past and dashed up the marble staircase to the office where she worked on the second floor. She went straight to her desk and took the cover off her typewriter. Her friend, Camille, a young French girl with carefully coiffed blonde hair, looked up from her typing and smiled conspiratorially. Camille had secrets; she was brimming with youth and energy and living ex-pat life to the full. Arielle was privy to those secrets; Camille's complicated love life involving several of the eligible bachelors in the Mairie, and more than one of the not so eligible married ones. But Arielle wondered what this morning's particular smile might signify. She knew that as well as a colourful love life, Camille had been taking other sorts of risks too. Risks of a more serious kind – to help the war effort. She was a spy and passed information on troop build-ups, military manoeuvres and whatever else she could find to Allied intelligence. When such information came across her desk, she would secretly copy maps and letters, official orders, pop them in her handbag and pass them to a contact over coffee and croissants at a café overlooking the lake. Arielle admired Camille's bravery, but had always been reluctant to get involved, afraid, as ever, to draw attention to herself. Added to that, she had never actually been approached to help out. She'd once heard a rumour that people of Annamite descent were not trusted to be spies, they were too likely to be working for their own cause, against the long-time occupiers of their homeland.

Now she winked in response, smiled back at Camille and began to type out the long document she'd started transcribing the day before. It concerned a survey for a drainage scheme in Hué province and was so tedious that she frequently had to stifle a yawn. As she worked, she kept glancing up at the double doors that led to the staircase, checking to see if her father was coming to see her. He sometimes did from time to time during the working day and she thought he might come this morning and tell her how his meeting with the governor-general had gone.

She'd been typing for half an hour when there was a series of loud bangs in the square outside accompanied by frantic screaming. Shocked, Arielle and Camille looked at each other with wide, terrified eyes. It was unmistakable. The sound of gunshots. Everyone in the huge office left their desks as one and dashed to the open front windows. Arielle squeezed in next to Camille and peered out. What she saw down in the square shocked her to the core. Under the elegant palms and ornamental orchid trees in the central gardens, swarmed Japanese tanks and dozens of soldiers on foot. From their uniforms, she realised that some were French and some Japanese. Both sets wore khaki uniforms but the Japanese wore berets and the French little pill box hats. They stood in loose lines, firing at each other, and the French, clearly taken by surprise, were outnumbered and outflanked. Many of them already lay on the square in pools of blood. Arielle put her handkerchief to her mouth, her heart pounding. The uneasy alliance between two rival forces must have come to an untimely end.

'We need to get out of here,' she said to Camille, her mouth dry. She moved away from the window towards her desk. Her movements felt clumsy and slow. Her first thought was for her father who worked on the floor below. They could find him on their way down.

'We can try to leave the back way,' said Camille uncertainly, fear in her eyes, 'But the streets might not be safe.'

'We'll have to try.' Arielle snatched her bag from beside her desk, but as she looked up, the double doors at the end of the office banged open and a group of Japanese soldiers burst into the room, brandishing machine guns, eyes blazing, faces contorted in anger and hatred.

'All French, come with us,' one at the front shouted and then the soldiers began lunging at people, grabbing them by their arms and pushing them to the centre of the room to stand in a quivering, terrified group. Camille was grabbed by one arm and propelled past the desks to the middle of the room.

'No!' Arielle tore at his uniform, snapping her nails. The soldier simply turned and pushed her roughly away, with such force she fell stumbling to the tiled floor. Gradually, she got to her feet. She must go to Papa. She began to run towards the doors, but they were guarded by two soldiers with machine guns.

'Cannot go,' one of them said. She wondered why they weren't taking her, but deep down she knew the answer. They must think that she was fully Annamese, not half-French. They wouldn't do this to locals, their aim was to ingratiate themselves with the civilian population.

'Please, I need to see my father,' she began, but the man simply shook his head and his eyes flicked away from her. From the other side of the room came gunshots. Instinctively Arielle screamed, the cry leaving her body involuntarily. A man, Pierre Thibaut, one of the officials Camille had been involved with, lay on the floor, blood spreading over his white shirt and pooling around him. He must have been putting up too much of a fight. The Japanese soldier who'd shot him, kicked his body casually. Arielle's eyes met Camille's. Her friend's face was drained of colour, all the life seemed to have gone out of her. She looked small and terrified.

'We go now,' one of the officers shouted and the crowd of workers moved slowly towards the door, prodded forward by machine guns. Arielle had one last glimpse of Camille's tear-stained face as she shuffled past her.

'Help me!' Camille mouthed as she was bundled from the room.

Yet again Arielle went towards the doors, thinking she might be able to slip out with the others and run downstairs. She was filled with anguish about what might have happened to her father. Was the same thing happening on the floor below? Was he being rounded up and carted off with his colleagues at gunpoint? But when she reached the doors again she was pushed away by the soldiers. 'You stay here,' one of them said, his face stony cold.

She was alone in the room now except for the soldiers and Pierre's body, face down in a puddle of blood. She shivered, not bearing to look at him. Instead, she went to the window again, her stomach churning at the thought of what she might see out there, terrified that Papa would be amongst those being herded out of the building. She gripped the sill and peered out, down into the square two floors below. Two dark green army lorries with hooped canvas tops were parked up outside. Her colleagues were being forced to climb onto the back of them, one at a time, pushed and prodded by Japanese soldiers. The queues moved forward, slowly, reluctantly. Where were they taking them?

She scanned both columns repeatedly, hoping against hope that she wouldn't catch sight of Papa. Her eyes lingered on one man who was shuffling along more slowly than the others, leaving a gap between himself and the man in front. Suddenly he peeled off from the column and made a break for freedom, running full tilt across the square towards the gardens. The next second a shot rang out and he slumped to the ground. Screams went up from the others in his column, but they were quickly prodded into silence by the soldiers.

One of the last people in the queue for the second lorry was Camille. Arielle's heart went out to her friend. Her blonde hair had come out of its pins and was tumbling around her shoulders. Her dress had a great rip down one side, exposing her pale legs. *Poor, poor Camille.*

But there was no sign of Papa. Arielle was beginning to to hope that he must have been spared, when another group emerged from under the front porch. Her heartbeat caught in her throat. There was Papa in the middle of the crowd. She let out a sob and leaned out of the window, hoping he would look up. She could hardly bear to watch as the group was pushed into line and prodded forward with guns and bayonets. Like Camille, like all the others, Papa looked diminished, stripped of all his dignity as he shuffled towards the lorry.

Arielle wrestled with an impulse to call out to him, only holding back because she didn't want to draw the soldiers' attention to him. Instead, she leaned out further and simply stared down at him, willing him to look up at her. He moved painfully slowly towards the lorry with the others. Finally it was his turn to climb up and over the tailgate. Arielle's eyes were filled with tears now and she could hardly bear to watch, but she kept her eyes fixed on her father as a soldier butted him with a machine gun and he put his foot on the first step. And as he did so, he looked up at the building, shading his eyes against the sun. Arielle waved frantically. It was only a spilt second and then he disappeared from view under the canopy of the truck, but before he did, she was sure he'd registered that she was there, by the way he hesitated momentarily.

Papa was one of the last prisoners to board, then the tailgates were slammed and the engines of the trucks roared into life. They circled the square and rumbled off, soon disappearing from view. Arielle stared after them and fear engulfed her. What would they do to Papa? Where would they take him? Papa was no longer young and quite frail. He suffered from asthma and high blood pressure. Did he have his inhaler with him? His medication? She could no longer support her body, or hold back her emotions. She turned away from the window and sank to the floor, tears streaming down her face.

3

HANOI, 1935

The stylish house on Boulevard Carreau was three stories high, set back from the wide, shaded road behind wrought iron gates which were flanked by a picket fence and a row of palm trees. The house was painted white, but the windows and doors had decorative black borders, and the shutters and balcony railings were painted black too. It was built to look grand and important, to house a grand and important man. The boulevard was on one of the most opulent and fashionable roads in the French quarter of Hanoi, but from the moment she climbed the steps and walked in through the front door as the mistress of the house, Arielle felt like an imposter there.

'You do like the house, don't you, my dear?' Etienne asked indulgently, squeezing her arm. She looked up at him from under her eyelashes hesitantly, already missing the slightly down-at-heel comfort of her father's townhouse. She swallowed and nodded, suddenly overawed by her surroundings and her new life, unable to speak. Perhaps what was troubling her was the thought of what was to happen during the night to come. Once that was over, she told herself, she might be able to relax and enjoy her new home.

Of course, she'd been to the house many times before. She'd visited with her father on numerous occasions during the past year, since Etienne Garnier had first moved to Hanoi and started cultivating the acquaintance of certain senior officials in the administration, including Arielle's father. At that time, Etienne had caused quite a stir amongst the French women at the officer's club in Hanoi; he was young and handsome, with his glossy dark curls and liquid brown eyes. He was urbane too and had a slightly mysterious past. Rumours circulated that he'd made his fortune in the French West Indies; Martinique and Guadeloupe, but nobody knew quite how. He charmed anyone and everyone in the small ex-pat community and he'd had no shortage of admirers.

Arielle's father, Georges Dupont, was as captivated by the newcomer as everyone else. He first came across Etienne when the younger man had applied for permits for the transportation of workers from Tonkin in the north of French Indochina to the rubber plantations in Cochinchina, south of Saigon. Etienne had wined and dined Georges at the Metropole Hotel to discuss the process, and since Georges was a widower, Arielle had been invited along too. She'd rarely been in the palatial dining room of the sumptuous hotel before, and the luxury had overawed her. She'd also been enthralled by Etienne, by his beautiful brown eyes and high cheekbones. She was drawn in by the way he looked at her, giving her his whole attention, as if she was the most important person in the room. To everyone else, including herself, she was an unsophisticated eighteen-year-old, who was barely out of school and had never left Indochina, whereas he was a well-educated Frenchman who had travelled the world.

Arielle had never been to the exclusive Officers' Club

which was central to all ex-pat socialising in Hanoi. Being half-Annamese meant she didn't qualify to be a member, but rumours filtered out via her old schoolfriends and the servants. Several of the French women who frequented the club, both married and unmarried, were falling over themselves to gain Etienne's attention, but he wasn't taking the bait. He'd confided in one or two of the men, over drinks and billiards, that he only had eyes for a young half-Annamese girl. People thought that very strange, almost perverse, when he could have his pick of the beautiful western women in Hanoi, but his disinterest in the club crowd only added to his attractiveness to them. Arielle didn't dare to hope that the subject of his attraction could possibly be *her*. After all, they were worlds as well as generations apart. He must be in his mid-thirties at least. What could he possibly find interesting about a gauche young woman like her?

But to her surprise and confusion, he *was* interested in her. He asked her father if he could call on them at home and take Arielle out one afternoon. Georges hesitated before giving his permission. He'd always been protective of his only daughter, particularly as he'd had to be both mother and father to her; her mother had died in a cholera epidemic when Arielle was only a baby. Georges had brought her up alone with the help of a series of kindly Annamese nannies, the last of whom, Trang, had stayed on as their housekeeper when Arielle grew a little older.

'I'm not sure about it, Ari,' he said after he'd told her about Etienne's wish to take her out.

'But why, Papa? He's a gentleman, he's kind and charming. Everyone likes him.'

'But he's so much older than you, and...'

'And?'

'I don't know. It doesn't seem quite proper somehow.'

But finally, he'd agreed; he could never deny Arielle anything she wanted, and like her, he'd been taken in by Etienne's charm. He could see no good reason why he should prevent them meeting.

Arielle had been a bundle of nerves as she waited in the front room for Etienne to arrive that afternoon. She'd stood by the window for several minutes before he was due, half-hidden behind the shutters, watching the front gate. Etienne was two or three minutes late and her mind had already gone through paroxysms of anxiety that he'd changed his mind and wouldn't come after all. How could she bear the disappointment and humiliation? But her heart leapt when she noticed a cyclo pull up on the road outside. A few seconds later the gate opened and Etienne came through, walking with a spring in his step across the front courtyard and up the steps to the front door. She rushed to open the door before Trang could get there, feeling her face flushed, her heart racing.

That day, Etienne had taken her to the botanical gardens. The Jardins Botanique were behind the beautiful, yellow-painted Palais du Gouvernement, which stood behind wrought iron gates and sentry boxes and was surrounded by mango trees. Arielle gazed in awe at the palace as they clambered out of the cyclo outside the front gates. She knew her father sometimes went there for meetings with the governor-general and the place had always fascinated her.

'I'll take you in there someday,' Etienne said, noticing her interest in the building. 'I know the governor-general personally.'

'Really?' she looked at him with renewed admiration.

'Yes, I've met with him on several occasions. He's very interested in my business, in supporting the flow of manual workers from Tonkin down to Cochinchina. It's in the government's interest to keep the plantations producing to their maximum.'

'Gosh,' she murmured.

But even then, she wondered what Etienne's job actually involved; what did it mean in practical terms to recruit and transport hundreds of people from one end of the country to the other? These people were desperately poor and had little education, plucked from their subsistence farms and tiny villages to travel far away for work. Were they well treated? Were they paid a decent wage? She'd heard rumblings of strikes on southern plantations against poor working conditions and low wages, and the resulting brutal reprisals from plantation owners. She'd also heard of uprisings amongst workers, stirred up by the burgeoning Communist Party. Was Etienne part of all that? She looked into his beautiful, soft eyes as he smiled down at her and couldn't believe anything bad of him. How could this gentle, courteous man be part of anything as evil as the cruel exploitation of poor workers?

Once inside the gardens, they strolled arm in arm under the shade of an avenue of banyan trees and went to sit on a secluded bench overlooking the lake. Conversation flowed easily between them; Etienne told Arielle about his upbringing in Marseille, where his father was a ship's captain, and how he'd travelled to Martinique and started bringing workers to the plantations there from other parts of the French Empire, such as Africa, La Reunion, Vanuatu and even Indochina.

'I've spent quite a number of the past few years on ships one way or another,' he said.

'It sounds romantic,' she said, thinking with envy of standing on the deck of a liner, the wind in her hair, the towering sky above, the endless horizon melting into the misty blue of the sea.

'Not really. It was a lot of hard work. I've been wanting to find somewhere to settle for a long time. And when I came to Hanoi, I knew it was the place for me. It's such a beautiful, sophisticated, vibrant city. And now I've met you and it's become even more special to me.'

She blushed and looked down at her hands. No one had ever spoken to her like that before and she had no idea how to respond.

Etienne took her on many outings over the next few weeks. They visited the ancient Temple of Literature, strolling through its courtyards between the statues, and in the shade of the stone cloisters, took a rowing boat out on Hoan Kiem lake, went to the Opera House to listen to an orchestra play Beethoven's Fifth Symphony. On each of these occasions Etienne behaved like a perfect gentleman, trying nothing more than holding her hand and giving her a peck on the cheek when he dropped her home.

One day he took her in his chauffeur-driven Citroën out of the city and north of Hanoi, all the way to the coast at Ha Long Bay. There, they took a boat out to sea, sailing between incredible limestone karsts, covered in tropical greenery, which reared up out of the water like magical rocks from an ancient myth. She'd been there before with her father when she was a child, but this trip seemed so much more romantic, and the beauty of the place was enhanced by that feeling of being completely alive, a feeling she only had when she was with Etienne. The boat, a converted Chinese junk, headed across the bay, threading between the rock formations, towards a large island where they moored up under the cliffs. They swam in the limpid blue water to the limestone caves that the sea had carved out of the cliffs and it was there that he kissed her for the first time.

Back on the boat, his chef had prepared them a lavish

meal which they ate by candlelight on the deck as the sun went down over the distant coast. Arielle knew her father had stipulated that they had to be back home that evening, but for the first time she wished she could have stayed longer with Etienne.

As they finished their devilled prawns, he took her hand over the table, looked deep into her eyes and said, 'Arielle Dupont, I have brought you here to ask you something important. I've fallen completely under your spell, and I'd like to ask you to marry me. Will you do me that honour?'

Arielle's mouth fell open and colour rushed to her cheeks. She was dumbfounded. They'd only met a dozen times at the most, including the times she'd accompanied her father to his house. They barely knew each other. She'd never considered marriage before. After all, she was only eighteen, but she was well aware that dozens of young women in Hanoi would give their eye teeth to be in her position. She swallowed hard and met his eager gaze.

'I had no idea you were going to ask me that,' she replied. 'Papa and I have been making plans for me to study at the Sorbonne in Paris.'

His face fell. 'Oh, I wouldn't want to stop you from completing your education, of course. We could marry first, then you could go to Paris next year, once my business is established. I could leave an overseer in charge and come over with you to get you settled.'

'Perhaps... I would have to speak to Papa.'

'Of course. And I intend to speak to your father too. You would need his consent to marry as you are under twenty-one, but I'm sure once he knows how happy I intend to make you, he won't stand in our way.'

Wasn't he making assumptions? She hadn't agreed yet. But she was enthralled by him and didn't want to offend him. She looked at him in the candlelight, admiring the chiselled lines of his face, the earnest look in his eyes. What was holding her back? How could she pass up such a tempting offer?

Later, as the boat plied its way back to Ha Long city over the dark water, snaking between the shadowy karsts, Arielle stood alone at the rail, looking up at the distant stars and thinking. What was making her hesitant? Etienne was a kind, generous, educated, not to mention wealthy, man. She enjoyed his company, and he wasn't going to stand in the way of her education. She was young, true, but she might not get another chance like this. And she couldn't help reminding herself, that if she turned him down, there were dozens of hopefuls waiting in the wings to snap him up.

Etienne came and stood next to her at the rail. He put his arm around her shoulders and nuzzled her neck behind her ear.

'Have you thought about my question?' he asked softly. She turned to face him, and in the light of the moon could see in his eyes how much her answer meant to him.

'I have,' she replied. 'And the answer is yes.'

THEY WERE married two months later at St Joseph's Cathedral, which Papa always said looked like a smaller and less ornate version of the Notre-Dame in Paris. Georges had been a little reluctant to agree at first, but after a couple of evenings at the club in Etienne's company, changed his mind and came round to the match.

The reception had been at the Metropole Hotel, and the whole ex-pat community was wined and dined and danced to a jazz band far into the night. Etienne had hired the best suite in the hotel for their wedding night, but they were both so exhausted when they finally fell onto the bed fully clothed at three o' clock in the morning that the wedding night would have to wait until the next day. It was the following morning that Etienne drove her the short distance to his home on Boulevard Carreau and she realised that her old life had gone for ever. A feeling of loneliness, and groundlessness swept over her as they entered the high-ceilinged hall, the servants smiling and bowing as they passed. It felt as if she had been cut from her tethers, like a hot-air balloon, and was floating, out of control, to an unknown destination.

Although she was nervous, the wedding night was not as bad as she'd feared. She and her schoolfriends had long speculated about what lovemaking involved and had pored over French magazines that gave advice to inexperienced women in such euphemistic terms that it had left them more mystified than before. Trang had spoken to Arielle about it the day before the wedding, but the old lady was so embarrassed, she couldn't meet Arielle's eyes, and all she said was, 'There may be pain, but not to worry, it will pass and the next time will be better.' There was a little pain, but Etienne was patient and loving and, Arielle wasn't surprised to find out, an experienced lover, and when it was over and she was snuggled up in his arms, she realised that Trang was right. The pain had passed quickly, and she could already tell that next time would give her pleasure instead.

But the next day Etienne had to leave for Haiphong to arrange the transportation of another group of workers down to Saigon. As he dressed in a suit and tie, she lay in bed and watched him.

'Do you have to go so soon?'

He laughed. 'If I didn't work, I wouldn't be able to provide such a beautiful home for you,' he said. 'I will be back on Wednesday, so it's not long.'

'I will miss you,' she said.

'Well, why don't you come along?'

She shook her head. 'I need to go and get my things from home... I mean my father's house. Get settled here.'

'Well, maybe next time then?'

'Maybe,' she said reluctantly. He came over to kiss her, then left her alone. She listened to his footsteps on the stairs, the bang of the front door behind him. She rushed to the window and watched him getting into the back of the Citroën and being swept away down the tree-lined boulevard.

His invitation had brought her up short. The truth was, she was a little nervous about finding out too much about Etienne's business. She'd accepted him at his word; the workers were treated well and earned good money on the plantations. They were transported in comfort, and without the opportunity he offered them, they wouldn't have the chance to go south and make money for their families. Instead, they would stay in Tonkin, in the north, in poverty, working their fingers to the bone to scrape a meagre living, their children unable to go to school, the cycle of poverty continuing on down through the generations. They'd discussed it on more than one occasion, over dinner at the Metropole, as they walked beside Hoan Kiem lake. She'd also tentatively asked her father.

'Oh, I'm sure Etienne is above board,' Georges had assured her. 'You needn't worry on that score. He's a man of honour. Not like some of the unscrupulous recruiters and traders out there. He is an educated, civilised man. He's signed assurances and conditions for all the transportation permits we've issued. He's paid all the fees promptly too. We've had no trouble at all from him.'

But still, she had niggling doubts.

Now, she got dressed in the bathroom adjoining their

bedroom and wandered down to the kitchen. The staff were all sitting round the table eating breakfast, as she walked down the passage she could hear their laughter and chatter echoing in the tall room. They put their forks and spoons down and hastily got to their feet as she entered, their chairs scraping on the tiled floor.

'Please. Don't get up,' she said in Annamese.

There was a short silence during which they all stared at her.

'Would madame like breakfast in the dining room?' one of the maids asked, stepping forward. 'What would you like? Croissants? Pains au raisins? Baguettes?'

'Oh no. Some of that beef pho you're all eating if you don't mind,' she smiled broadly at the group who looked back at her nervously. Two of the women were only a little older than herself she noticed. How she would love to have made friends with them, asked them to sit down with her and share her breakfast, but as she stood there, she realised that could never be. She was the mistress of the house and they were her servants and that gulf would always divide them.

With a sigh, she turned away and went into the dining room at the front of the house, where the ceiling fans whirred ceaselessly, high above the polished table. She sat alone, listening to the sounds of the city outside, the horns of the cars, bells of the cyclos, shouts of the pho sellers. Loneliness washed over her again, as it had when she'd entered this house as Etienne's bride less than twenty-four hours before.

How she missed her schoolfriends, many of whom had already returned to France, going on to further education or secretarial school or even finishing school. Papa had insisted on Arielle attending the French Lycée in Hanoi, where the majority of the pupils were well-bred French girls, the daughters of wealthy businessmen or diplomats. There were only a smattering of girls with Annamese blood, and after leaving school the previous year, they had all either gone on to university or returned to their families in other parts of Indochina. They'd all left in dribs and drabs over the past few months, while Arielle's attention had been consumed with Etienne and preparations for their wedding. And now she'd surfaced, she felt as though she'd been left behind.

She felt neither wholly in the French camp, nor the Annamese one. She sipped her noodle soup and thought about how little she knew of her native culture, even though she'd been brought up in the capital city of her homeland. She'd been raised as a French girl, even though she could speak the Annamese language fluently, but now she suddenly experienced a longing to understand her roots. Now she was here, in this quintessentially French mansion, the wife of a Frenchman, she was afraid of being cut off completely from her mother's culture.

Her mind went to her grandmother, Bà Ngoại, who lived in a tall house above a silk shop in the old town. Bà Ngoại had been at the wedding yesterday, with an old friend. But the two old ladies had sat in a corner, dressed in their best ao dais, silk tunics with silk trousers underneath, looking uncomfortable and terribly out of place. In the social whirl of the day, with so many people demanding her attention, Arielle had only been able to spend a few minutes speaking to them, and now the thought of them sitting alone and surveying proceedings with impassive stares, tugged at her heart strings.

Finishing her soup and dabbing her face with a napkin, she knew what she had to do that day. She would visit Bà Ngoại and ask her to show her the pictures she had of her mother as a baby. They would sip green tea and eat noodles in the comforting gloom of Bà Ngoại's tiny apartment, and listen to the clamour and shouts from the street market outside.

4

HANOI, 1935

As the cyclo rider pedalled her alongside Hoan Kiem lake and headed towards the Old Quarter of the city, Arielle felt the wind in her hair and with it, the anxieties of the morning begin to slip away. At least she had this. Whenever she tired of the sterile elegance of her new home, or of sipping cocktails and eating foie gras in luxury French restaurants, she could come here, to lose herself in the noise and clamour of the Old Quarter. Here, in the maze of thirty-six narrow streets, each named after the merchandise that was sold in its shops, the noise and atmosphere was an assault on the senses. Street vendors plied their wares on the pavements, men lugging sack barrows trudged to and fro with heavy loads, and you could pass stalls selling live eels or quails eggs or exotic vegetables, plumbing equipment, hand-made shoes or multi-coloured silks.

Bà Ngoại's house was on Hang Dao, or Rue de la Soie as the French had named it – Silk Street – and was, of course, above a silk shop. Bà Ngoại still owned the business but no longer worked there. The cyclo rider dropped her at the end of the street. There were too many obstructions to get closer to the house. Arielle paid him the few piastres for the ride, then shouldered her way between the people milling around near the open-fronted shops and colourful stalls that spilled off the pavement onto the street, past women in conical hats selling flowers from the backs of bicycles. She took care not to knock over precariously balanced piles of vegetables or bump into workmen carrying loads which bounced along from poles slung over their shoulders.

Bà Ngoại's house was old and crumbling. It was a classic "tube house", of which there were many in the Old Quarter. They were built with narrow frontages to avoid a French-imposed tax, but went back a long way from the street. Arielle glanced up at the first floor. Bà Ngoại often sat on her balcony watching the world go by, but today there was no sign of her, and the front shutters were closed, despite the hot and humid weather. Arielle waved hello to Diep, the silk vendor in the shop beneath the house, and climbed the narrow, wooden staircase that opened from the pavement beside it to knock on Bà Ngoại's door.

Bà Ngoại took her time opening it and when she did, Arielle's heart sank in dismay. Bà Ngoại's eyes were rheumy and bloodshot, and from her vague smile, Arielle knew that her grandmother had been smoking opium. She'd always dabbled, that was well known, ever since her husband died when Arielle's mother was small, and she'd been left with a young child, the business to run and her husband's gambling debts being demanded aggressively by the city triads.

Many of the local people had an opium habit. Arielle had read somewhere that opium dens had been encouraged by the French government over the centuries; the tax earned from keeping the population addicted filled their treasury coffers, and the drug kept the people docile and less likely to rise up against colonial rule.

'Are you alright, Bà Ngoại?' she asked, entering the apartment which was filled with the sickly smell of the opium pipe. There it was, in the corner, on the table beside Bà Ngoại's cushions, a curl of smoke rising from it to join the cloud hanging beneath the ceiling.

'I'm perfectly well thank you, child.'

'I wish you wouldn't, Bà Ngoại,' she burst out. The old lady shrugged.

'What else is there for me nowadays? My beautiful Tuyen is no longer with us. And now you have gone from me too, Arielle.'

'Oh, don't say that. I'm here now, aren't I?'

With a sigh her grandmother sank heavily into the cushions on the floor, crossing her legs nimbly in the lotus pose, despite her advanced years. She picked up the pipe again and took a heavy drag, her defiant eyes trained on Arielle. With a deliberate gesture, Arielle went over to the shutters and pushed them wide open, allowing the babble of the crowd from the street into the room. Then she sat down opposite her grandmother.

'You're here but you're not here,' the old lady croaked.

'Oh Bà Ngoại. That's the opium talking. It doesn't mean anything.'

Bà Ngoại regarded her steadily as she took another drag.

'On the contrary, my child. I speak the truth.'

'But whatever do you mean?' Arielle leaned forward, watching her grandmother's face. She had half a mind to leave straight away. She felt deflated. She'd been so looking forward to seeing Bà Ngoại, but clearly if she was in this state the conversation was going to go nowhere.

'I mean what I say.' Bà Ngoại tapped ash out into a little carved bowl. 'You may be here physically, Arielle, but spiritually and in every other way, you have left me. Since you married that Frenchman, you no longer have the right to call yourself Annamese.'

Arielle gasped at the brutality of the remark and shock and disappointment flooded through her. Her grandmother had just given voice to the niggling, guilty thoughts that had been plaguing her too.

'But my mother married a Frenchman,' she protested. 'Did you think the same of her?'

The old lady shook her head. 'He was a different kind of Frenchman. I could trust him. He was an honourable man.'

Honourable. Arielle thought of her father's words about Etienne. He'd said the same thing about him. Was it because he wanted to believe it, rather than because he knew it to be true?

'So, are you saying my husband isn't honourable?'

Still, those misty eyes bored into her. Could Bà Ngoại see into her mind? Could she see Arielle's own uncertainties, her own doubts?

'I'm saying that his profession isn't honourable, my child. Any man engaged in what he does needs to have made compromises, deep down inside his soul.'

'But that's not fair, Bà Ngoại. You don't know Etienne. He assures me that his company is professional and the best of its kind. People are well treated and get the opportunity of work they wouldn't get otherwise and to send money home to their families.'

The old lady let out a derisive snort. 'And you believe that? You're even more naïve than I thought.'

Tears threatened, but Arielle swallowed them down and kept her eyes trained on her grandmother's face. 'If you thought all this, why didn't you say so before the wedding?' she asked in a steady voice.

Bà Ngoại leaned forward, her eyes had cleared and were

suddenly deadly serious. 'Because your father forbade me from discouraging the match, that's why. He said he would stop helping me with my rent if I spoke out.'

For the second time in minutes Arielle's mouth dropped open. She was knocked back with the shock of this revelation.

'If you ask me,' Bà Ngoại went on, 'it's more than your father's career's worth to say anything against your precious husband. Garnier has the ear of the governor-general, and the governor-general keeps a very tight rein on all his officials.'

'But you just said Papa was an honourable man.'

'Oh, he's honourable all right. But he's a fool all the same.'

Bà Ngoại put her pipe down and leaned forward to take Arielle's hand. Arielle felt like snatching it away but was too deflated to do that. Instead, she let Bà Ngoại's leathery hand close around her own.

'Now, now. I'm sorry I've spoken so frankly, my child. I don't blame you for what you've done. You're young and impressionable, and he's a handsome man. I was young once and headstrong like you. I married a magnetic, handsome man, only to regret it bitterly afterwards.'

Arielle dropped her gaze away from her grandmother's.

'And you needn't take my word for it either,' Bà Ngoại went on. 'You should go with your husband on one of his trips and see for yourself sometime. Now put the kettle on the stove and let's have some green tea. Then later on I need to go along to the temple. Would you like to come with me?'

'I'd love that,' Arielle said, brightening.

A FEW HOURS LATER, when the fiercest heat had burned out of the sun for the day, and when Bà Ngoại was feeling herself again, they set off together for the Tran Quoc Pagoda on Ho

Tay, or West Lake. As they left the house, more stalls were setting up in Rue de la Soie, this time for the night market, and litter was being cleared from the road by a group of young street sweepers, barely more than boys. Arielle tucked her arm into her grandmother's and they walked to the end of the road to hail one of the passing cyclos on Hang Thung. While they walked, people bowed and smiled at Bà Ngoại. This diminutive old lady was a big personality, well-known and popular in the quarter. Arielle's heart swelled with pride to be walking beside her, despite their earlier difference of opinion.

Arielle hailed a cyclo on the street corner and, laughing together, they both squeezed onto the seat. The cyclo rider took off along the darkening streets on the fringes of the Old Quarter heading north and they were soon moving along the grid of streets built by the French, between rows of well-kept, white painted buildings where luscious date and almond trees lined the pavements. After twenty minutes or so, the road widened out and ahead of them was the West Lake.

The road carried on across the water. It was built on a bank between West Lake and a smaller lake on the other side and as they struck out across it between the two great expanses of water, both as still as mirrors, Arielle breathed in gratefully. The air here was clean and unpolluted, especially at this time of day, and there was a beautiful view of the golden sun dipping behind the buildings ahead, its reflection shimmering on the water. A little way along the road the cyclo rider stopped. Here was the entrance to the walkway that led from the road to the temple. It was flanked by two ancient banyan trees, their trunks gnarled with age. They would have to walk from there.

They made their way onto the promontory, and Arielle thought about how she used to love coming to the temple as a child. How she would relish the feeling of peace that would steal over her as she sat meditating beside her grandmother, the chanting of the monks from the adjacent monastery and the exotic smells of incense that floated on the air. But lately she'd hardly visited. At school the girls were encouraged to pray at the Catholic cathedral, and she'd gone along with that, neglecting her Buddhist roots. But now it felt as though her soul was yearning to be here.

They stopped at a street seller to buy lotus flowers, sticks of incense and candles to give as offerings, then carried on along the promontory towards the tall, multi-roofed pagoda, which soared into the evening sky ahead of them, with its many windows, each housing a white statue of the Buddha. Arielle drank in the beauty of the evening and, as she always used to when she came here, let the peace of this tranquil place seep through her.

They arrived at some elaborate double gates, set between yellow pillars, with a Chinese tiled roof and lettering down each side. A monk, dressed in saffron-coloured robes waved them on and they passed through the gates and left their shoes on a rack. Then they carried on along a tiled walkway between long, low buildings, which were the monastery lodgings. Beyond them was a square courtyard in front of an open-fronted prayer hall. The courtyard was dominated by one huge tree with spreading branches. The smell of incense wafted from a great cauldron in the centre of the courtyard under the branches of the great tree, where dozens of sticks of incense already burned.

'You know about that tree, don't you Arielle?' her grandmother asked.

'Of course, you've told me many times. It was grown from a cutting from the original Bodi tree in India where the Buddha first found enlightenment.'

Bà Ngoại turned to her, smiling with blackened teeth. 'You are a smart girl, Ari. You remember your lessons well.'

They moved on beyond the prayer hall to another square where the great red-brick pagoda soared above them, its eleven roofs jutting out from the walls at regular intervals, with the still, white Buddhas looking down impassively at them from each level. Arielle leaned back and stared up to the top of the pagoda where a marble lotus soared even higher into the sky.

In front of the pagoda was an altar, where more incense burned and people had laid flowers, candles and fruit as offerings.

'Come, let us meditate and pay our respects to the Buddha,' said Bà Ngoại, laying her lotus flower on the altar, stepping back and sitting down on the stone floor, lotus style. Arielle followed suit, laying her incense, candles and flower on the altar, then sitting down beside her grandmother. It was hard to force her unaccustomed legs into the lotus position, even though she was several generations younger than Bà Ngoại who managed it with ease.

Arielle closed her eyes and tried to settle her mind, allowing the chanting of the monks in the monastery, the discordant clang of the temple bells and the gentle voices of other worshippers to calm her down. They sat for ten or fifteen minutes and during that time, try as she might, Arielle couldn't empty her mind of thoughts. It kept returning to Etienne again and again. What was he doing now? Where was he? Had she been wrong about him and wrong to trust his assurances about his business? What did the future hold for the two of them? At last she heard Bà Ngoại getting to her feet, so she gave up the struggle to meditate, but she vowed to return to the temple. It felt good being here, connecting with her mother's faith, letting the calm of this spiritual place permeate her soul.

'Come, I need to go home now,' said Bà Ngoại. 'I am tired and I need my bed.'

'Me too,' said Arielle, a feeling of trepidation creeping through her at the thought of the huge, empty house she must go back to, alone but for the reticent servants.

They returned along the walkways to the yellow gateway where they put on their shoes and bowed their heads to the monk as they went through the gates. As they did so, a man stepped out from the shadows beyond the gate. He was dressed all in black and he came forward bowing his head respectfully to Bà Ngoại.

'Good evening, phu nhân – madame,' he said. Bà Ngoại stopped, a smile spreading across her face.

'Good evening, Xan. Nice to see you here on this beautiful evening. I hope you are well. This is my granddaughter, Arielle. Madame Garnier, in fact.'

The man turned his attention to Arielle, and she felt his serious, dark eyes sweep down her body, scrutinising her from head to toe, like the beam from a searchlight. He held out his hand and she took it, feeling the warmth and strength of his as she shook it.

'Good to make your acquaintance, Madame Garnier. I read about your wedding in the newspaper the other day. Your husband is ... an important man,' he trailed off but still he held her gaze. She looked away, the honesty in his look felt intrusive somehow.

'He is just a businessman,' she said, wondering how and why this man knew about Etienne or was interested in their marriage.

'Of course. Well, phu nhân, Madame Garnier, very nice to

see you. I must go and do my devotions now. But perhaps I will see you here again one evening soon?'

'You will, of course,' said Bà Ngoại, putting her hand on Arielle's back to usher her to the gate. As they walked away, Arielle felt those black eyes boring into her back.

'Who's that?' she asked. 'He's a bit intense, isn't he?'

'Oh, I often see him here,' said Bà Ngoại. 'He is a very nice man. But he has every reason to be serious. He is a communist. Fighting the corner of exploited workers all over Indochina. He is very passionate and serious about his cause.'

5

HANOI, 1935

W hen Etienne came home two days later, Arielle wondered why she'd worried so much. He was as loving and considerate as ever and they resumed the routine they'd begun during their courtship, spending time visiting the beauty spots of Hanoi, eating in chic hotels and cafés. Only now, instead of parting at the end of the day, they returned home together in the evenings, ate supper in the dining room prepared by Etienne's chefs, and retired early to their suite upstairs to make love.

During those days she focused on everything positive about him; his good looks and his charm, his kindness and generosity, and the way he so obviously cared for her. She put aside all those niggling concerns she'd had while he was in Tonkin, and by the time he'd been back for two or three days she was hardly giving her qualms a second thought. But on the fourth day, as they ate an early dinner at the Metropole Hotel, he said,

'Tomorrow I must set off early for Saigon, chérie. I have meetings with a group of plantation owners down there. There is some trouble brewing amongst the work force.'

Arielle didn't know what to say in response. Suddenly all the pleasure of the last few days had melted away in a single sentence. "Trouble brewing amongst the work force" sounded so sinister, she had to ask about it.

'What do you mean, trouble among the work force?'

He looked at her sharply. 'Just what I say. There are communists infiltrating the rubber tapper gangs. Demanding more pay, shorter hours, more days off. The plantation owners are looking to me to help them deal with it, as it was me who sent the workers to them.'

'And what *will* you do about it?' she asked quietly, dreading the answer.

Etienne shrugged moodily. 'I'll think about that on my way down there on the train. I need to find a way of rooting them out. Whatever it is, it won't be easy... or pleasant. Situations like this aren't good for business. I could get my permits revoked if this sort of thing is allowed to carry on. I might need to speak to your father, tee him up about it...' he mused.

Arielle's nerves tingled and she put her fork down. The mousse au chocolat which she'd been devouring with pleasure until a moment ago no longer tasted quite so appealing. Her father was so above-board, so honourable, as everyone said, she hoped that Etienne wasn't planning on asking him to authorise or sign off on anything less than proper. She'd noticed over the past couple of days, when she'd been round to the townhouse to collect clothes and belongings, that Papa had been looking a little preoccupied when he came in from work. Did it have something to do with this?

'Hey,' Etienne said gently, slipping his hand over Arielle's on the table. 'Don't look so downhearted. You don't need to trouble yourself about this. Let me take care of the business so you can relax and enjoy yourself.'

She tried to force a smile. Didn't he realise that she couldn't just put this sort of thing to the back of her mind?

'Look, why don't you come with me down south?' he went on, 'You wouldn't need to concern yourself with that unfortunate business at all. We could stay in Saigon for a few days, take in the theatre. How about it?'

She shook her head. She didn't want to go anywhere near the plantations if there was unrest and if reprisals were being taken against communist infiltrators.

'I'll come another time,' she promised. 'When I'm a bit more settled. I need to get used to my wonderful new home first.'

Etienne departed again the next morning and after she'd waved him goodbye from the balcony she turned back into the bedroom with a sigh. Just as before, the house felt terribly big and lonely, but perhaps a bit less so this time. Amongst the things she'd fetched from her father's house were paintings, silks, carvings and ornaments – traditional Annamese artefacts that made her feel at home. Bà Ngoại had also given her some bright silk cushions, which she'd scattered on the cream velvet sofas in the drawing room. She'd noticed Etienne's look of surprise when he'd seen them there, but he hadn't said anything.

Thinking about it now as she wandered through to the marble-tiled bathroom and turned on the shower, why should he be surprised that she wanted some reminders of her Annamite roots in her new home? Had he assumed that she was more French than Annamese and that she'd left that side of her behind completely? She sensed, in the way he sometimes spoke about the plantation workers and the locals in general, that he scorned some elements of Annamese society. So, had it come as an unwelcome shock to him that her Annamese roots were important to her? She stepped into the shower and let the soothing warm water splash over her. She realised that those roots *were* becoming more and more important to her, the more time she spent amongst the French and in this house which was a temple to French fashion and style.

Stepping out of the shower she wrapped herself in a fluffy towel and went to the wardrobe to pick out her clothes for the day. She found a beautiful bottle-green ao dai and pulled it out. She remembered buying it on Rue de la Soie well before Etienne came into her life. She'd loved it as soon as she'd set eyes on it and had bargained long and hard with the shop-keeper to get it at a price she could afford.

While Etienne had been around, she'd dressed in western clothes, in the chic copies of Chanel and Dior dresses that the tailors in the Old Quarter had run up for her in the weeks before the wedding. But now he'd gone, she wanted to wear something traditional. She slipped on the tunic and trousers, loving the feel of the smooth silk against her skin. Staring at herself in her mirror she realised that dressed like this she looked as though she didn't have a drop of French blood in her veins. What would Etienne think if he saw her like this?

After breakfast, of pho soup once again, she left the house and set off along the boulevard, hailing a passing cyclo as she walked.

'The Tran Quoc Pagoda please,' she said, getting in. Ever since she'd been to the temple with Bà Ngoại, she'd been hankering to go back there. She wanted to sit cross-legged before the altar and meditate in the fresh breeze that wafted over from the lake, to clear her mind of worrying thoughts and to feel some connection with the other people worshipping there. She'd been longing to listen to the temple gongs and the chanting from the monastery and to breathe in the scent of the incense and the smoke from the candles.

The cyclo rider dropped her at the temple entrance and,

just as she'd done with her grandmother, she went straight to one of the stalls that were grouped around the start of the walkway and bought flowers and incense to give as offerings to the Buddha. Then she set off along the walkway towards the temple. As she neared the elaborate, yellow gates she remembered the unsettling encounter with the mysterious-looking man when she and Bà Ngoại had been leaving the temple the last time. She realised then that the chance meeting hadn't been very far from her thoughts during the course of the past few days. The way his serious, all-seeing eyes had bored into her had made a lasting impression. She shivered now thinking about it, despite the fierce heat of the morning sun that was burning the mist off the surrounding water. She couldn't help looking around for him now. Was he there lurking under the trees still? But the shadows under the branches were empty and she walked on through the gate, bowing to the monk, and left her shoes on the rack beside him.

This time, being alone here, Arielle felt a little self-conscious as she laid her flowers on the altar, lit her incense from a candle, and joined the other people who were kneeling or sitting on the marble tiles in front of it. She closed her eyes and tried to concentrate on her breathing, remembering the lessons she'd learned as a child. This time she was able to keep her mind from wandering for a little longer than she had before, focusing on the birdsong in the surrounding trees, the gongs and the sound of chanting from the monastery, breathing in the soothing smell of the incense. She sat for ten minutes or so and, feeling so much lighter of soul as she got up, she felt a little encouraged that her efforts had been worthwhile. If she came here regularly, perhaps meditation would soon come as naturally to her as it did to Bà Ngoại.

But as she began to retrace her steps to the gate, she wondered what Etienne would say about her renewed interest in Buddhism. It had never been discussed during their courtship, and she realised that she didn't want to talk about it with him. It was similar to the way she'd felt looking at herself dressed in her green silk ao dai in the bedroom mirror. She would keep it to herself; her own little secret that she would be able to indulge whilst he was away from home.

She approached the temple gate and went to take her shoes from the rack. When she was putting them on, she heard someone behind her.

'Good morning, Madame Garnier.'

It was a gentle, male voice, and even before she'd looked up she knew who it was. Inexplicably she felt the colour rush to her cheeks as she turned and looked straight into those dark, serious eyes.

'Good morning,' she replied and shook the man's proffered hand.

'Are you not with your grandmother today?' he asked.

'No, I came alone. She usually comes here in the evening. Sometimes she goes to a temple in the Old Quarter, though.'

'She is a courageous and intelligent lady,' the man replied. 'I know her well. She is a keen supporter of our cause.'

Arielle looked at him in surprise. She knew Bà Ngoại was a communist sympathiser, but she'd had no idea that she actively supported the party. She vowed to ask her about it the next time she saw her.

'Would you like to go for a cup of tea?' the man asked.

She hesitated. Was it quite proper for her, a newly married woman, to go for tea with a complete stranger? What if someone were to see them and news of it were to make its way to Etienne?

'I'm not sure,' she hesitated.

'Well, let us walk to the road together while you make up your mind,' he said with the trace of a smile on his lips. So, they walked side by side through the gate and along the tiled walkway towards the main road.

'May I ask, what does your husband think about you coming to the temple?' He asked, inclining his head towards her when they had gone a few paces. Arielle was a little shocked at the question and her immediate reaction was to be affronted, it seemed such an impertinent thing to ask, but she quickly realised that that was because it had touched a raw nerve. It was exactly what she had been thinking about herself in the minutes before they'd met.

'I'm not sure. He's away from home at the moment,' she replied, trying to keep her voice non-committal.

'Yes, I am aware of that.'

Again, she stared at him. 'How are you aware? Do you know my husband?'

He laughed. 'No. I don't know him personally, but I know *of* him. I make it my business to know the comings and goings of certain Frenchmen. Your husband is one of those.'

Arielle stopped. 'And may I ask why?'

The man cleared his throat and went on in a careful tone, 'Now I don't want to criticise your husband, but what I will say is that his line of work leads people like me to take a close interest in what he's doing.'

'His line of work?'

'Well yes. He is in the business of profiting from the labours of poor Indochinese people. I, and my fellow communists take a great interest in that.'

Arielle stared at him. 'Now wait a minute,' she protested. 'That's a bit strong. You and I don't know each other at all, but you already see fit to criticise my husband.'

'My apologies if I've offended you, Madame Garnier, but I only speak what I know to be the truth.'

They walked on in an awkward silence, soon reaching the food stalls on the pavement beside the road.

'Would you please accept my apologies for offending you? And as a gesture of goodwill, madame, would you permit me to buy you that tea?'

He sounded so formal and sincere that Arielle couldn't help softening and smiling. She looked around at the locals milling about, some passing on the pavement, others simply going about their business. She was a stranger here. No one was taking any interest in her or would notice who she chose to take tea with. And after all, she had all day, and apart from possibly paying another visit to Bà Ngoại, she had nothing else to fill the time with.

'Alright,' she said, relaxing. 'But please, don't call me madame. My name is Arielle.'

'And I am Xan,' the man said, a rare smile flashing across his face. It enhanced his chiselled cheekbones. She saw that his teeth were perfectly white and straight, contrasting with many of the Annamese men she knew whose teeth were stained by betel nut and tobacco. This man must be an educated, civilised person. Perhaps he even came from a noble family.

'Come – let us sit at that far stall under the trees. I know the lady there and she makes an excellent cup of green tea.'

He guided her past several tea stalls towards some low chairs and tables at the furthest stall in the row. It seemed out of the way and more private than the other stalls they passed. Had he done that on purpose? Did he realise how nervous she was about being seen with him?

The old woman in charge of the stall hovered around Xan, bowing and smiling. He was obviously an important customer. He ordered a pot of green tea which the woman brought quickly in a large pot with small earthenware cups.

'It is very nice to finally make your acquaintance. Your grandmother often speaks of you,' Xan said, pouring the tea once the woman had retreated behind her counter.

'Really?' she smiled, looking at him, thinking fondly of Bà Ngoại. Dappled sunlight played on his features. He was watching her steadily.

'Oh yes. She is clearly very proud of you. She had high hopes of your going to the Sorbonne.'

'Well, I'm still going,' Arielle said, a little defensively. 'I have deferred my place for a year.'

'That's good to know. An intelligent young woman like you should make the most of such opportunities. Is your husband prepared to do without you while you take your degree?'

'Oh, he's planning on coming with me,' she said, and as soon as she'd said it, she wondered if she was telling this man too much.

'Really?' there was interest in his voice but when she looked into his eyes she realised that he was regarding her sceptically.

'Yes. He is all for me completing my education.'

There was a short silence during which the voices of others taking tea at the other stalls floated over to them, the tonal rise and fall of the Annamese language, the engines and horns of vehicles on the road and the distant gongs from the temple.

'Do you know much about your husband's business?' Xan asked, breaking the silence.

Arielle drew herself up, that prickle of defensiveness rising in her again. This man was very impertinent. She was beginning to regret having agreed to take tea with him.

'I know that through his efforts poor people in Tonkin get the opportunity to work on plantations in the south and to send money home to their families. I understand he takes great care of his workers.'

'And you believe that?' he asked, his eyes on hers. She dropped her gaze to the table, stirred her tea and watched the clear liquid swirling round in the cup. His comment echoed what Bà Ngoại had said, but Bà Ngoại had said it with snorting derision. Xan was saying it with deadly seriousness. This was somehow far more effective and more chilling too.

'I believe my husband to be a truthful, honourable man and he has assured me as much. I take him at his word. I have no reason to doubt him.'

'He is lucky to have such a devoted and trusting wife,' Xan said, sipping his tea. She wondered if he was mocking her, but there was no trace of irony in his tone.

'If you get a chance, you should go with him to the plantations in the south, or north to the port of Haiphong. You will then be able to see for yourself the conditions workers are transported in and how they are treated by his overseers.'

Again, the bald impudence of his comment made her pause. She took a deep breath and replied.

'He has asked me to go with him on many occasions, actually, so I'm sure he hasn't got anything to hide.'

'Well, you *should* go,' Xan urged her. 'Then you will understand our concern.'

Arielle didn't want to hear any more. She drained her cup and stood up. 'I'm afraid I must be getting home now,' she said. 'I have things to attend to. But thank you for the tea.'

Xan got up politely and took her hand. 'I'm sorry you have to go so soon but thank you for taking tea with me. Perhaps we will meet again, here at the temple?'

'Perhaps,' she said, shaking his hand and moving away from the table. As on the previous occasion, she could feel his steady, dark eyes on her back as she walked away.

Their conversation filled her mind as she rode on the back of a cyclo towards the French quarter. She went over and over what had been said. Why had this mesmerising, fascinating man suddenly come into her life? And why was he so interested in getting to know her? It was obvious, when she thought about it. She was a route to finding out about Etienne's business, so she mustn't be drawn further on that. And what on earth was she doing anyway, married less than a week and already feeling herself drawn to another man?

They were passing through the Old Quarter now and she stared absently out at the shops and stalls. But even the vibrant clamour of these streets couldn't divert her mind from the encounter with Xan. She thought about his advice to go with Etienne on one of his trips and remembered Etienne's invitations. It would be easy to go with him. After all he had asked her many times. And perhaps a visit would put all those doubts to rest, and she would be able to face this sort of questioning with a clear conscience. And as the image of Xan's face passed across her mind, she realised it would be good to be with Etienne rather than alone here in Hanoi, vulnerable to chance encounters with mysterious strangers.

6

SAIGON, 1935

The city of Saigon was as beautiful as Arielle remembered from her childhood trips here with her father. She and Etienne arrived at its elegant, white-stuccoed railway station after a forty-hour journey from Hanoi. During the trip they had dined in the first-class railway car and spent long hours relaxing in their luxurious compartment. For a large part of the journey, the railway ran beside the coast and Arielle stared out at the palm-fringed beaches and rolling breakers that glinted under a vast sea-blue sky.

It was a fortnight after her encounter at the Lake Pagoda with Xan. His words had played on her mind day and night, and when Etienne had returned from the south, she'd told him that she wanted to accompany him on his next trip. He'd looked gratified at that suggestion and had taken her hand and kissed her.

'I'm so pleased you've come round to wanting to share that part of my life with me, my darling,' he said. 'I will have to go again very soon, though. I came to some arrangements with the owners and managers regarding the communists on the plantations, but our strategies have to be tested, and I will need to return to assess how they are working,' he'd said cryptically. She'd shuddered at those words, wondering what "arrangements" and "strategies" really meant, but she didn't have the courage to ask.

A chauffeur was waiting to meet them at Saigon station in a big, black Peugeot, ready to drive them through the city to the Majestic Hotel, one of the grand old colonial buildings near the docks on the riverfront. The Majestic was tall, at least six stories, occupying a corner plot, with grand arched windows along the lower floors and an elaborate entrance. As they walked into the elegant lobby, where planters and their wives lounged in chairs under whizzing fans, reading French newspapers, several people looked up and stared openly at Arielle. The hostility in the room was almost palpable.

'They're obviously not used to seeing people with Annamese blood staying here,' Arielle whispered to Etienne.

'Don't take any notice of them. You're as French as they are, underneath,' Etienne said, squeezing her arm, but she wasn't sure it was quite the answer she wanted to hear.

They spent three days in the city. The first evening, Etienne took her to the opera house to see Madame Butterfly. Arielle wasn't sure she enjoyed the opera, all those grating, high-pitched voices and the deafening sound of the orchestra. It exhausted her, but she acknowledged that it was a spectacle that everyone around her seemed to embrace enthusiastically. Over the next few days, Etienne took her on a whistle-stop tour of the beautiful buildings of the city; the Post Office, the Cathedral, the Hotel de Ville, and the Palais de Justice, all of which looked as though they could have been built on the banks of the Loire, but for the tropical greenery and palm trees surrounding them and the rickshaws and cyclos plying to and fro in front of them, bringing clerks, officials and advocates to and from work.

In the evenings, they dined in the hotel dining room amongst the potted palms, trying to ignore the malicious stares from other guests. It made Arielle feel bitter and angry. And as the time they had to leave for the plantations drew closer, she became increasingly nervous. She was dreading coming face to face with the reality of how Etienne made his money. In contrast, Etienne seemed relaxed about the impending trip, although occasionally he let slip his concern about the communists who were infiltrating the tappers gangs. From his occasional comment about them, Arielle gathered that he wasn't quite as nonchalant as he was trying to appear.

The day they were driven south in the big Peugeot the weather was as hot and steamy as Arielle had ever known it in Indochina. Etienne sat in front beside the driver. Arielle wore a short-sleeved cotton shirt and wound the windows down in the back of the car. She leaned out and watched the scenery rolling by as they moved through the spacious tree-lined streets of the French centre of Saigon, and out through the less wealthy outskirts, past shabby, cramped housing and on through the poverty-stricken suburbs where skinny children played in drains that ran alongside the road, and people existed in shacks built of wood or corrugated iron. Then they were out in the open countryside. Here the land was flat and the road straight, running on and on through avenues of tall, shady trees, through villages of one-storey dwellings that straddled the road, where children, playing in the red dust, stopped and stared at them with huge, curious eyes. And on past paddy fields, where farmers in conical hats waded knee deep in water, and past wide, sluggish rivers and lakes nestled amongst palm trees, the water reflecting the bright sunshine.

After driving for about an hour, they turned off the main road onto a dirt track, where the surface was so rutted that the driver had to slow down to walking pace. It was cooler here, and shadier. The red earth road ran between rows of grey-green rubber trees, their silver trunks planted in rigid, straight lines. Arielle strained to see signs of human life here, but there was none.

'These are young trees,' Etienne explained. 'They need to grow for seven years before they can be worked.'

After a kilometre or so the car stopped. They had reached a security gate and a uniformed guard asked to check their identification. While Etienne produced the paperwork, Arielle was shocked to see that on either side of the gate, between two rows of rubber trees ran a high fence, topped with coils of barbed wire.

'What's happening, Etienne? What is this place?' she asked, alarmed.

He turned and smiled reassuringly. 'It's just the security for the rubber estate, chéri.'

'But why the barbed wire? It looks more like a prison than a plantation.'

Etienne gave a hollow laugh. 'It's just to discourage the workers from leaving,' he said grimly. 'It's quite standard on plantations of this size.'

She watched in silence as the barrier rose and the car eased past the security post. The guard saluted as they passed. 'But you said they were well treated,' she murmured.

'Of course they are well treated,' he said and from the way he spoke she could tell that his patience was wearing thin. 'They are stirred up by malign forces, putting ideas into their heads, telling them they are exploited and that they deserve more. That's why we have come. You know that.'

The car slid on, past the high fence and on through the endless rows of trees. Arielle sat back on the leather seat, dismayed at this turn in the conversation and by Etienne's tone of voice. They drove for another ten minutes, before she spotted a row of workers halfway down an avenue of taller, darker trees. Some were hammering at the trees with tools, others were holding cups tied round the trunks, watching the contents.

'Each tapper has to tap at least three hundred trees per day,' Etienne said, a note of pride in his voice.

'Three hundred? And what if they don't?' Arielle asked, staring back at the thin-looking workers, with bare feet and bare heads, clad only in loin cloths.

'Their pay is docked of course, or they lose their time off.'

'That sounds rather harsh,' she murmured.

They were approaching a group of buildings now which loomed up out of the trees, looking alien in this landscape of uniform greenery. Some of the buildings appeared new – built of shiny, corrugated iron. It looked and felt like the industrial area of a modern city, not at all how she'd imagined this place in the middle of nowhere. She'd expected something more rustic, like a primitive village, simple and small-scale, with thatched huts and animals rooting about in the mud.

They drew alongside a windowless barn-like structure. 'That's the barracks for the male workers,' Etienne said with a note of pride in his voice. It's newly built. All modern conveniences.'

'Except windows,' Arielle muttered, appalled that men could be housed here, without light or air, like animals waiting for slaughter.

'What are those places?' she asked, pointing to a series of small, thatched huts on some open ground behind the barracks.

'That's the workers' village,' Etienne replied. 'If they come here from the north with their families, they can live there.

Some of the women work on the plantation too. The village is perfectly adequate, and there is a school for the children.'

Arielle stared at the huts. They looked tiny and cramped and were built close together, opening out onto red, dirt roads.

Opposite the barracks was a vast shed, with huge wooden doors that were closed.

'That's the latex shed,' explained Etienne. 'The liquid latex from the trees is pressed into sheets, then hung up to dry.'

He asked the driver to stop.

'I just need to nip into the shed and see if Bertrand, the manager, is about,' he told Arielle. 'Wait here. I won't be a minute.'

He got out of the car and vanished round the side of the building. Arielle sat there, the heat building in the car, wishing she could see inside the sheds. And as if someone was listening to her thoughts, one of the great doors began to open. A worker was pushing it aside on rollers. From where she sat, Arielle could see inside. Huge ladder-like racks were being moved about inside the giant building by workers. They were like oversized laundry racks with square white sheets hung up to dry on every rung. Other men were pushing wooden crates on sack barrows. A row of sack barrows came out of the building and were taken out and across the yard, where the workers unloaded the crates and stacked them in a pile. Like the tappers working on the trees, these men were also half-naked and walked on the bare earth and concrete of the shed without shoes. Their ribs were clearly visible and their cheeks looked hollow, even from this distance.

When they'd deposited their loads they brought the barrows back past the car. A couple of them glanced inside, but seeing Arielle quickly looked away. Then they disappeared inside the shed and the door was pushed shut again.

Arielle realised that she'd had a rare glimpse inside the

workings of the latex shed. Then Etienne appeared round the side of the building.

'Bertrand isn't here,' he said. 'Out on his rounds of the plantation. I'll catch up with him later on. Drive on please, to the guest house.'

The car moved on, leaving the latex sheds behind. Beyond it was another, smaller building. This one had windows.

'That's the hospital,' Etienne explained. 'With so many men working here, there are bound to be some who become ill and need medical attention. As you see, no expense is spared to care for the workers.'

The car rolled on, past more one-storey buildings, that looked like offices, then past a row of houses, brick built with balconies and narrow front gardens.

'That's where the overseers live,' Etienne explained.

Beyond the houses, the dirt road plunged back into the trees again.

'The guest house is a little way away from the main buildings. It's next to the manager's place. They are both attractive houses. I think you'll be very comfortable staying here.'

Arielle said nothing. She was thinking about the bone-thin workers she'd just seen, sweating their days away labouring out on the plantation or in the sheds, returning to a meagre hut in the village or to a windowless barracks to sleep once their work was done. She began to understand why the communists might be welcomed here. But what troubled her most, was that Etienne seemed to genuinely think that the workers' conditions were good.

Soon the trees opened out into a large clearing. There, complete with well-tended gardens, stood two white-painted houses, with shuttered windows and wide verandas, shaded by a spinney of tamarind trees. The car turned into the gravelled driveway and they scrunched up it between low hedges, behind which white rose bushes were in full bloom. Uniformed gardeners were watering the immaculate lawns with hoses. It was a scene of beauty and tranquillity, so different from the place where men sweated and laboured their days away, but yet so close.

At the end of the drive, they drew up in front of the smaller of the two houses.

'This is the guest house,' Etienne announced. 'Bertrand Martin, the manager lives next door. As I said, he's out on the plantation at the moment, doing his rounds. I'll introduce you to him later on.'

Arielle got out of the car and mounted the wooden steps to the veranda of the guest house. As she did so, she glanced across at the other house and paused, surprised. There on the veranda sat a native woman. She looked a little older than Arielle herself. She was dressed in a shabby green ao dai and she looked thin and pale. She was staring at Arielle quite brazenly, her eyes steady and serious. A shiver passed through Arielle at the strange encounter.

'Who's that, Etienne?'

Etienne cleared his throat. 'Oh, that's just Bertrand's live-in housekeeper,' he said quickly. 'Come on inside. I think you'll like the house.'

The chauffeur heaved their suitcases across the veranda and in through the front door and Etienne paced around the large reception room opening the shutters, letting the sunshine stream in to cast strips of bright light across the polished wooden floorboards. The room was indeed beautiful, with chintzy sofas and white painted furniture with pastel prints on the walls. A wide, wooden staircase rose up from the centre.

'The kitchen staff will have made us lunch by now,' said Etienne. 'Would you like to take it on the veranda?'

'Yes, but is there somewhere to freshen up first? I feel a bit sticky from the ride.'

'Of course. Come on upstairs.'

He showed her through a light, airy bedroom and past a four-poster bed draped with lace hangings, to a large, marble-tiled bathroom.

'Here it is. I'll see you out on the veranda,' Etienne said, closing the door.

As she splashed cold water on her face at the sink, she happened to glance out of the little window. It looked out over the side of the house in the direction of the manager's residence. With surprise, she noticed that the girl was still there, sitting in the same spot as before. She was no longer staring at the guest house, though, but instead was absorbed in a brightly coloured magazine, flicking through the pages. That was strange. Why would the housekeeper be sitting on the veranda reading a magazine, and why would she be dressed like that? Surely the servants here wore uniforms. Then a thought occurred to Arielle and she realised that Etienne must have been speaking in euphemisms yet again. Perhaps the young woman wasn't a housekeeper at all. Perhaps she was the manager's native love interest. It was well known that Frenchmen far from home took local girls as their mistresses, even living openly with them and having children. Some of these men were even married back in France.

Arielle dried her face and went back downstairs to Etienne, her mind filled with thoughts of the strange looking girl on the veranda. What must her life be like, kept here on the plantation with nothing to do but satisfy the needs of a strange foreigner? Where did she come from? How long had she been here?

Etienne took her out to the front veranda where two male servants dressed in white tunics were laying the table. They

bowed as she approached and she addressed them in
Annamese; 'There's no need for that,' she said, but their eyes
flicked towards Etienne, clearly unsure whether to take that
order seriously.

'What did you say?' Etienne asked.

'I told them not to bow to me,' she replied. 'It is enough
that they serve us, without having to scrape and bow too. It's
humiliating for them.'

Etienne sat down at the table with a heavy sigh. 'You
shouldn't confuse them. They've been trained to bow to guests
here. Now they won't know what to do.'

Arielle shrugged and sat down opposite him. From where
she sat, she could see the edge of the green silk ao dai
belonging to the girl on the veranda of the planter's house. It
distracted her, put her off her food – chicken chasseur and
green salad – and stopped her from concentrating on what
Etienne was saying.

'Are you listening to me, Arielle?' he asked later as they
were being served dessert of Chantilly cream. 'You seem very
distracted.'

'Oh, I'm sorry, but I'm a little tired from the journey,' she
said, trying to put the girl out of her mind and to give him her
full attention.

'Well, that's fine, because I need to go down to the office
and speak to the manager this afternoon about the communists. It's an unpleasant business, probably best if you don't
accompany me. So, you can rest up if you like.'

Arielle nodded slowly, regretting having said she was tired.
The long, boring, empty afternoon stretched out before her.
She would have preferred to go with him, even if the discus-
sion was about "unpleasant" things.

'Then this evening Bertrand has invited us round for

dinner. He's a nice chap. You'll like him, I'm sure. And tomorrow, we will take you on a tour of the plantation and the factory. It's state of the art. You'll see what excellent work is done here and what great opportunities the workers are given.'

When Etienne had departed for the office in the car, Arielle went upstairs, shut the shutters in the bedroom and lay down on the big bed under the ceiling fan. The mattress was soft and comfortable. She closed her eyes, but sleep wouldn't come. Despite the fan, the heat was oppressive and the sound of cicadas in the garden seemed louder here than in Hanoi. They were magnified in the silence. Her mind wandered to the girl on the veranda again, but she must have eventually drifted off, because she was awoken by Etienne moving about in the room.

'Are you awake, Ari? We need to start getting ready.'

She sat upright, startled, rubbing her eyes. He'd opened the shutters and the sunlight was streaming in, red and golden from the setting sun.

'I had no idea I'd slept for so long,' she said, swinging her legs over the side of the bed and standing up. Her suitcase was on a stand under the window.

'Shall I wear an ao dai?' she asked. 'I put one in, just in case.'

Etienne stopped and stared at her. 'Why would you do that?'

'I just thought... if... well if the "housekeeper" as you called her, is there, perhaps she will be wearing one. I thought I might keep her company.'

He came up close and took her chin in his hand, pinching it, turning her face towards his. 'Don't ever say that,' he said, his eyes blazing. 'You are *not* like that woman. She has nothing. She *is* nothing. She's kept by a lonely Frenchman for her

body. You are much more than that. You're an educated
woman and you're as French as I am.'

'But I'm not quite, am I?' Arielle said, defiantly, looking
straight up into his eyes. 'You're forgetting that I'm half-
Annamese. You always seem to want to forget that fact.'

'But you're not, though. You're not to me. You are worlds
apart from those native women who have nothing, who have
to use their bodies for money. You're not like that. And you
never will be.'

He let go of her chin and rifled in the suitcase, pulling out
a black silk evening dress.

'Wear that,' he said throwing it on the bed. 'And never
compare yourself to a woman like her again.'

Shaking, she picked up the dress and went into the bathroom and locked the door with clumsy hands. She turned the
taps on full so that water was thundering out, then sat down
on the side of the bath and burst into tears.

BERTRAND MARTIN WAS A BURLY, dark-haired Frenchman with
a bushy beard. He greeted them on his veranda wearing a
crumpled, linen suit. He had small eyes in a fleshy face and
Arielle felt them resting on her body for a little longer than
was comfortable.

'Come in, come in,' he said. 'We're going to dine out here,
mosquitoes permitting. It's cooler than inside the house. The
servants have set some coils burning.'

He clicked his fingers and a male servant appeared in the
doorway, bowing obsequiously. He was shabbily dressed,
unlike the servants in the guest house, and Arielle saw that his
eyes were downcast, his shoulders drooping.

'Drinks?' asked Bertrand. 'We don't have a huge selection,

but how about an Indochine martini with ginger? Or gin and tonic?'

They both chose gin and tonic and Bertrand clicked his fingers at the servant who bowed again and scuttled into the dark interior of the house.

'Do take a seat,' Bertrand waved them to the cane table, already set for supper. As Arielle sat down she noted that it was laid for four people, but there was no sign yet of the mysterious mistress. She peered into the gloom of the house, hoping to catch a glimpse of the young woman who'd so fascinated her earlier.

Bertrand cleared his throat, seeing her curiosity. 'Oh, Maki will be down in a minute. She's just getting dressed. That always takes for ever...'

Etienne laughed knowingly, settling himself at the table.

First the drinks appeared on a wobbling tray, then, after the servant had retreated to the kitchen again, the girl stepped out from the shadows.

'Ah, don't be shy, Maki,' Bertrand boomed ushering her towards the table. 'Come and meet our guests.'

She came forward and Arielle noticed, to her surprise, that Maki too was wearing western clothes this evening. She was dressed in an up-to-the minute, close fitting black taffeta evening gown, trimmed with silver lace at the bodice. It was a little too dressy for the occasion and contrasted sharply with Bertrand's shabby suit.

Close up, she looked younger than Arielle had imagined. Her face, though thin and sallow, was childlike under the thick makeup. She smiled and curtseyed.

'Very nice to meet you,' Maki said in heavily accented French, shaking first Etienne, then Arielle by the hand. Then she sat down quietly at the remaining place where the servant had already thoughtfully placed another gin and tonic.

Food was brought to the table and as everyone tucked into delicious gỏi cuốn shrimp rolls, the men started talking about the price of rubber and the difficulties of production. Maki ate her food in silence and with great concentration, rarely looking up from her plate. The silence between them began to feel a little awkward and Arielle racked her brains, trying to think of a suitable topic to introduce in conversation, but for several minutes was stumped. By the time the next course came, fried pork with noodles, she remembered having seen Maki on the veranda reading earlier in the day.

'Do you like magazines?' Arielle said and Maki looked up from her plate and stared at her wide-eyed.

'Oh yes. I love to read about film stars, celebrities, royalty. I'm always reading.' And for the first time she smiled, a wide smile, displaying huge, gappy teeth which instantly gave her face character.

'Me too,' Arielle confided, not saying that her reading matter was more likely to include literary greats for her studies than the gossip columns of magazines.

'Who's your favourite film star?' Maki asked, taking a large forkful of noodles and twirling it around her fork expertly. Arielle had to think hard.

'Oh, I'm a bit out of touch, but I love Rita Hayworth.'

'Me too,' said Maki warmly. 'But my favourite is Jean Harlow. This dress is copied from one she wore in *The Girl from Missouri*. Bertrand took me up to Saigon to see it at the cinema a few weeks ago. I had the dress made there too.'

'How lovely. Did you like Saigon?'

Maki's eyes lit up. 'I love it. Such a beautiful city. We've been before, though. Bertrand has taken me many times to see movies there. Sometimes we go into the local town where there's a small cinema, but Saigon is better.'

Arielle asked her which movies she'd seen, and Maki

reeled off a list of the latest Hollywood hits. One by one Arielle asked her about them. Maki had an incredible memory, rattling off details of plot, stars, locations. Somewhere along the line they had stopped speaking French and lapsed into their native tongue. It felt natural to do so especially as the two men were deep in discussion about the difficulties of recruiting and controlling coolies on the plantation.

During a lapse in the girls' conversation, Arielle heard Bertrand say, 'We need to toughen up though, Garnier. Severe punishments are definitely in order. Going easy on those communist bastards isn't going to solve this problem.'

Shock waves went through her and she turned back and looked into Maki's eyes which were also deadly serious. Suddenly Maki grabbed her hand and leaned forward and whispered something to her quickly in Annamese.

'People are dying on this plantation,' she said, her voice breathless and strangled. 'I've seen it with my own eyes. Come to see me tomorrow and I'll tell you everything.'

7

BIÊN HÒA PROVINCE, COCHINCHINA, 1935

Arielle spent a restless night on the four-poster bed shrouded behind the lace curtains. Etienne had drunk far too much whisky at the meal at Bertrand's and he went straight to sleep, snoring loudly beside her. The room was hot and airless, despite the fan which just seemed to push the stifling air round and round. The whirring of cicadas from the plantation sounded even louder than it had in the afternoon. She lay wide awake, staring into the darkness. Visions of bone-thin coolies working from morning to night on the plantation or in the factory sheds passed through her mind. The look in their sad, vacant eyes haunted her and the thought of their malnourished bodies forced to labour on, with no chance of escape from the endless toil, tore at her heartstrings.

She must have drifted off eventually, but it felt as if she'd only just closed her eyes when a servant came into the room with a tray of tea.

'What time is it, Etienne?' she asked, forcing herself awake as the servant left the room. There were no chinks of morning light creeping between the shutters yet.

'Five o'clock,' Etienne said in a blurry voice, taking a sip of tea. 'Bertrand wants me to accompany him on his morning rounds. He's got something important to show me, apparently.'

There was something in his voice that made Arielle look at him sharply. It sounded ominous for some reason, particularly in the light of the conversation she'd overheard about punishments. He avoided her gaze, got out of bed and went straight into the bathroom. She lay there listening to the sound of him splashing in the shower, wondering why his words had bothered her, and what that "something important" might be.

After he'd left, she fell into a deep sleep and when she finally awoke, bright sunlight was streaming through the chinks in the shutters. She sat up quickly, annoyed with herself for oversleeping. She'd intended to get up early and go and see Maki as soon as it had felt right to do so. But now the opportunity might be lost. She forced herself out of bed and into the shower, where the cold water felt deliciously soothing on her sweat-drenched body. She dressed carefully in a simple cotton summer dress and went downstairs. The servant was waiting at the bottom of the stairs to tell her that breakfast was waiting for her out on the veranda.

As she munched her way through croissants and pains aux raisins, and sipped café au lait, she listened to the cicadas and the whooping of distant monkeys and mused on how strange it was to be eating as if in a Parisian café, here in a clearing in what had been deep jungle a couple of decades before. How strange that warm croissants and baguettes were actually available in the middle of nowhere. She beckoned the servant and asked him, in Annamese, where they came from.

'We bake them in the kitchen, madame. Especially for

guests,' he said proudly, for the first time meeting her eye and smiling a genuine smile, displaying betel stained teeth.

'Please thank the cook for me,' she said, and he nodded again. As she ate, her gaze wandered over to Bertrand's house to see if Maki was up and about, but there was no sign of her. The shutters were closed, the ceiling fans on the veranda were still.

'Is there anyone around next door?' she asked the servant who still hovered in the doorway. His smile immediately vanished, and he shook his head, frowning deeply.

'The woman not up yet. Sometimes she does not get up until noon,' he said, and Arielle felt the disapproval radiating from him. She couldn't think of what to say in response, but as she searched for the right words, she noticed the black Peugeot appearing through the gap in the rubber trees and coming towards the house. Her heart sank. Etienne was back already, and she hadn't had the opportunity to go and see Maki yet. She drained her coffee and wiped the crumbs from her dress. Perhaps she would get a chance to go next-door later on.

'Are you ready?' Etienne asked, calling from the bottom of the steps. 'Bertrand is going to take us on a tour of the estate and the factory.'

'Yes. Are we really going in the car though? The factory is only just through those trees. Surely we could walk?'

'We do need the car. It's terribly hot today and you don't want to get all sweaty walking. And we might be going to some far-flung parts of the plantation, so we'll need to be driven. And besides, it wouldn't do for the coolies to see us walking about like they have to.'

'Whyever not?' she asked, going down the front steps and sliding onto the leather back seat as the driver held the door open for her.

'Don't be naïve, Ari. They need to know who's master.'

She glanced up at the chauffeur, embarrassed, wondering if he'd understood Etienne's words, but the man just carried on staring ahead of him, and his face was as impassive as ever.

The chauffeur got into the driver's seat, drove the car back to the factory sheds and stopped outside the first one. It was the building they'd passed the day before where Arielle had seen barefoot workers in loincloths pushing the latex racks around. But today the huge doors were closed. Bertrand stood waiting for them in front of the building.

'Bonjour!' he said heartily, pulling the door of the car open for Arielle to get out. 'I'm so pleased you want to look around the plantation. Nothing gives me greater pleasure than showing someone how we work. Come on inside.'

He took Arielle firmly by the arm and walked her inside the shed, in between the racks of drying latex that she'd seen the day before. A group of workers stood beside one of the racks bowing and smiling. There were two women and two men. She stared at them, unable to smile at first. These workers didn't look either sick or malnourished. They looked happy and healthy and were dressed in white overalls and wide black trousers, with rubber shoes on their feet.

'You see how happy they are for you to see their work?' Bertrand asked and she nodded slowly, deeply puzzled. She noticed him exchange a quick, knowing look with Etienne. It was barely perceptible and as they walked on through the pristine-looking factory sheds, she wondered if she'd imagined it, and if she'd also imagined such a different scene as they'd passed by the day before.

'I'll show you the various processes we use to refine the latex. Come...' Bertrand went on, moving her gently forward by pressure on her arm. 'First we bring it in from the plantation in tanks. Then it is poured from those tanks into flat containers to solidify. Here...' he waved his hand in the direction of a series of low, tiled baths in which lay white latex. They walked slowly past them. The sickly-sweet smell of raw latex hung on the air. Arielle looked around her, still mystified. There was no one tending the tanks. How odd that there were so few people around. The factory was all but deserted.

Bertrand ushered her on into another part of the factory.

'Once it has firmed up a little, it is pressed through rollers into flat sheets.'

Several sets of heavy-duty metal rollers stood on rough, wooden tables. Most were standing idle, but two were being used. Two women were sitting at the tables operating the rollers by hand, threading the sheets of latex through the wringers. Like the other workers they had just seen, these women looked fit and healthy and were dressed in uniform. They smiled and nodded as Arielle passed by.

'The next process is to add chemicals and hang it up in the rear part of the shed and for smoking. That process is called pre-vulcanisation. Once again it is hung up to dry on racks. Then it is smoked further to turn it into rubber.'

Bertrand pointed in the direction of some huge doors at the rear of the shed.

'Unfortunately, I cannot show you inside that part of the factory. It is extremely hot, and the atmosphere is very unhealthy.' He turned towards her smiling, spreading his hands out wide.

'So that's it. You've seen everything here. Now, do you have any questions, otherwise we can press on outside to see the plantation itself.'

'That was very interesting indeed, Bertrand,' Etienne cut in. 'I don't suppose Arielle has any questions, do you, Ari?'

She could tell from the tone of Etienne's voice that he was warning her not to ask anything, but she couldn't stop herself.

'Well, there *is* just one thing I'd like to ask. And that is, why are there so few people about? I thought a factory like this would be full of workers. We've only seen about five people.'

'Oh, some of them are taking a well-earned rest in the canteen. It is lunchtime here. They start very early in the morning, you see.'

'Could we possibly see the canteen?' she asked on an impulse and could feel Etienne's blazing eyes on her face.

'I'm afraid not, Madame Garnier. We like to give our workers at least some privacy.'

It was difficult to challenge this, and she felt momentarily wrongfooted, so she kept silent and followed him out to the car. The driver leapt forward to open the doors and all three of them got in, Bertrand in the front seat. He told the driver to drive on, past the workers' village and up another track between lines of trees. The car skidded and bumped on the rough ground as it went.

'These are the most mature trees on the plantation,' Bertrand was saying. He went on to talk about the age of the trees and how they were planted, but Arielle wasn't listening to him, she was wondering whether the memory of what she'd seen in the factory shed the day before was accurate, or if she'd built it up in her mind to be something more than it was. How could that be? She glanced at Etienne, he was looking at Bertrand, listening intently to what he was saying. It felt as if this was some sort of collusion between the two of them, and in that moment she knew she wouldn't be able to raise the matter with Etienne either.

The car pulled off the road and into a clearing.

'Let's see some trees being tapped,' Bertrand said eagerly, getting out of the car.

They followed him for ten minutes or so through the trees. The ground was rutted with weeds and fallen leaves. Despite the shade it felt hot and sweaty, and Arielle found herself batting away flies and mosquitoes constantly.

'Here!' Bertrand stopped by a tree to which a wooden bowl was hanging by a hook. The trunk of the tree had a wide strip of bark removed, like a wound on its trunk, and latex was crawling round the bottom of the groove and dripping into the cup. 'All these trees have been tapped this morning.' He waved down the line of trees, all of which had cups hanging on their trunks.

'Where are the tappers?' Arielle asked in dismay.

'Oh, they've moved on from here. They are deep inside the plantation by now. Way beyond the road. So, I'm afraid we won't get to see them today. They will return here later to empty the cups.'

Arielle stared at him, thwarted once again.

'Come on, let's get you back to the house now,' he said. 'It's awfully hot out here.'

Wordlessly, she turned round and walked slowly back to the car, the two men following behind. Anger simmered in her heart, but she sensed that she must hide it. There was no point protesting or asking anything more, she knew that now. The whole tour had been a ruse to stop her asking awkward questions, perhaps to ensure she went back to Hanoi with stories of how well workers on the plantation were treated. She'd seen through the charade, but she was well aware that there was no point challenging what she'd just been shown.

8

BIÊN HÒA PROVINCE, COCHINCHINA, 1935

W hen she got back to the house, Arielle went straight upstairs, took a shower, and lay down on the bed under the fans. Etienne had returned with Bertrand to the offices. She was so tired from having slept so little the previous night that she drifted off to into a half sleep. When she opened her eyes, Etienne was creeping around the room.

'What are you doing?' she asked.

'I'm just getting changed out of these sweaty clothes and packing a few things. I have to go to the other plantations in the area to speak to the managers there. I didn't want to wake you. I'll be back tomorrow evening.'

'Why didn't you say so before?' she asked in surprise, propping herself up on her elbows.

He sat down beside her to do up the buttons on his shirt. 'To tell you the truth, I didn't want to bring up the subject of the communists again. I know it upsets you.'

'But you haven't even told me how you dealt with them on this plantation yet,' she said.

'Ah,' he said, looking away from her as if he needed to

concentrate hard on doing up the buttons on his sleeve. 'They've all gone now. They were arrested, taken away by the police. They won't be coming back.'

'So have police been here since we arrived?' she asked in disbelief.

'Yes. They came yesterday afternoon in fact.'

'But... but... I heard Bertrand saying that the communists needed to be dealt with. Yesterday evening, at dinner.'

'You must have misunderstood, chéri,' he said, kissing her lightly on the shoulder. 'Those communists are long gone. They won't trouble us again. Not on this plantation, at least.'

'But Etienne...' None of this made sense. Her fears were being dismissed again.

'Please don't question me about it, Arielle,' he said, his voice suddenly sharp. He got up from the bed. 'I've told you the position. You need to accept what I say. Now, I have to leave if I'm going to get to the next plantation before dark. As I said, I'll be back tomorrow.'

She watched from the bedroom window as Etienne ran down the steps and into the waiting car. Dressing quickly, she hurried down the stairs and out of the house. She needed to speak to Maki as soon as she could. She ran the short distance to the manager's house and up the wooden steps to the veranda.

'Hello,' Maki said smiling. She was sitting in a planter's chair, a magazine on her lap. 'I thought you would come when I saw your husband leaving just now. Sit down. Do you want a drink?'

'Some tea would be wonderful,' Arielle sat down breathlessly in the other chair.

After the servant had laid a china teapot and cups on the cane table between them, Maki leaned forward and said quietly, 'I asked you to come and see me because I sensed you would want to know what is really happening here on the plantation. And the truth about what your husband is involved in.'

She poured the amber-coloured liquid into two cups and handed one to Arielle.

'I do,' Arielle replied. 'I am sure he's not telling me everything. He and Bertrand took me on a tour of the factory and the plantation this morning but there were no workers about. They obviously didn't want me to see how thin and sick the workers look. But I saw yesterday when we went past the sheds and was shocked. Etienne doesn't know that, though.'

'It's true,' said Maki, her eyes deadly serious. 'When visitors come here, Bertrand often takes them to the factory when the workers are on a break. They get people from the office to stand in for them.'

Arielle nodded. 'Yes, there were a few people there. They looked well dressed and healthy. Not how I remembered the workers from yesterday at all.'

'Men here are malnourished and work incredibly long hours,' Maki replied. 'The overseers beat them if they don't work hard enough. Malaria is rife too and nothing is done to stop it. Many people die here on the plantation and their deaths are covered up.'

'That's terrible,' Arielle was horrified, unable to swallow her tea for a few seconds. Then she forced it down and asked, 'But how do you know all this?'

'From my father. He works on the plantation in one of the tappers' gangs. He and my mother live in the workers' village. I was born up in the north, in Tonkin, before they came here, but I've lived here most of my life. I've seen the plantation grow bigger and bigger around me. It was once small, just a few acres of young trees, but rubber is so successful there's no end to the expansion.'

Arielle looked at her with renewed respect. 'That's fascinating. So did you meet Bertrand when he came here as manager?'

Maki laughed, a humourless laugh.

'Young native girls aren't safe here on the plantation. When the French overseers see someone pretty in the village, they pluck them away from their family and take them to their houses to use for sex. My mother was clever. She made sure that the first Frenchman to notice me was the new manager. So here I am.'

Arielle's mouth dropped open in surprise. 'I had no idea. So, you're not here by choice then?'

'I suppose I am now. I've got used to him over the years. He's not unkind to me, despite the way he runs the plantation. I don't have any choice but to stay with him.'

Arielle looked at Maki with pity and then checked herself. Was this really so different from her own story? On the surface it was, but now she was discovering more about the man she'd married, she realised that every day with him was now a compromise for her.

'Do you know what they've done to the communists?' she asked. She was fearful of the answer, but she had to know. 'Etienne told me that they'd been arrested and taken away by the police.'

'That's a lie! I'll show you what happened to them, and while we're at it I'll show you what the factory is really like, and the tappers' lines. If we go now, we will be back before it gets dark.'

She drained her tea and Arielle did the same. Her heart began to beat fast. Now she might find out what Etienne and Bertrand had been hiding from her.

'You will need this,' Maki told her, handing her an umbrella from a stand beside the front door. 'To keep off the sun. And are your sandals comfortable? We will be doing a lot of walking.'

They walked the few hundred metres to the factory shed. As they walked, Maki explained that there had been trouble with communists on other plantations a few years before. In 1930 there was a strike on the Michelin plantation at Thuân-Loï in the same province. Conditions for workers were very harsh and the communists had established themselves on the plantation. They'd persuaded the workers to take strike action for better pay and conditions. The strike became violent, and the French military were sent in. The ringleaders were eventually arrested and sentenced to long prison terms.

'I think I might have read about that in the newspaper,' Arielle murmured, thinking that at the time it had felt so far removed from her own life. Now it felt so close.

'So, you see, the management are terrified of another strike like that. It means they lose money, but more than that, it could spread discontent to the whole of Indochina. So, they will stamp out any hint of communist feeling in the harshest possible way.'

They had reached the latex shed by now. This time the great doors stood open and, just as Arielle had seen the day before, the workforce of half-naked, emaciated men, was hard at work, shifting crates, moving racks of drying latex, feeding sheets through the rollers. The scene was noisy, smelly and chaotic, contrasting starkly with the controlled activity she'd been shown earlier that day.

'Stand here,' Maki said, and drew Arielle back into the shadow of the doorway. 'We don't want to be spotted by the overseers.'

They stood there for a few minutes, and as they watched, one of the workers knocked a pot of liquid latex over on the floor. Within seconds a Frenchman was upon him, hitting him with a whip, shouting obscenities. Even from where they stood, the girls could see that the Frenchman's eyes were narrowed in hatred, flecks of spittle flying from his mouth. The worker cowered on the floor, yelling in protest, until the Frenchman seemed to grow tired of the sport and sauntered away. As soon as he'd gone the worker scrambled to his feet, grabbed a filthy cloth from a nearby sink and began to scrub the latex furiously from the concrete floor. Another worker stopped to help him, and they exchanged brief glances of despair, but no one else seemed to notice.

Arielle moved forward instinctively, but Maki held her back.

'This happens all the time,' Maki said. 'The overseers are brutal men. There is no check on their behaviour. They beat the tappers who haven't reached their quota every day. I've seen it happen.'

'But that's terrible,' said Arielle, feeling the blood drain from her face. 'We should help that poor man.'

'It wouldn't do any good. It would only get him into more trouble and Bertrand and Etienne would find out that I'd brought you here.'

Arielle bit her nail, frustrated that she couldn't do anything about the injustice she'd just witnessed.

'I will speak to Etienne,' she said. Maki laughed bitterly.

'What good would that do? He knows already. He may try and convince you he has the workers' interests at heart, but I've seen him watching while beatings happen.'

Arielle looked at her but said nothing. She was shocked, but not surprised. It was what she'd half suspected for a long time now.

'I have something else to show you,' Maki said, tucking her arm inside Arielle's. 'Come. It is beyond the far sheds.'

Maki led her behind the factory shed to some waste

ground and there, Arielle was surprised to see the ruins of several other buildings, left to rot and decay. Wooden roofs were caved in, walls green with moss, jungle plants growing in abundance, sprouting from inside the buildings.

'These are disused latex sheds,' Maki explained. 'The plantation got too big for them, so the owners built a new one in front.'

'Is this what you wanted to show me?'

Maki shook her head, picking her way around a tumbledown wall. A bright green snake darted out from between the broken bricks and slithered across their path. Arielle jumped and let out a little squeal.

'Hush! They will hear us. Snakes are common here. That one is venomous, though. Tappers come across venomous snakes all the time in the plantation. Many tappers are killed by their venom. But no one cares. Tappers' lives are cheap.'

Arielle felt a shiver run right through her.

Beyond the farthest disused building and between that and the first line of rubber trees that marked the edge of the plantation, was a long, wide strip of land. No bushes or trees grew here. Some of the land was covered in coarse grass, but in one corner it was just bare, red earth. Arielle shaded her eyes to look.

'What is this place?' she asked, puzzled.

'Can't you see? Look more closely,' said Maki, pressing her forward. Arielle took a few more steps and then stopped with a gasp of surprise. Underneath the grass were oblong mounds of earth. Dozens and dozens of them. Some were marked with simple stones, others by stumps of wood, but many mounds were not marked at all. Flowers were scattered on some of them, some of which looked quite fresh, others were drooping and decaying in the heat.

'It's a graveyard,' she said, and Maki nodded.

'This is where they bury the workers who die.' Maki put her face close to Arielle's, her eyes deadly serious. 'Did you know that on this plantation there is a death rate of 15% of the workforce every year? The French simply replace them with more poor labourers from Tonkin, with the help of your husband. Without him and others like him, they wouldn't be able to do it. They'd have to take better care of the workers.'

Arielle stared at her, stunned, trying to process what Maki was saying.

'That's hundreds of young men dying here every year. Senseless, needless deaths.'

'What do they die of?' Arielle asked in a small voice.

'Of starvation, overwork, or malaria. Some die in accidents too. Some kill themselves through despair.'

'But that's... terrible...' Words seemed inadequate to express the shock and revulsion that Arielle was feeling. She shaded her eyes and peered across the neglected graveyard. It stretched on for acre after acre behind the buildings. She shuddered, thinking of how many men must be buried here. How many young lives wasted and forgotten in the pursuit of greed and profit.

'I need to show you something on the other side of this field,' Maki said, taking Arielle's hand and beginning to walk along the edge of the graveyard. They walked beside the derelict buildings on a path which must have been worn in the grass by families visiting the graves of loved ones. Arielle walked hesitantly. She was terrified of stepping on a snake.

They reached the end, where new graves lay. The grass had not yet had a chance to grow on them. There were at least ten very fresh-looking mounds.

'Some of these are workers who died where the jungle was being cleared. They are still expanding the plantation and it's very dangerous. Men die there nearly every day.'

'And the others?' Arielle asked.

'They are the communists. Four of them. Bertrand kept them in a locked room in one of these old buildings and early this morning they took them out to a remote spot on the plantation and beat them to death. I heard about it from my mother earlier today.'

'And Etienne?' she could hardly bear to ask.

Maki nodded. 'It was him who persuaded Bertrand to give the order.'

Tears sprung to Arielle's eyes at the words. She was so shocked she couldn't speak, she could hardly even process what she'd just heard. Here was the evidence that her husband was a brutal, cold-hearted killer. What was she doing with that man who she thought she loved? How ever could she go on with him?

Four days later, Arielle got out of a cyclo in front of the temple entrance and paid the rider. The Tran Quoc Pagoda with its red roofs soared above her on its promontory out on the lake. A warm feeling of peace and wellbeing stole over her. Just being here in this tranquil, spiritual place made her feel instantly lighter. As usual she bought some lotus flowers and incense from one of the stalls near the entrance, then she walked towards the elaborate gateway, bowed to the monk as she went through, took off her sandals and carried on down the tiled walkway towards the pagoda. She looked up at the majestic temple building as she went, but her mind was elsewhere. She was thinking, as she had done constantly over the past few days, of her visit to the graveyard on the plantation with Maki, and of the shocking revelations she'd encountered there. The calm that had begun to permeate her mind at the sight of the temple dissipated as she allowed her thoughts to wander back to that morning.

When they'd left the graveyard, Maki had led her into the trees, and they walked on through the plantation for a long time. Maki seemed to know where she was despite every line of trees looking exactly like the last one to Arielle. Each avenue was bathed in the grey-green light cast by the rubber trees, and all had a bed of dead leaves and short grass underfoot. Very soon Arielle was completely lost, and without Maki she sensed that she would have wandered for ever down those regimented lines of forlorn grey trees, each with an identical gash on its trunk.

After they'd been walking for half an hour or so, Maki took her arm and said, 'Stop... Can you hear that?'

They stood stock still and listened. At first all Arielle could hear was the rustling of the leaves in the faint breeze, but soon she realised that there were other, different sounds coming from a hundred metres or so ahead. They were the sounds of human activity; of chopping and sawing. The occasional raised voice floated through the trees towards the two girls standing there in a pool of grey light.

'What's happening?' Arielle asked.

'Come. You'll see,' Maki said, taking her arm once again.

At the end of the line of trees they stepped out of the gloom. Arielle realised they'd finally reached the edge of the plantation. She blinked at the sudden sunlight and at what she saw there. In front of them was a scene of constant movement and activity. Dozens of coolies dressed only in loincloths were working there clearing the jungle, chopping at trees and foliage with axes, clearing creepers and bushes by hand, hauling tree trunks with chains towards a great pile on the edge of the clearing. A Frenchman sat on a tree stump, his back to Arielle and Maki, a gun in a holster at his hip and a whip on the ground beside him. He was smoking a cigarette and the smoke floated over to where they stood. From time to time he stood up, waved the whip and yelled at the workmen in a harsh voice, telling them to hurry up, to work faster, to stop slacking.

'They are clearing the jungle,' Maki explained, 'to plant more rubber trees. There is no end to the demand for rubber for the west.'

'Look at those poor workers,' Arielle murmured. 'They are so thin.'

It was true. These men all looked malnourished; like the men she'd seen in the latex shed, their ribs were visible beneath their skin. Their bodies all glistened with sweat and many bore cuts and bruises.

Just then, a giant teak tree that two men had been chopping at with an axe began to tilt to one side and fall towards the ground. One of the men shouted urgently, but not quickly enough for another group who had been clearing some creepers near the tree to move away. The tree crashed down, slicing through the undergrowth, bouncing slightly as it landed. An agonised yell went up. Three of the men had managed to jump clear but another had been crushed under one of the bigger branches. He lay there on the forest floor screaming in pain.

The overseer got up, threw down his cigarette and marched over to the scene, shouting at the men who had cut down the tree, yelling at them to move the branch. Soon five men were straining and panting, trying to shift the great tree enough to pull the man out. It took them ten minutes of frantic effort, then finally the unfortunate man was pulled out by the arms. He was still crying and screaming in pain.

'Why didn't you get out of the way?' the overseer yelled at him, then he said impatiently to the others, 'Take him to the hospital, then get back here straight away. We need to finish this patch today.'

Four men carried the injured man across the clearing towards where Arielle and Maki stood watching in horror.

'Quick, get behind this tree.' Maki drew Arielle into the shadows, and they watched in silence as the men struggled past them. They were close enough to smell their sweat and hear the sound of their laboured breathing. Arielle was shocked to see that the man they were carrying was badly injured, one of his legs was completely crushed, the shinbone jutting out at an angle from the skin. His face was white and tears were streaming down his cheeks. A wave of nausea passed through her at the sight of the crushed leg, but she took a deep breath and fought it back. What right had she got to feel sick in the face of what had just happened?

When the men had moved on, Maki said, 'This sort of thing happens every day. This is the most dangerous place on the plantation. The French don't care for the safety of the workers. They know they can replace injured or dead men easily. And they do that with the help of men like your husband.'

Arielle hung her head, guilt and shame filling her heart for being associated with Etienne and his business.

Now, walking towards the pagoda to make offerings to the Buddha, she still felt the pain of that shame as keenly as she had that morning. After she'd seen the truth of working conditions on the plantation, she passed the rest of her stay in the guest house in turmoil. When Etienne returned from his trip to the other plantations, she could hardly bear to look at him, let alone allow him to touch her. She pretended she was feeling unwell and asked him to sleep in the other bedroom. It wasn't far from the truth. She felt sick to the core and lay awake staring into the darkness, imagining the four communists, their skin covered in cuts and bruises, cowering on their knees, chained together in a clearing in the middle of the plantation, being beaten to death with clubs and sticks by Bertrand's henchmen. Had Bertrand and Etienne been there watching, egging them on? She went hot and cold at the thought that her husband, the man she'd loved and committed her life to, could have done something like that.

But now she forced those memories to the back of her mind. She needed to focus on being fully present when she made her offerings at the altar in front of the pagoda. She stepped forward and laid the flowers beside the gifts of food and flowers that were already there. Then she took a stick of incense, lit it from one of the candles flickering there and put it in a pot for its scent to mingle with the perfume of the other sticks already burning there. She stepped back and sat down to meditate. It was harder than ever to still her mind that day, and no matter how hard she tried to focus on her breathing, shocking thoughts kept thrusting themselves to the forefront of her mind. She persisted for a long time, dimly aware of others coming to make offerings and sit beside her. Finally, she gave up and got to her feet, vowing to return the next day to try again.

As she left the temple area and walked towards the gate, someone touched her arm. She knew who it was before she turned to look and sure enough it was Xan. He was peering at her with that intense, concerned look of his.

'Good morning, Madame Garnier, how are you today?' he asked rather formally, his eyes grave. 'You look a little pale. Are you unwell?'

She shook her head. 'No, not unwell.'

She began to walk towards the gate again, unsure what to make of the swirl of emotions that meeting him again had set off in her heart.

'Not unwell, but troubled perhaps?'

She fell silent and dropped her gaze to the ground ahead of her. How perceptive he was, or was it so obvious that anyone would have noticed? She shrugged. What was the point in hiding it?

'I noticed you haven't been here for a few days. Have you been on a business trip with your husband, perhaps?'

Miserably she nodded, hanging her head.

'Would you like to join me in the café for tea again?' he asked. 'It might help to talk about it.'

She stopped and looked into his eyes. He was right. It would help to talk. She was bursting to speak to someone about what she'd seen, but who could she tell? At least this man would understand. So once again she followed him past the tea stalls to the one at the far end, where tea was served by the smiling proprietor. When Xan had poured and handed Arielle a cup, he said, 'So, tell me about it. You went to the south, didn't you? Tell me what you saw there.'

She began to speak, and once she'd started, the words she'd been bottling up for days tumbled from her lips. She told him all about the working conditions she'd observed, the state of the workers, the beatings, the graveyard and the accident in the jungle. And as she spoke, he sat there nodding gravely, occasionally shaking his head or clicking his tongue in disgust. When she'd finished, he held his hand up to her cheek and wiped away a tear. Until that moment she hadn't realised that she'd been crying.

'Thank you for telling me this, Madame Garnier. You are aware now, aren't you, what sort of man your husband is. That knowledge must be very painful for you to bear, but you don't need to worry anymore. I think I know how to help you.'

9

HANOI, MARCH, 1945

Arielle crouched on the boards underneath the windows of the first-floor office in the Hanoi Mairie for a long time, her back against the wall, sobbing uncontrollably. She was alone in the cavernous room apart from the two Japanese guards on the door and the body of Pierre Thibaut which lay in an expanding pool of blood just a couple of metres from where she crouched.

She couldn't stop thinking of Papa's face as he'd been shoved up the steps and into the back of the lorry by the Japanese soldiers, the fear and despair in his eyes as he'd glanced up at her at the window for one last time. She'd tried to convey to him as their eyes locked together that she would do everything she could to find him, to get him released and bring him home again, but had he understood? She thought about Camille, too, her clothes dishevelled, her blonde hair tumbling about her shoulders, being prodded along with the rest of the French office-workers at the point of a bayonet. Arielle felt helpless, terrified, and very alone. Part of her wished that the soldiers had taken her too. Then maybe she would have been able to stay with Papa so he wouldn't have to face what was coming alone. Whatever would happen to him? He was weak and frail. He should have retired a long time ago and have been safe at home instead of here in the HQ of the French Colonial Government when the soldiers arrived. But he loved the work and had insisted on carrying on.

She lost track of time and had no idea of how long she'd sat there, tears streaming down her face, but eventually it dawned on her that the guards were still on the door for a reason. Did it mean that the rest of the soldiers were intending to return? Suddenly, she realised that she should try to get home before they appeared. Later, she would try to find out where Papa and the others had been taken. Once she'd resolved to make a move, she wanted to be out of the building as quickly as she could. She scrambled to her feet, and, keeping her eyes averted from Pierre's body, made her way between the desks to the double doors where the guards stood. Her heart was hammering as she drew closer. She could already see the staircase beyond, only a few steps to freedom.

One of the guards put out a hand to stop her as she tried to pass.

'Where you go?' he asked sternly.

'I need to get home,' she said without looking into his eyes. Her voice was tremulous with fear.

'You can*not* go,' the soldier said pushing her back into the room.

'But why? I am Annamese, not French. I am surely free to leave here?'

He shook his head. 'You are not free,' he said, and she wondered what he meant.

'Please,' she began, a sob catching in her voice. 'There is no reason for me to stay...' but even as she said that she heard the sound of an engine outside, footsteps on the front steps and the doors to the building being torn open violently, slamming against the walls. Then came the sound of boots on the stairs. Several Japanese soldiers appeared at once, and she sensed from the swaggering way they walked, by the fact that they were followed by a retinue and by the way the guards on the door stiffened and stood to attention, that these were important men.

She stood aside as they swept into the room. The man at the front was stony-faced and held a rigid, commanding air. He wore a peaked cap and elaborate uniform, decorated with many coloured medals. The two others were half a step behind him, followed by four ordinary soldiers in khaki uniforms and simple caps, their rifles drawn.

The three officers stopped in the middle of the room and conferred briefly, then one of them turned and shouted at the guards on the door, pointing to Pierre's body. The guards sprang into action, hurried to where the body was, picked him up by his hands and feet and dragged him unceremoniously out of the room. The commanding officer wandered around the room briefly, running his hand over typewriters, over papers left on desks, occasionally picking something up and peering at it closely. Finally, he settled himself behind the biggest desk in the room and swept everything off the surface. Papers, pens, ink pots, paper clips, photographs, all tumbled to the floor. He barked some orders to the soldiers who immediately rushed over and dropped to the floor to remove the clutter. The other two officers also found themselves desks in the room. Arielle watched, pressed against the wall, her heart beating fast, dreading the moment when they would notice her standing there.

It came when the commanding officer lifted his eyes from the desk and looked around the room. They widened as he caught sight of Arielle.

'Come here, girl,' he said in broken French. Slowly,

shaking from head to foot, she walked towards him. 'Vite, vite,' he said and she sped up, stumbling over an upturned chair.

'Who are you?' he asked, and she knew that it would be fatal to give her proper name, which would give away the fact that she was half French.

'My name is Tuyen, sir,' she said thinking quickly, 'Tuyen Nguyen.' She gave her mother's name, saying a hasty prayer to her long dead mother, asking her to understand.

'What do you do here?'

'I am a secretary, sir. I type letters mainly, and I file papers.'

'I need a secretary,' he said. 'One who can speak both French and Annamese. You can do that, I assume?'

She nodded slowly, not able to look him in the face, a sinking dread in her heart. How could she work here for this man? For the enemy? She'd heard many tales of Japanese brutality and cruelty over the years they'd occupied Indochina.

'You will be my secretary, Miss Nguyen. I am General Nishihara, Commanding Officer of all of Tonkin and Annam. Make no mistake, you are honoured to be offered to work for the Imperial Japanese Army.'

She had no idea what to say in response, but realised he was pausing, waiting for some acknowledgement of his words. She bowed her head, hoping he would read this as a respectful gesture.

'You may go home now and tomorrow morning you will report to me here at eight o'clock sharp. Where is your home, Miss Nguyen? Tell me your address.'

Haltingly, she began to give her address, but after she started, she wondered if the general would know that the street was in the French district? Should she give a false address, or the address of Bà Ngoại's old apartment in the Old Quarter instead? She decided that wasn't a good idea.

Although her grandmother had passed away, Arielle didn't want to bring any trouble to her neighbours. So, she gave her own address. She watched as the general wrote it down in Japanese script.

'Eight o'clock tomorrow,' he said, peering at her without expression. 'If you don't come, my soldiers will hunt you down and bring you here, so don't be tempted to try to run away.'

She stared at him, her mouth open, about to protest, but deep down she knew that any objections would fall on deaf ears and may make things worse for her in the long run. But there was one thing she needed desperately to find out. She knew she was taking a risk to ask and that doing so could backfire on her, but she couldn't go home without at least trying.

'Sir,' she began, 'I'm wondering if you are able to tell me where my colleagues have been taken?' She tried her best to keep her voice steady, to look him in the eye rather than dropping her gaze to the floor as she would have preferred. Once again, her heart was beating hard and the blood surging in her ears.

'Colleagues? You mean the French office workers?' there was incredulity in his tone. 'I do not know, and it does not matter. They are enemies. Do not ask again. It is not your concern.'

'Some of them are old and unwell, sir,' she said, knowing it was probably risky to push this, but unable to stop herself.

The general thumped on the table with his fist.

'What do you care? The French are colonists. They mistreat your people.'

She hung her head, not trusting herself to reply.

In the end he said, 'The Japanese Imperial Army treats its prisoners well. They will be looked after.'

It would arouse suspicion to persist, she sensed that she'd

already gone further than was wise, so, she simply bowed again and turned away from him. Collecting her bag from beside her desk, it crossed her mind how much had changed since she'd arrived at the office this morning in her carefree state, thinking it would just be another humdrum work day. Still trembling, she walked to the door where the guards still stood, rifles cocked. As she crossed the room, she did her best to avoid stepping on the broad streak of blood left on the boards when Pierre's body had been dragged across the room.

Outside in the square, she stepped over broken barriers and bushes that had been uprooted and destroyed in the brief battle between French and Japanese forces. Glancing to the other side, she was relieved to see that the bodies of the French soldiers had been removed at least, but there were still patches of dark blood on the paving stones where they had fallen. Setting off towards home, she saw that there was evidence that fighting had taken place everywhere in these streets. Debris and rubbish were strewn about, damaged vehicles blocked the roads in many places, and shopkeepers were hard at work sweeping up broken glass and mending shopfronts.

As she walked, picking her way through the debris on the pavements, she tried to figure out what to do about Papa. She was no closer to finding out where he, Camille and the others had been taken, but she couldn't go on without knowing. Making her way through the devastated streets, as her heart stopped pumping quite so fast, she realised that she was weak with hunger. She had no idea how many hours had passed since she'd eaten breakfast, but from the position of the sun above the buildings she guessed that it was probably late afternoon.

Turning in at the end of her road, she half expected the townhouse to have been damaged in the fighting, with broken windows or doors kicked in, like so many buildings she'd passed on the road. But there it stood, with its pale yellow walls, deep pink bougainvillea climbing over its black wrought iron balconies. Her heart leapt to see it there and she ran the few steps along the road to the front door and let herself inside.

'Is that you, Arielle?' It was Trang, the old housekeeper. Arielle ran into the kitchen and threw herself into Trang's arms, tears of relief streaming down her face.

'The Japanese have seized the Mairie,' she sobbed. 'They came with guns. Papa and everyone else were taken away by the soldiers in a lorry. I don't know where they took him.'

Trang gasped in shock and shook her head at the news, but she put her arms around Arielle and ushered her towards the kitchen table.

'Come and sit down my child. I will bring you some hot soup. You look very pale. What a terrifying time you must have had. Your poor, poor father too.'

Arielle did as she was told. She sat down at the table and watched Trang at the stove ladling soup and noodles into a bowl. Just the sight of the old lady going about her work brought back memories of her childhood and comfort to Arielle's frazzled mind. Trang was the nearest thing she'd had to a mother down the years and Arielle loved her unconditionally. They'd grown even closer since Bà Ngoại passed away peacefully just before the war. Trang brought the steaming bowl over and put it on the table, then she sat down opposite Arielle.

'Eat, little one,' she said gently, and once Arielle had started spooning the nourishing liquid into her mouth, Trang leaned forward and looked into her eyes.

'I think I might know where your father and the other French workers could have been taken,' she said. 'There was a lot of talk of it in Hang Da market earlier when I went to buy vegetables. Some of the stallholders had been speaking to people who'd seen where the Japanese took the prisoners.'

Arielle put her spoon down. 'So where, Trang? Tell me where they went?'

'To the Citadel at Thang Long. There has been fighting all over Hanoi, all over the country, my child. Many, many French and colonial soldiers have been captured and imprisoned there. They are being held by the Japanese in that old building. It is possible that your father was taken there too.'

'Poor, poor Papa,' Arielle murmured with a shudder, thinking of the grim, stone building with its fortified towers and walls, with only narrow slits for windows, surrounded by fences topped with coiled barbed wire. However would he cope in that cold, forbidding place? How would he survive, old and frail as he was?

'I must go to him,' she said, standing up, but Trang grabbed her hand.

'Sit down child. Do not be hasty. You need to eat first and think carefully about what you're planning. These are dangerous times. Ask yourself this; would going there put you and your father in more danger than you are in already?'

Arielle thought about the Citadel again. She'd been there once on a school trip aged twelve or thirteen. She and her classmates had been shepherded around the building and the starkly formal grounds by Mademoiselle Touran, their strict history teacher. 'The first buildings here were built by the Ly Dynasty in 1010,' the teacher had barked. 'Hardly any of that remains. It was the seat of Vietnamese emperors until the capital was moved to Hué in the early 19th century.'

Arielle had wandered around the ancient buildings, awestruck by the sense of history evoked there, trying to imagine elaborately robed courtiers and mandarins wandering through its courtyards and passages. But it was hardly more than a ruin, inhospitable and stark, not the sort of place that an old man could easily survive imprisonment. Tears stung her eyes just thinking about it, but Trang was right. Impulsive moves could put both her and her father in more danger than they were in already.

But then an idea struck her.

'Perhaps I could take some food there in a caddy. I could say that I was a servant, see if they would give it to Papa for me.'

The old lady's face became serious while she thought about the proposal. 'I suppose that's not such a bad idea,' she said after a pause. 'Perhaps I will cook up your father's favourite chicken broth.'

WHEN THE CYCLO drew close to the heavy, wooden gates of the Citadel, Arielle was dismayed to see that they were shut and barred, with four Japanese soldiers guarding them, rifles drawn. She asked the cyclo rider to wait for her a little way down the road and walked along the pavement towards the soldiers, carrying the tiered caddy of broth, still steaming hot, that Trang had cooked and ladled in a few minutes before. Her knees were quaking as she approached the gates, but none of the soldiers so much as turned their heads to look at her. She went up to the first one and said, her voice shaking with nerves, 'I have brought this food for my master, Monsieur Dupont. Is he inside? Could you give it to him please?'

The soldier briefly glanced in her direction.

'No Français,' he said, then shouted something in Japanese and waved her away from the gate.

'Please,' she said. 'Please. Give this to Monsieur Dupont. I beg you.'

The soldier's eyes darted from side to side and then, to Arielle's surprise he put out his hand and grabbed the handle of the caddy, snatching it from her.

'Will you give it to Monsieur Dupont, please?' she repeated.

'You go now,' he said, putting the caddy on the ground and thrusting his rifle towards her. She turned and fled back to the cyclo and scrambled onto the seat.

'Back to Boulevard Rialan. Quickly please.'

As the cyclo rider sped her through the devastated streets, her heartbeat gradually began to slow down. She went over and over the brief but shocking encounter with the soldier. Had he understood who the food was for? Would he give it to Papa? Or would he eat it himself, or even empty the broth down a nearby drain and kick the caddy under the bushes? She guessed she would never know, but she had to hold on to the hope that her father had received the food and while that hope remained, she would keep on taking it to him.

After a restless night, she rose early the next morning and dressed as demurely as she could. She was so worried about what the coming day might bring that her hands were clumsy and her routine took a lot longer than usual. Trang had stayed the night to keep her company. She must have got up early to cook Arielle pho soup with noodles for breakfast. The delicious smells floated upstairs to the bedroom, calling her down. But when she got downstairs and sat at the table to eat, Arielle found it difficult to force the breakfast down, her stomach was so churned up with nerves. She was grateful to Trang and didn't want to offend her, so she did her best. When she'd eaten as much as she could, she picked up her bag and slipped on her sandals ready for the walk to work. Trang gathered her in her arms and hugged her tight.

'Good luck, my child,' she said, and from the sound of her voice, Arielle could tell that the old housekeeper was as apprehensive as she was about her work at Japanese HQ.

She took her usual route to work and was struck by how much had changed in the past twenty-four hours. Gone was the hustle and bustle that was normal in the Hanoi rush hour. The streets were virtually empty now. No stallholders were out on the pavements setting up shop, shouting about their wares; it seemed that people were terrified to come out of their homes. Those who were out were still clearing up from the battle, sweeping debris from the road, pushing damaged vehicles off the carriageway, mending broken windows, clearing away shrubs that had been uprooted in the struggle. Normally the streets were choked with traffic, but today few vehicles passed her – only a couple of lonely cyclo riders touting for trade.

She approached the Mairie walking along the side of Hoan Kiem lake. From a distance the building looked just as it always had – an imposing, white stucco reminder of the strength and dominance of the French imperialists. But no more, she thought. Indochina had new masters, its former leaders banished into captivity. As she drew closer to the imposing building, her heart began to beat faster. The Mairie was guarded by Japanese soldiers at every entrance and several armoured vehicles were drawn up on the courtyard outside. There was no doubting the military strength of the new rulers.

A soldier stopped her at the door, barring her entrance with his rifle.

'Papiers,' he barked.

She realised that her papers were in her real name, not the name she had given the general, so she couldn't give him those without revealing her French identity. Thinking quickly, she shook her head and spread her hands out indicating that she had none.

'Why you here?' he asked, frowning deeply.

She replied quickly, 'I am here to work for General Nishihara.' She tried to mime typing in the air with her hands. He nodded curtly and spoke to his colleague who disappeared inside the building. When the soldier returned a few minutes later he nodded her through.

'Tomorrow you bring papers,' said the first soldier sternly and as she passed him and started up the steps towards the office, she wondered how she'd be able to achieve that.

General Nishihara was seated behind the great desk when she entered the high-ceilinged room on the first floor. The streak of blood from where they'd dragged Pierre's body across the parquet floor had been cleaned away and the room was tidy now. In fact, the general and his colleagues looked so at home, quietly poring over papers on their desks, it was almost as if they had always been there.

'Here girl,' said the general, motioning her to his desk and handing her a sheaf of handwritten notes. 'Type these papers up for me. My French is not good, so I expect you to make it better.'

As she took the papers from him, she noticed with dismay that his eyes lingered on her breasts, despite her having dressed in a blouse which buttoned up to the throat and a calf-length skirt. She'd heard many stories of native women assaulted by Japanese soldiers, but she'd hoped that the general would be above that. Seeing his lascivious look now was a reminder to her that she needed to be very careful.

Throughout that day, many communications about troop movements in Indochina crossed her desk and she realised that what Trang had told her the previous day had been true. The fighting between the Japanese and the French colonial army wasn't confined to Hanoi, but had spread right through the country, to all the major cities, regional capitals and French garrisons. She knew from rumours that had been circulating around the Mairie for weeks, that although the Japanese had allowed the French to retain power when they'd invaded in 1940, they'd recently grown suspicious of their allegiances and were worried about an Allied invasion. So that must be why they were seizing back power in a well-co-ordinated coup. From what Arielle read in the general's papers, she knew that it was called Meigo Sakusen or Operation Bright Moon and she realised that it wasn't quite over yet. The French were putting up strong resistance in some cities and along the northern frontier with China.

All day she typed away, trying to keep her head down and not draw attention to herself, but once, when she went to use the bathroom along the corridor, general Nishihara was waiting for her when she came out. He came towards her, that lecherous smile playing on his lips again.

'Thank you for your work, Miss Nguyen,' he said. 'I can see already that it is good.'

He stepped closer trapping her against the wall with his great bulk and to her horror he put his hand on her breast. For a second she was frozen with terror and revulsion, but then anger took over and with an effort she slid out from behind him and ran as fast as she could back to the safety of the office, her heart in her mouth. When he strolled back in a few minutes later, casually adjusting his jacket, it was as if nothing had happened. He brought some more reports to her desk for typing, just as he had been doing throughout the morning and spoke to her in an expressionless voice.

The day wore on without further incident and watching the clock at the end of the room, Arielle wondered when she would be allowed to leave. But at six o'clock sharp all the officers got up from their desks and began to gather their belongings.

'You may go now, Miss Nguyen,' the general said as he swept past her on his way out. 'Be back tomorrow morning, eight o'clock sharp.'

Sighing with relief she pulled the cover over the typewriter and went to the window to check that the three men had climbed into their waiting limousines, before leaving the building herself.

Instead of going straight home, she hailed a passing cyclo and asked him to take her to West Lake and to the Tran Quoc pagoda, hoping against hope that it would have escaped damage in the battle and the attention of the Japanese forces. Over the past ten years she'd developed the routine of visiting the pagoda several times a week to meditate and present offerings to the Buddha. And even though her grandmother had now passed away, she still went there alone. Her faith had grown and developed from those shaky beginnings in 1935 and now she welcomed the peace and sense of belonging that the temple and its community offered. She bought lotus flowers and incense as usual from the stallholder who was now an old friend, and made her way towards the pagoda in the fading light, pausing to exchange a few words with the monk on the gate and to remove her shoes.

But as she walked along the promontory towards the pagoda, a stranger approached her. He touched her arm and drew her aside.

'Madame Garnier? I need to speak to you urgently.'

A shiver went through her. How did he know her name? This was all horribly familiar and gave her an instant sense of déjà vu. For a bewildering second the thought had crossed her mind that this man was Xan. But it couldn't possibly be Xan. She knew that really.

'We know you are working for the Japanese,' the man said. There was something threatening in his tone that set her nerves on edge.

'Not through choice,' she replied drawing herself up. 'If I don't do what they say, they will punish me. My father has been taken to prison and I don't want him to suffer...'

'It's all right. It is a good thing,' the man said, patting her arm again. 'Keep on working for them. It is useful for us.'

'And who are you?' She looked at him, trying to remember if she'd seen him before. He was in his forties, his face heavily lined, a jagged scar running down his forehead. She would have remembered if she had.

The man smiled briefly, but there was no humour or warmth in his eyes. 'We are the Viet Minh,' he said. 'Our aim is to free the Vietnamese people from colonial rule, either French or Japanese. We want you to help us. You are working for General Nishihara, aren't you?'

She nodded slowly, wondering how they'd found that out so quickly.

'That's good. Now, we want you to bring us information from his headquarters. Anything you see about Japanese troop movements, battle plans, maps. You must surely come across such things during your work.'

She stared at him, her heart pounding. This would put her in even more danger than she was already in.

'I'm not sure...'

The man now squeezed her arm – a little tighter than was necessary. He came closer and hissed, 'You don't have a choice about this, Madame Garnier.'

'Really?' she asked defiantly, annoyed by his presumption, trying to step away from him. 'And what if I refuse?'

He put his face close to hers and whispered in her ear, 'You forget. We have very close links with the communists, and many of them were around here ten years ago and know what happened then. We know your secret, Madame Garnier. Your dark secret, and we're quite sure you wouldn't want that information to go any further. Especially not to your new Japanese masters, would you now?'

She looked into his cold black eyes, horrified at his words.

'Meet me here tomorrow at the same time and make sure you bring all the information you can from Japanese HQ. Failing in this task is not an option. As I've explained, there would be severe consequences for you. Look upon it as a chance to serve your country. You should feel honoured to be given the opportunity.'

With that, he turned on his heel and walked away from the pagoda, pausing only briefly to slip his shoes on at the gate, then, nodding to the monk, he strode on through the archway and disappeared from view.

Arielle turned away and hurried on towards the pagoda, shockwaves still coursing through her, tears blinding her eyes. The lotus flowers hung limp in her hands, she'd crushed the stalks without realising it during the brief exchange with the man. What a fool she'd been, thinking that everyone had forgotten what had happened. She'd lived such a quiet life in the French Quarter with Papa that she'd been lulled into a false sense of security. But she should have known they would never forget what had happened back in 1935.

Reaching the pagoda, she laid the flowers on the altar and with shaking hands lit her stick of incense. Then she stepped back and sank down into the lotus position to meditate. But after the day she'd had and the terrifying encounter with the man, it was impossible to clear her mind. She bent her head forward and gave in to the thoughts that had plagued her on and off for almost ten years and once she'd invited them in, the memories came flooding back unchecked.

10

HANOI, 1935

After Arielle and Etienne returned from their trip to the plantations in the south, her days fell into a regular routine. If Etienne was working in Hanoi, he would leave the house early to go to his office and Arielle would be left to spend the day on her own. There was little to do in the house. Her pile of books was gathering dust in her wardrobe, but she had no inclination to study. Etienne had gently rebuffed all talk of her going to the Sorbonne the following year, putting up objection after objection, so after a while she hardly dared to bring the subject up. If there was no chance of going to university, what was the point in reading the books?

Unlike when she'd lived at her father's house, here she had no household chores. Etienne's servants were polite but unfriendly, and their obvious awkwardness discouraged Arielle from going anywhere near the kitchen. How she missed Trang, with whom she used to chat for hours while they chopped onions and garlic at the kitchen table.

So, during those days, she found herself setting off to take the short walk through the French Quarter back to her childhood home far more often than was natural for a newlywed. She was drawn to the comfort of the big old kitchen and the homely living room with its bright pictures and floor cushions, where she could relax and be herself. Mostly, she visited during the daytime, and Trang would give her the latest gossip from the neighbourhood, but sometimes, if she stayed late in the afternoon, Papa would return from the office. He was often distant with her, his eyes preoccupied with that faraway look she knew meant he was worried about something.

'What's wrong, Papa?' she asked one day.

'Oh, nothing my dear, nothing really. It's just that things at work are a little tense at the moment.'

'Oh really?'

'Hmm. Nothing for you to worry about though.'

'But if you're worried, I'm worried too. I don't like to see you unhappy, Papa.'

'You don't need to worry about me, my darling,' he said, patting her hand and for a time she left the subject alone. She didn't want to press him if he didn't want to speak about it, but at the same time, she felt a wave of sadness that her father wasn't confiding in her. They'd always been so close. But then, as she was reflecting, she realised that she was keeping things from him too. So far, she had not had the courage to tell him about what she'd seen on the rubber plantation, of the horrors that had unfolded there. She wasn't sure what was holding her back. Was she shielding Papa from the shock of knowing the truth, or was she subconsciously protecting Etienne? She didn't analyse her motives too closely, but she did know that what she'd seen there haunted her night and day. Hardly an hour passed without the vision of those cowed, desperately thin workers entering her thoughts, their skin blemished with cuts and bruises, their cheeks hollow, toiling away in the jungle or in the latex sheds.

The only person who did understand, and with whom she could speak freely was Xan. She met him almost daily now on her visits to the pagoda on the lake and they usually took tea together after making their offerings to the Buddha. He encouraged her to talk about what she'd seen in the south, and she knew that he took that information away to report it back to his comrades in the Communist Party. It didn't matter to her. She was glad that the information she was giving him might be a catalyst for change. When she spoke about what she'd seen on the plantation, she saw the fury in his eyes and his fists clench on the table.

'They killed the four communists,' she said quietly. 'I saw their graves.'

'I knew all those men,' Xan muttered, his voice unsteady with emotion. 'They were all incredibly brave. They were willing to die for the cause. Their deaths shouldn't go unpunished.'

She wondered what he meant by that and sipped her tea quietly. The force of his reactions unsettled her, but she understood that he felt passionately about the plight of the plantation workers. The four communists had died in the most brutal manner, beaten to death, murdered in secret there on the plantation, without any sort of trial or a chance to defend themselves.

'I'd like to meet your husband,' Xan said suddenly, and she put her cup down and looked into his eyes.

'Why?' she asked, surprised. 'What good would that do?'

'I'd like to talk to him, to point out the error of his ways. Get him to understand that the workers he's exploiting are human beings, with their own loves and dreams, hopes and fears. They deserve to be treated with respect and they deserve dignity. I'd like him to understand that.'

She swallowed. She knew exactly what Etienne thought

about the coolies on the plantations. He held them in contempt and had even expressed the view that they were less than human, that their lives were expendable.

'So, would you be able to introduce us?' Xan asked, looking earnestly into her eyes.

'Oh, I don't think that would be a good idea,' Arielle replied quickly with a shudder, her heartbeat speeding up. She could imagine Etienne's reaction to someone like Xan; he would treat him with arrogance and disdain. 'I doubt that he would agree to meet you. And if he did, I don't think he would take any notice of what you have to say.'

Xan shook his head in dismay. 'How can you go on living with someone like that? You've seen what his work involves with your own eyes. What more proof do you need?'

'I don't know. I can't explain,' she said, hanging her head. She couldn't bear to look into Xan's eyes and see the disappointment there. Her deepening friendship with him meant more to her every day. She depended on these meetings to be able to speak her mind, to offload her anxieties. He was strong and decisive, and she admired his high principles and everything he stood for. She was vaguely aware that she was getting too fond of him, but then nothing felt right in her life at that moment. After all, she'd committed to spend her life with a man who was no better than a slave trader. It was hardly surprising that she was drawn to this enigmatic man who was her husband's opposite in every way.

'If he asks you to go with him again,' Xan went on, 'you should definitely do so. It seems you might need reminding of what is happening on those plantations. You ought to go to the north with him too, to Tonkin, to see what methods he employs to persuade people to leave their homes and go down south for a life of toil.'

Later, as they parted at the temple entrance, he drew her

close and brushed his cheek against hers, before leaving her and walking quickly away. It left her heart racing and her head spinning with confusion as she stood on the pavement waiting for a cyclo. She watched him make his way down Than Nien Road, in the shade of the plane trees, his head held high, his shoulders proudly square. Already her heart ached at the parting, and she couldn't wait to see him the next day.

That evening, at dinner, Etienne said, putting aside his newspaper, 'I need to travel up to Haiphong tomorrow, chéri, so I'll be away for a few days again I'm afraid.'

She looked up. In some ways this was good news. It would be good to be relieved of the strain of being with Etienne for a while, of the ordeal of sleeping with him at night, when his touch sent her flesh crawling, but she'd run out of excuses to refuse his advances.

'Unless you'd like to come with me, of course,' he added. 'It was good having you with me when you came to the plantation. And if you did come, you wouldn't have to be alone here.'

She thought about Xan's words, urging her to go with Etienne on his trips. This was surely the perfect opportunity. 'Alright,' she said. 'I'll come.'

'Good. We'll need to be up quite early. I want to catch the seven o'clock train.'

Panic swept through her then. There was no time to let Xan know that she was going to be away for a few days. He would go to the pagoda in the morning, expecting to see her there. What would he think when she didn't turn up? Would he assume that his brief kiss on their parting had scared her off? How could she let him know that she would be away? She didn't even know where he lived. All these thoughts swirled through her mind, but as she finished her meal, she had an idea.

'I need to go and see Bà Ngoại,' she said to Etienne, getting up from the table.

'What, now? It's dark outside. Surely you shouldn't be going into the Old Quarter at this time?'

'It's just that... I promised I would visit her tomorrow. She'll wonder what has happened to me. She hasn't been well lately.'

Etienne sighed and picked up his newspaper again. 'Well, go if you must,' he said impatiently. 'But get Tek to take you in the car. It would be safer that way.'

She ran up to her room and scribbled a quick note to Xan explaining that she was going away with Etienne to Haiphong for a few days. Then she went out onto the drive and asked Tek, the chauffeur to drop her on the edge of the Old Quarter. When they arrived at the end of Rue de la Soie, she asked him to wait for her there.

She left the car behind and made her way through the cobbled streets. The night market was in full swing. Colourful street stalls were lit up with oil lamps and candles and the streets were crowded with shoppers and stallholders, the air filled with the smell of charcoal fires and cooking spices. She hadn't seen Bà Ngoại for a couple of days and, as she elbowed her way through the crowds, she hoped the old lady wasn't smoking opium again. Each time they met Arielle did her best to persuade Bà Ngoại to give it up but without success.

'I'm too old for it to harm me now, child,' Bà Ngoại always said. 'Leave me be. Let me enjoy my last years. I will die soon anyway.'

As usual she waved at Diep, the woman in the silk shop beneath Bà Ngoại's apartment as she passed, climbed the narrow, wooden staircase and knocked on her grandmother's door. There was no response. She tried again and when there was no answer, she tried the handle and let herself into the apartment. Switching on the light, she wandered around, hoping that Bà Ngoại wasn't ill, lying unconscious somewhere in the dark, but it didn't take her long to discover that the place was empty. Bà Ngoại's opium pipe stood empty beside an ashtray on the little table, but apart from that the rooms were clean and tidy. She closed the door and went down to the silk shop and asked Diep if she'd seen her grandmother. The woman looked away.

'She went out earlier,' Diep finally admitted in a quiet voice.

'Do you know where she is? I need to see her this evening. I want to give her a message.'

Diep carried on folding lengths of silk, her face impassive. She didn't reply.

'Please, I need to see her,' Arielle persisted. She knew that she could leave a note for Xan with Diep to give to Bà Ngoại, but she didn't want to do that, she wasn't sure she could trust her, especially not now that Diep was being so unhelpful.

'I'm sure she wouldn't mind your telling me, Diep,' Arielle pleaded. 'She doesn't have secrets from me,' she said, not quite sure, in the present circumstances, that this was completely true.

'All right. I will tell you, but please don't tell her it was me,' said Diep. 'Go to the junction of Rue des Paniers and Rue de Balances. On the corner is a doorway. Go through it and down some steps to a cellar. You will find her there. She often spends her evenings there. But please, I beg of you, don't tell her I told you.'

With a feeling of dread in her heart, Arielle hurried away from the silk shop and on through the busy streets, pushing her way between the stalls and the shoppers, ignoring the shouts and cries of the vendors, until she reached the street corner. There was an old building there, on the end of the terrace of shophouses, facing diagonally to the road. The door was unvarnished and worn, and when she put her hand on the handle, it felt sticky and dirty. She had never been anywhere like this before but she knew that there were many of these establishments tucked away on street corners in Hanoi.

Tentatively, she turned the wobbly handle and pushed the door open. From the sickly, sweet smell that wafted up the steps towards her she knew without a doubt that she was about to enter an opium den. It broke her heart that Bà Ngoại had been reduced to this. Smoking alone was one thing, but frequenting these seedy, desperate places was quite another.

The stairwell was badly lit and the steps uneven and she had to feel her way down by the damp walls. At the bottom, she found herself in a low-ceilinged lobby with doors opening off it. She pushed one open at random and stepped into a fuggy hall filled with a haze of smoke. It was a cavernous room and everywhere around, people lay on low wooden beds, puffing on pipes or completely spaced out, their glazed eyes staring towards the ceiling. Most of the people here were old, or prematurely old, with shabby clothes and haggard features. It tore at Arielle's heart to think that Bà Ngoại was one of these people. She wandered between the beds, looking for her grandmother. An ancient Chinese man with a wispy beard and bloodshot eyes came up to her with a pipe, but she shook her head.

'I am looking for my grandmother,' she said. 'Her name is Hoa Ahn Dao. Do you know her?'

The old man nodded and beckoned her across to the other side of the room. Bà Ngoại was reclining on one of the beds puffing away on a pipe, but her eyes were still focused and clear.

'Bà Ngoại!' Arielle rushed up to her. 'Why are you here?'

Her grandmother's expression fell and she took the pipe from between her lips. She struggled to sit up and the old man seized one of her arms and hauled her into a sitting position.

'Why are you here, Granddaughter? Who told you I was here?'

'I just guessed,' Arielle lied, sitting down on the hard bed beside her. 'When I saw you'd gone out, I had an inkling that you might have come to one of these places. Why do you do it, Grandmother?'

The old lady shook her head. 'It takes me away from everything. Besides, it is legal. The government encourages it, there is nothing to stop me.'

'It's legal because the government get taxes from opium, Bà Ngoại, surely you know that? You've fallen into their trap. It ruins lives. It's ruining your life, can't you see that?'

Bà Ngoại looked into Arielle's eyes and took her hand. 'My life is almost over, child. It doesn't matter anymore. I've lost my daughter and I've lost you too, to that slave trader. I've nothing to keep me going other than this.'

She sank back onto the cushions and her eyelids began to flutter. She was fading fast.

'Bà Ngoại, I've been meeting your friend, Xan at the temple lately. Could you give him a note from me tomorrow morning? Here...' she took the hastily scribbled note from her pocket and pressed it into Bà Ngoại's hand. 'I have to go away to Haiphong tomorrow, but I will be back in a couple of days. Could you give this to him, please?'

A smile spread slowly across Bà Ngoại's lips. She took the note and put it inside her trouser pocket.

'Of course I will give it to him, Ari. I'm so pleased you've been meeting him. I told him you would help him.'

'Help him? You told him I would help him? What with? Why?'

But Bà Ngoại was slipping away now, her eyelids flickering, her body was growing limp and she was sinking into a stupor. Arielle got up, propped Bà Ngoại's pillow behind her head, kissed the old lady on the forehead, and walked back through the opium hall towards the door. What did Bà Ngoại mean by her words? Had Xan only befriended her because he thought he could use her? Disappointment flooded through her. She'd thought they were friends, that he enjoyed her company, but perhaps he was only showing her friendship for the information that she might bring him about Etienne and about the plantations.

Hardly noticing her surroundings, she went out through the warped door and climbed the broken staircase towards the street, trying to come to terms with what she'd just heard. The indignation she'd first felt was quickly fading though. Did it really matter anyway if Xan was using her? She liked his company and she admired him too. It was enough to be able to meet him at the temple and spend time with him. She was flattered by the attention from such an intelligent, high-minded man. What did it matter if his motives weren't quite as pure as she'd first imagined?

11

HAIPHONG, TONKIN, 1935

At six forty-five the next morning, Etienne's shiny black Citroën nosed its way through the jumble of cyclos, handcarts and bullock carts that clogged the entrance to the elegant white building that was Hanoi station. The chauffeur leaned out of the window and banged his hand on the car door, yelling at cyclo riders, bullock cart drivers and coolies to make way for his vehicle. At last they drew up at the front steps of the station building. The chauffeur took their cases from the boot, and they followed him across the crowded concourse towards the train waiting at platform 3. He waved their tickets at the collector and walked down the train to the first-class compartments where he handed the suitcases to a uniformed guard.

Once inside the carriage, Arielle settled back on the plush upholstery and closed her eyes. She hadn't slept well the previous night, what with worrying about Bà Ngoại and Xan, and her usual recurring anxieties about Etienne. Perhaps the train journey would give her a chance to catch up on some rest. Etienne opened some papers on the table between them and started poring over them. Arielle glanced down at them and realised that they were transportation permits from the colonial government and that her father's signature was at the bottom of each.

Seeing her looking, Etienne said, 'Your father has been less than helpful over these past weeks. I've had to use significant persuasion to get him to sign off on these.'

'Significant persuasion? What does that mean?' she asked, her scalp tingling with alarm.

'I've had to pay him a couple of visits at his office, and I've had to get the governor-general involved too. Your father came up with some cock and bull story that I hadn't complied with the terms of previous permits. It was partly true, but I really thought that he and I had an understanding... what with him being family. The governor-general soon put him straight on the matter, I can tell you.'

'Oh dear...' she murmured.

That explained why Papa had looked so preoccupied over the past few days and weeks. And it explained too why he was reluctant to talk about it. Clearly, he didn't want to share anything with her that might infer criticism of her husband.

'Oh dear is a bit of an understatement,' Etienne snapped. 'My whole reputation, and my whole business rests on these permits. How can I supply the plantations in the south, which are crying out for extra labour, if I don't have them? It's not the time for a nit-picking attitude.'

'I'm sure Papa has just been doing his job. He is very conscientious,' Arielle countered.

'A bit *too* conscientious in my book,' Etienne muttered. 'I thought marrying his daughter would put paid to his attitude problems, but clearly not.'

'What?' she felt the colour drain from her face.

'Well, it stands to reason. There had to be some benefits.'

'*Some* benefits?' she asked, her mouth dry with shock. 'To what?'

'To marrying someone of mixed race, when I could have had my pick of all the French women in Hanoi.'

'Etienne!'

The shock of his words took the breath from her body. Had he married her in order to curry favour with her father? Surely not. He'd been in love with her, and at that time she'd been in love with him too, in her own naïve way. Or had his courtship all been an act, to secure closer links with an official at the heart of the colonial regime? That seemed more and more likely now. Added to that, this was the second time in less than twelve hours that she'd found out that someone had been getting to know her for reasons other than the pleasure of her company.

Anger and hurt coursed through her. She had half a mind to get off the train and run home to Papa's house, but the train was already moving, sliding out of the station and on through the centre of Hanoi, running parallel to the Boulevard d'Henri Orleans, where the stationary traffic stood steaming in the early morning rush hour, past the great Citadel with its high, forbidding walls, then on along a high embankment above rickety buildings and rubbish strewn streets. On past ware-houses and slum dwellings, their wooden roofs rotting and covered in moss. The engine gave a great blast of the horn and then they were crossing the Red River, rumbling across a great bridge of iron girders. The sound of the wheels on the metal bridge was deafening. Arielle stared out of the window. A road ran beside the railway track across the bridge. Carts, cyclos and motor scooters clogged the highway. Below swirled the Red River, its water stained red-brown by the silt washed down from the delta.

Soon they were across the river and running between flat

paddy fields fringed with palm trees, where farmers waded in conical hats. Beyond the emerald-green plane, far, far in the distance, Arielle could just make out the grey shape of the mountains in the early morning mist. She looked out at the flat rice paddies, thinking how similar the landscape here was to the fields around Saigon, that they'd driven through on their way to the plantation. But how much more she knew now than she had then.

She clenched her fists, trying to suppress the anger she felt at Etienne's admission. She wasn't just angry with him though, she was angry with herself. How could she have not realised that he only wanted her to get to her father? And how had Papa not seen it either? They had both been equally blinded by Etienne's charm, designed to draw them in and to throw them off the scent. This new knowledge made her even more determined to get to the bottom of Etienne's business, to find out exactly what he was up to in Haiphong and to take that information back to Xan. That way, at least some good might come from her unwise marriage.

The train journey only took a few hours. Once they were underway, a steward brought them coffee and croissants, but apart from that, Etienne barely looked up from his papers. Arielle spent most of the trip wrestling with her thoughts and worries, and before long they were rolling through the scattered outskirts of Haiphong and arriving with a blast of the horn into the pretty, yellow-stucco station near the port.

Etienne flagged down two rickshaws. Unlike in Hanoi, the rickshaws here were wooden handcarts with iron wheels, pulled by barefoot coolies who ran between the shafts like a horse. Arielle felt a pang of guilt as she climbed into hers and lodged her suitcase beside her on the seat. This was altogether different from the cyclos in Hanoi, where the rider pedalled instead of ran. She vowed to tip the man heavily when they arrived at the hotel.

The Hotel d'Europe wasn't far from the station. It stood on a quiet, leafy road, the Boulevard Paul Bert. It was a gracious, old colonial building, covered in blossoming bougainvillea, and had a huge, covered terrace overlooking the peaceful street.

As soon as they were settled in their spacious room, Etienne put on a clean shirt and picked up his briefcase.

'I have to go out now and meet my recruiters at the docks. They have chartered a ship which will set off for Saigon later today, so there are a few formalities we need to go through. Transporting eight hundred workers that distance by sea is by no means straightforward.'

'Can I come with you?' Arielle asked. Now was a good opportunity to see what Etienne's business involved here in Tonkin.

But he shook his head. 'Best not. It's a bit unsavoury around the docks. And it can be dangerous too. No place for a pretty woman. I won't be long. Why don't you take lunch on the terrace while I'm out? The food is actually very good here. They do excellent shellfish straight from Ha Long Bay.'

When he'd gone, Arielle showered quickly in the anti-quated bathroom, then she pulled on an old ao dai that she'd slipped into her suitcase at the last moment. It was faded brown cotton, the sort that female workers wore, practical and comfortable but completely unremarkable. She used to use it for cleaning and cooking at her father's house. She covered her hair with a black cotton headscarf and left the room. In the cavernous lobby with its noisy fans, she asked the man on the desk for a map of the city and for directions to the docks. He gave her a strange look, before directing her to take the Boulevard de Beaumont at the nearby crossroads. 'Then walk

straight ahead, up that road for half a kilometre. The docks
are straight ahead of you. You can't miss them.'

She left the hotel and walked quickly along the shady
boulevard. It was the hottest time of the day and the sun was
high in the sky, but it wasn't as hot or sticky here as in Hanoi.
There was a gentle breeze blowing in from the South China
Sea. She looked about her as she walked. The French quarter
of Haiphong was elegant and peaceful, with beautiful villas
shaded with plane trees. It was so much more relaxed here
than in Hanoi. But as she neared the docks, that relaxed
feeling began to desert her. She needed to keep her wits about
her and well out of sight if she wasn't to be spotted by Etienne
or one of his recruiters.

She came to the end of the road and the docks spread out
in front of her. She stopped and took a deep breath. They
stretched as far as the eye could see, all along the riverfront
towards the distant sea, with lines of customs sheds, go-downs
and warehouses on one side and hulking ships moored to the
dockside on the other. Out on the wide river, sailing ships
stood at anchor surrounded by an army of junks and fishing
boats, their colourful sails fluttering in the breeze. On the
dockside, under the occasional giant crane that swung huge
bits of cargo from ship to dock, dozens of coolies in conical
hats bent under the weight of crates and barrels, scurried to
and fro loading and unloading the ships by hand.

The smell of the sea wafted over, mingling with the
earthier smells of the dockside; rotting fish and open drains.
The whole place was filthy, the surface covered in oil slicks
and puddles of dirty water. Shading her eyes, she looked for
anything that might resemble human cargo, but could see
nothing. She began to pick her way along the dockside,
keeping a careful eye out for Etienne and his men.

At one point she almost bumped into a worker, carrying a

heavy box on his back, a cheroot dangling from the corner of his mouth.

'I'm sorry,' she said as he took a sidestep to avoid her. He barely glanced at her, his bloodshot eyes squinting with stress, his brow wrinkled into a frown. As he rested his load on the ground momentarily, she said, 'Could I ask you a question?'

He nodded briefly, his eyes darting over to the ship where no doubt his master was supervising with a rod of iron.

'Do you know where I can find the ship that's taking people to Saigon to work on the plantations?'

The man removed his cheroot and pointed further down the docks.

'The St Germain, fourth ship along. But they're not taking women,' he replied before hoisting his load onto his sweating body and tottering off towards his ship, back bent under his load, the muscles in his legs bulging as he trotted.

Keeping to the shadow of the buildings, Arielle moved slowly along the dockside in the direction the man had indicated. She passed three massive cargo ships which were being unloaded with a great deal of noise and commotion, before stopping short and pressing herself into a doorway. There it was, the ship with the words *St Germain* painted in white lettering on the prow. It was an old hulk that looked as if it had seen better days.

Her heart beat faster when she caught sight of Etienne. He was standing by the ladder on the side of the ship, talking to two other Frenchmen. On the dockside swarmed a great crowd of male workers. They looked as though they'd been plucked straight from the paddy fields of the Red River delta. They all wore conical hats and rough, workmen's clothes. Some were even dressed in loincloths and walked without shoes. They were being herded onto the ship by a group of local overseers, who used sticks to guide them towards a ladder on the side. Occasionally, if a man stepped out of line, he would receive a sharp prod or even a rap on his back.

Arielle stood watching as dozens of men climbed the ladder, urged on by the overseers. If a man climbed too slowly, the stick would be brought down on his ankles. She swallowed hard and drew herself back further into the doorway. Etienne had stopped speaking to the other men now and had joined in with the overseers, pushing workers onto the steps, yelling at them if they weren't quick enough. Worker after worker mounted those steps and disappeared over the rail, no doubt destined for the bowels of the ship. There were few portholes in the side of the hulking vessel, but through them, even from this distance, Arielle could see the overcrowding within. It must be unbearably hot in there, she thought. It was hot enough out here on the dockside. Could a ship that size really take eight hundred men? She dreaded to think of the conditions on board.

She waited and watched for a long time, transfixed with horror that Etienne could be supervising something as brutal as this. Gradually, the crowd of workers thinned out and at last the entire group had been squeezed onto the ship. Then there was some commotion on board and one man was bundled off the ship and pushed onto the ladder. He missed his footing and fell, sprawling onto the concrete dock. Etienne and the overseers surrounded him. They were all yelling at him and Arielle gasped to see one of the overseers bring a whip down on the man's back. He hit him ferociously several times, leaving red strips across his back. Another bound the man's hands and feet with rope and then he was pushed towards a warehouse across the quay and ushered inside, the great doors slamming behind him. With a shudder Arielle noticed that the name GARNIER was painted in huge letters on the front of the building. Shame washed over her at her association to this contemptible business.

The ship's engines rumbled into life and the old vessel shuddered and shook. Three or four sailors, who, like the workers were clad in loincloths and bandanas, untied the ropes from the quay and sprang back on board, then the ship edged away from the quayside and out into the still waters of the Cua Cam River. There was no one standing on the docks to say farewell to the travellers. Poverty must have prevented their relatives coming to see them off. Arielle felt a pang of pity for those hundreds of men, embarking on a journey full of hope, which would ultimately bring them hardship and suffering on the plantations in the south. She watched the listing vessel as it moved off into the current and out towards the South China Sea, smoke and steam belting from its funnels. It looked so dilapidated and overloaded that she wondered whether it would actually make it to Saigon.

Etienne and the other Frenchmen disappeared into the Garnier building where they'd dragged the defenceless man a few minutes before. Arielle watched the ship as it made its way between the other vessels on the water and out to sea. Soon it was just a black speck on the horizon, disappearing from view. She just stood there, in the shadows of the buildings, going over and over what she'd just witnessed, trying to come to terms with the horror of it all.

12

HAIPHONG, TONKIN, 1935

A s she waited in the shadows of the warehouse, watching the old ship disappear over the horizon, Arielle saw Etienne and the two Frenchmen, who must be his recruiters, emerge from the building. She watched them lock it up and walk away along the dockside in the opposite direction. She guessed they were heading for one of the fleshpots of Haiphong that would inevitably line the streets of the red-light district behind the docks. They would be celebrating the transportation of another shipload of unsuspecting peasant workers. She wondered how much Etienne had received for his part in this despicable trade, shuddering to think that as his wife she was now a beneficiary of that blood money too.

When she was sure the men had gone, she hurried over to the building. Looking around to check that no one was watching, she tried the door that opened onto the dockside. It was locked, but scouting around, she noticed a passageway at the side of the building. She made her way down it and found another door opening onto it. Rattling the handle, she put her ear to the door. A voice inside was shouting; 'Help! Help me!'

She turned the handle again, trying her best to tug the door open, but to no avail. Leaving the door, she carried on along the side of the building. Looking up, she saw that there was an open window, high up, a little way along. She went to the end of the alleyway and looked around for something to stand on. Right at the back of the warehouse, on a pile of rubbish, she found a discarded workmen's bench. It was dilapidated and rickety, but she managed to drag it round to the window and prop it up against the wooden wall. She hoisted herself up onto it, lifted the window and peered through. It took her a few seconds to get used to the gloom on the inside. When her eyes adjusted, she could make out what appeared to be a great, cavernous room inside, lined with shoddily constructed bunk beds several tiers high. The smell that rose and greeted her through the open window was rank with human faeces. This must be where the workers had been kept before they were put on the ship, with little or nothing in the way of food, water or toilet facilities.

Gradually, as she was able to see more, her eyes were drawn to a large structure lining the walls at the back of the building. With shock she saw that it was a cage, the bars stretching from floor to ceiling and in that cage stood the man she'd seen being beaten off the ship. It was him who was clinging onto the bars and shouting, 'Help me!'

Looking around her to check no one was watching, she hoisted herself higher and managed to get a leg inside the window. Then, with supreme effort she squeezed her whole body through and dropped to the ground inside the building. She ran up to the prisoner inside the cage and he stopped shouting, astonishment in his eyes.

'I'll try to get you out,' she said, rattling the cage from the outside. It was clearly locked, and she looked around wildly for the key. It was nowhere to be seen, but beyond the barn-like area where the workers had been housed, she noticed that there were some one-storey rooms in the front of the building. She ran across the filthy floor towards them and, as she'd guessed, they were offices, with windows overlooking the docks. The rooms were untidy, cluttered with rubbish and broken furniture, with papers, documents and maps spread out over every surface. In one of the rooms was a dilapidated old bureau. With one eye on the window to check for Etienne and his men, she began going through the drawers in search of the key. It had suddenly become vital for her to release the prisoner. At least then she'd have done something, rather than just stood and watched dumbly as the workers were taken away to meet their brutal fate. Eventually, she found a bent biscuit tin and inside that was a large, rusting key.

She ran back to the cage and the man stepped back as she tried the key in the lock. It was stiff, but after a few attempts it turned in the lock and the cage door swung open.

'Come on,' she said urgently, and they ran together to the side door of the building which was only secured by bolts. The man pulled them open and then they were both in the cluttered alley at the side of the building.

'I can't thank you enough,' the man said, taking both her hands in his and looking into her eyes.

'No need to thank me,' she said. 'I couldn't believe what I saw when they were loading that boat. Why did they lock you up?'

'I am a communist,' he admitted, 'We are trying to help the workers on the plantations in the south. They discovered me somehow. Perhaps somebody betrayed me, I have no idea.'

'You need to get away from here as quickly as you can,' she said. 'And I must go now too. But what is your name? I have a friend in the Communist Party in Hanoi. His name is Xan.'

'I am Lin,' he said. 'And I know Xan. He is a good man. You are fortunate to be his friend. Send him my best regards.'

'I will. Now you must go.'

She watched him run down the alley and disappear into the road at the end, before following at a more sedate pace. She reached the rutted service road that ran behind the warehouses and followed it until she reached the boulevard. Then she retraced her steps to the Hotel d'Europe and slipped in quietly through the lobby and up to her room.

There, she got out of the old ao dai, rolled it up and slipped it into the lining of her suitcase, then went into the bathroom and got into the shower. She gasped when she saw the grazes on her stomach and thighs that she must have got when she climbed into the window. It would be difficult to hide them from Etienne, so she needed to think of a plausible explanation for them. She showered quickly and dressed in one of her French cotton dresses, then went out to the terrace and ordered tea and baguettes.

She was still sitting there, reading a book, when Etienne arrived an hour or so later, his face full of thunder.

'What's the matter, chéri?' she asked innocently.

'Bloody communists! We found one trying to board the boat south and locked him up in the warehouse. We went off for a swift drink and by the time we came back, the wretched man had escaped. He must have had help. He couldn't have done it on his own. I'll need to get the gendarmes onto it.'

He sat down heavily in the chair opposite her, his face sweaty, his shirt dishevelled.

'Poor darling,' she said, reaching out and squeezing his hand. 'What a bore for you. Shall I order you some cognac? It might help to relax you after your difficult morning.'

TWO DAYS LATER, back at home in the French Quarter of
Hanoi, Arielle couldn't wait for Etienne to leave the house for
work so that she could go to the pagoda and find Xan. She
needed to tell him what she'd witnessed on the docks. She
and Etienne had returned from Haiphong on the evening
train the day before, and she'd spent yet another restless night
thinking about the fate of the men she'd seen so brutally
despatched on the rusting old vessel to Saigon. Would they
have arrived there by now? She imagined them stumbling off
the boat, bewildered, forced by violent overseers onto crowded
trucks that would take them straight to the plantations to
begin their lives of endless toil.

From the bedroom window, she watched Etienne climb
into the black Citroën and be driven away by the chauffeur.
She showered quickly and dressed in a pale blue silk ao dai,
full of anticipation of the morning to come. But before she
could go to the temple she knew she had to look in on Bà
Ngoại. The sight of her grandmother slipping out of
consciousness in the smoke-filled opium den had never been
far from her thoughts since she'd left her there two days
before.

The cyclo rider dropped her at the end of Rue de la Soie
and she walked the rest of the way to Bà Ngoại's apartment.
Stallholders and hawkers were getting ready for the day,
putting up their wooden stalls, setting out their produce, chatting and laughing in loud, boisterous voices. Arielle smiled.
She loved being in Hanoi in the heart of the bustling Old
Quarter. How different this was from her peaceful but sterile
surroundings of her home on the Boulevard Carreau.

Diep looked away hastily as Arielle passed the silk shop
and headed up the stairs to Bà Ngoại's apartment. Perhaps she
was worried that Arielle had let slip to Bà Ngoại who had
given away her whereabouts the other evening. Arielle

mounted the stairs and knocked. After a long pause, Bà Ngoại opened the door in her dressing gown.

'What are you doing here so early?' Bà Ngoại asked blearily.

'I came back from Haiphong last night and I wanted to check how you were. Last time I saw you, you were a bit... well, you weren't yourself.'

Bà Ngoại frowned. 'Oh, in the opium hall. You shouldn't have gone there, Granddaughter. It is no place for a young girl like you.'

She held the door back and motioned Arielle inside.

'I'm pleased to see you're alright, Bà Ngoại,' Arielle said, casting an eye around the apartment. There were no opium pipes in evidence that early in the morning. 'I just wanted to check that you had given the note I gave you to Xan.'

'Is that really why you came?' Bà Ngoại asked sharply, her voice suspicious. Without waiting for an answer she bustled over to the stove and put the kettle on.

'I was about to make my morning tea so you might as well join me.'

'Of course that wasn't the only reason I came,' Arielle said, sitting down in front of Bà Ngoại's low table. 'You know I worry about you.'

'There's no need to worry about *me*. You need to worry about yourself my girl,' Bà Ngoại said, clattering about in her cupboards.

'Worry about myself?' Arielle asked, puzzled. 'What do you mean?'

Bà Ngoại put two teacups down on the table as the kettle came to a whistle.

'Just what I say,' she said, taking it off the hob and filling the teapot. 'You need to worry about yourself. My life is over, but you are young and have your whole life ahead of you. And look how you are spending it. That would cause me sleepless nights if I were you.'

Arielle fell silent and watched as Bà Ngoại poured the amber liquid into the cups and sat down nimbly opposite her. Visions of the men being pushed and prodded and harried onto the old ship, of Etienne wielding his stick at men as they climbed the ladder, of the forlorn graveyard at the rubber estate, of the bone-thin workers in the latex shed and on the plantation. She knew exactly what Bà Ngoại meant. Suddenly, Bà Ngoại's leathery hand closed over her own.

'Think about what you are doing, Ari,' Bà Ngoại pleaded, her voice serious for once. 'There are ways you could bring some good out of your situation. You know that, don't you?'

Arielle nodded, tears oozing from her eyes and running down her cheeks.

'I gave your note to Xan, by the way,' Ban Noi reassured her, 'and I had tea with him at the pagoda. He is a good man, Arielle. He is passionate about his cause. And you could help him so much by telling him everything you know.'

'He wants to meet Etienne,' Arielle whispered. 'But I'm not sure that's a good idea.'

'Not a good idea? Of course it's a good idea. Whyever wouldn't it be?'

Arielle frowned, wondering about the answer. She hadn't quite understood her own reluctance to agree to this plan, other than being quite sure that Etienne would insult Xan and that nothing good would come of it.

'I don't know why you protect him,' Bà Ngoại huffed.

'Protect who?'

'Your wretched husband, of course. Who else?'

Arielle shrugged and fell silent. In her own mind she had been protecting Xan against being insulted and humiliated by

Etienne. She hadn't considered that perhaps, subconsciously, she was also protecting Etienne against Xan.

'After all, you don't owe him anything,' Bà Ngoại said, slurping her tea noisily. Something in her tone made Arielle look sharply at her.

'What do you mean by that?'

'Nothing Ari. Other than you really don't owe him anything.'

Bà Ngoại got to her feet. 'Now, if you don't mind, I need to go and get washed and dressed. So, why don't you get off to the temple now? I know you're itching to get there to see Xan, and now's the time he usually goes there to do his devotions. Don't let me hold you up.'

As usual the cyclo rider dropped Arielle at the entrance to the temple and she joined the crowd of morning worshippers as they ambled along the promontory towards the pagoda. She usually came a bit later than this, so the place seemed busier than usual. While she walked, she scanned the crowd for signs of Xan. A couple of times she thought she'd seen him and her heart sped up when she caught sight of a man dressed in black, walking tall and proud, or another with the same glossy black hair, shaved at the back and sides. But each time she was disappointed. Perhaps Xan wasn't coming today? Had he given up on her?

Her mind wandered back to what Bà Ngoại had said about not owing Etienne anything. Bà Ngoại was right, of course, but the words seemed to have a particular significance. What exactly had Bà Ngoại meant by them? Puzzling over this, Arielle made her way towards the pagoda, past the great bodhi tree and the prayer halls, where the temple gongs were clanging, and the smell of incense floated on the morning air. She finally arrived at the altar in front of the soaring pagoda where she had to wait in line to place her flowers and light her candle. Afterwards, she found a space and dropped to the ground in the lotus position. There, she settled her mind and closed her eyes to meditate. She found it relatively easy to focus her thoughts today, surrounded by others doing the same, and she sat in the same position for half an hour or so, until the stiffness in her legs compelled her to stand up and stretch. She glanced around her at the crowd of silent sitters, and saw him instantly, in the back row, sitting perfectly still, his eyes closed in deep meditation.

She wandered to a bench at the side of the courtyard, in the shade of a frangipani tree and waited for Xan to finish. She couldn't help her eyes from wandering repeatedly over to look at him, although it felt a little like prying. She took in the lean shape of his body, his chiselled cheekbones and the lines on his face that added to his appeal. A thrill went through her as she recalled the heat of his cheek against hers when he'd kissed her the last time they'd met here.

At last, he opened his eyes, blinked several times and stood up, stretching his arms and legs. Then, just as she had done, he shaded his eyes and scanned the crowd. Eventually he turned his gaze in her direction. When he saw her watching him, he broke into a smile and came over quickly.

'So, you're back,' he said shaking her hand. 'I wasn't sure from your note which day it would be.'

'Yes. We came back last night.'

'Come, let us walk to the café. You can tell me all about what you saw in Haiphong.'

They walked side by side in silence for a while. Arielle was struggling to find the right words to begin telling him about the horrors she'd seen, when Xan spoke.

'I take it you saw them loading workers onto the latest transport ship to Saigon?' he said.

She nodded. 'It was awful, Xan. Those poor, poor men,

beaten and forced on board. They looked like prisoners… or slaves. The conditions must have been unbearable inside the ship. It was so hot and overcrowded.'

He stopped and put his hands on her shoulders. 'So now you know,' he said, looking into her eyes. 'You know what your husband's business involves. You've seen the plantations and you've seen the transport ships.'

She nodded and then she remembered the communist. 'There was a man they forced off the ship and locked up in the warehouse. I managed to release him. He said he knew you. His name was Lin.'

'Ah yes. I know him well,' Xan smiled. 'How brave of you to help him. He is an excellent comrade. He has been working amongst the villagers in Tonkin, trying to make them aware of the false promises that are made to them when your husband's men and others like them come to recruit them.'

They began walking again and Arielle waited for Xan to go on.

'They are promised a good home, excellent pay and short working hours. When they get there, as you've seen, nothing could be further from the truth.'

She shook her head, a lump in her throat. How could Etienne preside over such dishonesty, such exploitation? It was still hard for her to believe, even though she'd seen the evidence with her own eyes.

'I found it hard to take in, Xan, but as you say, now I know the truth.'

They had reached the café now and sat at their usual table. The smiling proprietor brought them their usual order of jasmine tea and put it on the table between them.

'So, are you ready to help us now?' Xan asked.

'Yes,' she said looking back into his eyes that were fixed on hers. 'Tell me what you want me to do and I'll do it. I don't need any more convincing.'

Xan poured out the tea and handed her a cup. He leaned forward, 'As I told you before, I would very much like to speak to your husband.'

'Alright,' Arielle replied, her heart sinking, all the old worries about the meeting rising to the surface.

'But I've changed my mind about how that might happen,' Xan went on. 'I don't think it's necessary for you to introduce us. I think that would add complication and he would wonder how we know each other. I think it would be better if you told me in advance where he would be at a certain day and time, and I could approach him myself. That way, you could stay out of it.'

Arielle thought for a moment. That sounded a far better plan than her introducing the two men, but there was something in Xan's tone that made her hesitate.

'What's wrong?' he asked. 'You hardly need to be involved. You can just call me at my HQ if he goes out and I will approach him somewhere discreet.'

'You know that nothing you can say to him will persuade him that he is doing anything wrong, don't you?' she asked. 'He thinks the French are superior, that they have every right to exploit the natives in Indochina and extract whatever wealth they can from them.'

'I just want to tell him a few home truths. Point out the error of his ways. You need not concern yourself with the details. Your role would be just to let me know when he's going out and where he's going.'

She sipped her tea uneasily. 'I often don't know where he goes when he goes out in the evenings,' she admitted. 'He never tells me. It's probably to the Officers' Club where I'm not allowed.'

Xan leaned back in his chair and eyed her steadily. 'You don't owe him any loyalty you know.'

'You sound just like my grandmother. That's exactly what she said to me earlier this morning. And ever since she said it, I've been wondering what she meant.'

Xan leaned forward again and looked earnestly into her eyes. 'I have something to tell you about your husband and I'm going to tell you this for your own good. If I thought you really loved and respected him, I wouldn't think of doing this, but I want you to understand exactly what sort of man you married.'

Shock washed through her. Didn't she know everything now? What was this?

'Your husband has a mistress,' Xan said quietly.

Her hand flew to her mouth in shock and disbelief.

'She's a Romanian woman, one of the hostesses who works in the red-light district. He's been seeing her ever since he came to Hanoi. Since well before you were married.'

Arielle couldn't reply. She thought of Etienne's harsh words on the train to Haiphong which had made her wonder for the first time if he'd married her to get to her father. Now she knew for sure. The shock of the revelation had made everything around her go into a state of suspension. She hardly heard the chatter of the customers in the lakeside cafés, the bells and horns of vehicles passing on the road and the birdsong in the trees above. She even forgot that Xan was sitting opposite her, his compassionate, concerned eyes resting gently on her face. She sat for a long time in silence, letting the full impact of Xan's words sink in, coming to terms with the full extent of Etienne's betrayal. When finally she was ready to speak she looked up at Xan and said,

'I'm glad you told me. And of course I will help you. Like you say, I don't owe him anything.'

13

HANOI, 1935

On her way home from the pagoda, partly to delay her return to the house on Boulevard Carreau, Arielle decided to drop in at her father's house to see Trang. After Xan's shocking news, she was craving the comfort and warmth of her old home. But to her surprise, poor Trang looked careworn and unhappy when Arielle walked into the kitchen. The old lady was sitting at the table, hunched over, her head in her hands.

'Whatever's wrong?' Arielle asked, rushing forward and putting her arms around Trang's shoulders.

'It's your father,' Trang said. 'He's not at all well. He's had a relapse of malaria, but there's something else.'

'Is he awake? I'll go and see him.'

Momentarily putting her own cares aside, Arielle took the stairs two at a time and went into her father's bedroom at the front of the house.

'Are you alright, Papa? Trang said you have malaria again.'

Her father often suffered relapses of the fever which he'd first caught as a young man when he was new to Indochina.

They usually occurred when he had been working too hard, was anxious, or at a low ebb.

'It's nothing to worry about, Ari,' Papa said weakly, struggling to sit up in bed. 'Trang shouldn't have alarmed you.'

'Can I open the windows? It would be good to get some fresh air in here.'

'Of course. Go ahead, but please shut the shutters again would you? I can't seem to bear the sunlight.'

She threw open the windows which opened onto a wrought-iron balcony at the front of the house, then drew the shutters back to shade the room. A light breeze was blowing outside and the sounds of traffic on the street and the birds in the trees floated into the room.

'Now, tell me what's wrong.' Arielle went over to her father and sat down in the chair beside the bed.

'Oh, it's nothing really, just a bit of fever.' But Arielle was not convinced. He looked thin and drawn, his skin lined and sallow.

'I've noticed that you've been looking a bit troubled lately. That's probably why you've become ill. Is it something to do with work, Papa?'

He sighed and looked away.

'You know, Etienne said something about some transportation permits,' Arielle went on. 'Did he put pressure on you? Is that what's been troubling you?'

Her father opened his eyes and with a great sigh looked pleadingly into hers. 'I wasn't going to mention it to you, Ari.'

'So it is that! What happened? What did he say?'

'He made some applications to transport more workers south. But there are limitations on numbers; there are conditions on how many he can take on each ship. He's not complied with the conditions of previous permits... I happened to raise the matter with him and he got... well he got very angry I'm afraid to say. He said some dreadful things.'

'Such as?' Arielle leaned forward and took her father's hand. It felt clammy and cold to the touch.

'I don't want to repeat them,' he said, looking pained. 'There were threats, and insults. For some reason he has the ear of the governor-general. When he wasn't getting any joy with me, he went to see him, and I was ordered to issue the permits without further investigation. I'm now under disciplinary proceedings by my superiors. It's all very worrying.'

'Oh Papa.'

Tears sprung to Arielle's eyes. On top of the shock she'd just had, this was too much. She couldn't bear her father to be troubled and unhappy like this. His professionalism and integrity were everything to him. It must have been agonising for him to have them questioned like that. She put her arms around him and hugged him tight.

'I went to Haiphong with him this week and you are right,' she said. 'Too many workers are crammed into that ship. They are whipped and yelled at and treated so badly. I saw it with my own eyes.'

'He took you to the docks?' her father said, shock in his tone. She shook her head.

'I wanted to see what was going on. I went alone and watched him and his men loading the ship. They were so brutal. I couldn't believe my eyes.'

'Oh Ari. I'm so sorry,' Papa said, squeezing her hand.

'Sorry? Sorry for what?'

'That you aren't happy with your new husband. I can see it in your eyes.'

'You're right. Since I began to find out what his business really involves, I've started to regret marrying him.' She didn't want to add to Papa's pain by telling him about Etienne's unfaithfulness.

'It's my fault. I'm so sorry for encouraging the match with Garnier. For allowing myself to be taken in by him. I see now that he was just manipulating both of us.'

'It's not your fault Papa. I hardly needed any encouragement. Please don't spend another moment feeling guilty. Now, do you need me to bring you anything to eat or drink? I want you to stop worrying and to get better.'

Now she knew what to do. As she went down to the kitchen and helped Trang make broth for her father and carried it to his bedside, and as she left the house and walked through the peaceful streets of the French Quarter back to her home, her thoughts hardened yet further against Etienne. Seeing her father brought to his knees like that had brought home to her even more the destructive effects of Etienne's business and she wanted no part in it.

Xan had given her a number to call to let him know when Etienne had left the house, but she decided not to do it that evening. She would wait until tomorrow. That evening she had other plans.

ETIENNE CAME HOME EARLIER than usual, but he looked preoccupied as he stepped out onto the veranda where she was sitting, her face turned towards the late afternoon sun. Inside she was in turmoil, the bitterness she'd been feeling since Xan had made his revelation was eating her up. She looked at Etienne with revulsion as he approached.

'Are you alright?' she asked, seeing his expression. He sank down into a cane chair opposite her.

'There were a few problems on the transport down to Saigon,' he said. 'When they unloaded the ship they found that a few of the coolies had died on the voyage. It means we couldn't supply the plantations with the numbers we'd promised.'

'That's terrible,' she said, the blood draining from her face, forgetting her own troubles for a moment. She imagined the bodies crammed so tightly into the hold that men were unaware that there were dead amongst their number. 'How did they die?'

He shrugged as if this was the least of his concerns. 'The crew didn't give them enough water. Some of them suffocated.'

'Oh Etienne!' Her mind flew to the image of the men being forced up the ladder and onto the ship. Wave after wave of them. And her glimpse through the porthole at the over-crowding within. It wasn't surprising that some men couldn't have survived those conditions.

'The boat was very overcrowded,' she murmured without thinking. Etienne stared at her.

'It was not overcrowded... and anyway, how on earth would you know?'

Colour flooded her cheeks at the foolishness of what she'd just said.

'I *don't* know,' she said quickly. 'What I meant was... what I really meant was... that if men died of suffocation, the boat must have been overcrowded.'

His eyes were on her face now, his brow knitted into a suspicious frown.

'The boat wasn't overcrowded at all,' he repeated slowly as if explaining something to a child. 'It has plenty of capacity. It's all down to those fools loading it incorrectly and not making sure the passengers were given water. They will be severely punished, I can tell you. They've lost me money and they've damaged my reputation.'

Arielle fell into a troubled silence while Etienne got up and went through the French windows into the dining room and poured himself a generous measure of whisky.

'Ask the servants to serve dinner at seven this evening,' he said, leaning in the doorway, draining his first glass. 'I have to go out later on.'

Later, they sat opposite each other in stiff silence at the long dining table underneath the chandeliers and whirring fans, eating chicken casserole and rice. Etienne had continued to drink more than usual, and Arielle was busy with her thoughts. Each time she glanced across at him she imagined him in the arms of his lover. She could hardly bear to look at him. Her appetite had deserted her, so she had to make a pretence of eating her food. Etienne wolfed his down with copious quantities of wine, then pushed his plate away and stood up.

'I'm off now,' he said. 'Don't wait up for me.'

'Where are you going?' she asked, keeping her voice innocently neutral. She knew where he was going, and she also knew he was about to lie to her.

'I need to go back to the office to attend to work matters. To do with the ship. Like I said, I'll be late.'

With that he walked unsteadily out of the dining room. She heard him putting on his jacket in the hall and leaving the house with a slam of the front door.

As soon as he he'd gone, she sprang into action. Glancing out of the dining room window, she saw that Etienne was waiting on the pavement, scanning the passing traffic for a cyclo. She dashed into the downstairs cloakroom and changed as quickly as she could into the old ao dai that she had worn in Haiphong, then she put on a conical straw hat, just like female workers in Hanoi all wore. Then she left the house via a side door and emerged from the front gate onto the pavement just in time to see Etienne flag down a passing cyclo. She watched as he spoke briefly to the rider, jumped into the seat and the cyclo pulled out into the traffic.

A few seconds later an empty cyclo came pedalling along the boulevard. Arielle waved it down and told the rider to follow Etienne. The man gave her a strange look but began pedalling quickly down the road in pursuit. She sat forward, her eyes glued to Etienne's head bobbing along a few lengths in front. Her cyclo was gradually gaining on his. She tapped the man on the shoulder.

'Don't get too close,' she said. 'I don't want him to know we are following.'

The man shrugged and eased his pace a little. They were heading north now, out of the French Quarter, and were soon moving alongside the Hoan Kiem lake along the tree lined Avenue Beauchamp. Lights from the string of streetlamps that lined the lake danced on the water, and the sky was so clear that the reflection of the full moon cast a rippling white circle in the middle of the lake. Despite her anxiety to keep up with Etienne, she couldn't help drinking in the beauty of the warm evening.

Halfway along the avenue, opposite the grim walls of the Citadel, Etienne's cyclo turned sharply into a side street on the right.

'Make sure you don't lose him,' she said and her cyclo rider sped up and took the turn into the side street at break-neck speed, almost throwing her out of the back seat. She clung on tight with both hands and suppressed a scream. She didn't want him to slow down. As it was, they were several metres behind Etienne, and in the dark it was difficult to see him, especially in these crowded, narrow streets when other vehicles pulled across their path. They followed him down a maze of side streets, where gaudily dressed women wandered

the pavements, blowing kisses and shouting crude invitations
to passing men. Most of these women looked Annamese, but
there were some Europeans plying their trade here too. In the
doorways, stout older women, heavily made up, the
mamasans of the brothels, watched over their charges. Arielle
had never ventured this far into this quarter before. Her father
had always told her that these streets were unsafe, rife with
crime, and to keep away from them, and now she saw why.

Etienne's cyclo turned again, this time into a narrow alley,
and came to a halt.

'Stop here,' Arielle said and the cyclo rider pulled up at
the end of the alley. From the light of the street lamps, Arielle
watched Etienne get down unsteadily from the back seat of
the cyclo, pull some coins from his pocket and pay the rider,
who then moved off down the alleyway.

Etienne pulled a bell-rope beside a door and after a few
seconds the door was opened by a woman. Even in the dark
Arielle could see that she was tall, as tall as Etienne himself,
and had luxuriant blonde hair. She put her arms out and
pulled Etienne towards her. He staggered into her embrace
and the door slammed behind him.

'We go now?' the cyclo rider asked. Arielle was smarting
with shock and humiliation. She was shaking so much that
she couldn't answer immediately, but in the end she nodded
dumbly. The man turned the cyclo round and headed back
the way they had come, but as they travelled back through the
seedy streets of the red light district, Arielle realised that she
couldn't bear to go home. She didn't want to be alone this
evening. When they reached the end of the side street and the
cyclo was about to turn left along Avenue Beauchamp towards
the French quarter, she put her hand on his shoulder.

'Take me to Rue de la Soie instead,' she said. She knew
that Bà Ngoại might already be sinking into her opium stupor,

but it still would be good to be in her comforting presence this evening. She asked the cyclo rider to stop at the end of the road as usual and paid him handsomely for his evening's work. He beamed at her as he took the notes she offered him, then pedalled off into the night. She watched him disappear into the throng of evening traffic thinking how strange it was that this man had been with her during one of the most monumental and important discoveries of her life, and now he had melted away into the darkness and she would never see him again.

She wandered through the market to the silk shop and up the stairs to Bà Ngoại's apartment.

Bà Ngoại opened the door as soon as Arielle knocked. She had her bag on her shoulder. 'I was just going out, Grand-daughter. What do you want?'

'Can I come in for a minute Bà Ngoại? I've just had a bit of a shock.'

'Of course,' Bà Ngoại said, her face full of concern. 'Come on in and sit down. I will get you some snake whisky. That should set you straight. Tell me what happened.'

Arielle wandered into the apartment and slumped down on the floor cushions in the corner. Suddenly her body felt so heavy she could barely support it.

'What is it, child?' Bà Ngoại asked, sitting beside her and handing her a glass of golden liquid. She took a sip and it burned her mouth like firewater, and coursed down her throat and into her stomach, searing her insides as it went. But once it had settled, she started to feel the effects; her limbs began to feel relaxed and she sank back on the cushions.

'I've just followed Etienne into the red light district and discovered him with his Romanian prostitute,' she blurted.

'Oh, my poor child!'

'It was what you were hinting to me, wasn't it, when I came

earlier? Xan told me Etienne had a mistress but I wanted to be sure. And now I am.'

Bà Ngoại gripped her hand. 'I'm so sorry, Ari. You don't deserve this. He is a terrible husband and a wicked man... Did you think any more about what Xan has asked you to do?'

Arielle nodded and took another sip of the whisky. 'I will do it tomorrow. Tomorrow, if Etienne goes out, I will tell Xan that he's gone and that he's probably gone to the red light district.'

'But why don't you tell him this evening? You know where your husband is, after all. He might not go there tomorrow.'

Arielle thought for a moment, about the shock and humiliation that had left her reeling, less than an hour before. Perhaps Bà Ngoại was right.

'But I need to call Xan. I don't know where he is. And there are no telephones around here.'

'You can send a note to his headquarters. It isn't far from here. One of the boys from the market will be glad to take it for you for a few piastres. Shall I bring you paper and a pen?'

Arielle nodded. Why not this evening? Why not let Xan speak to Etienne in the dead of night when he was on his way home. It might bring him up short, remind him of his responsibilities.

Bà Ngoại handed her pen and paper and she leaned on the low table and wrote quickly while Bà Ngoại went down to the market to find a messenger.

Dear Xan,

I followed my husband this evening and he is with his Romanian woman in the red light district. It is halfway along an alleyway, the third turning off the Rue Bourret as you go from the citadel. If you want to speak to him he is there now and I think he is planning to stay until late.

Yours, Arielle.

She folded the note and, hearing footsteps in the apartment, looked up. A grubby boy of seven or eight years old stood in the doorway with Bà Ngoại. Arielle beckoned him forward and handed him the note. Bà Ngoại gave him some instructions and he was off, out of the door in a flash, his bare feet pounding down the concrete steps.

Arielle went over to the window and watched the boy pushing through the milling crowds at the market stalls, until he disappeared from view at the end of the road. Then she turned back into the room and saw Bà Ngoại's triumphant look.

'Well done, Ari. You have done the right thing for sure.'

She sank back down on the cushions and reached for the whisky glass again. Had it been the right thing to do? What did Xan really want with Etienne? She took another gulp of the fiery liquid and closed her eyes, for once wanting to forget everything that was happening to her.

14

PARIS, 1946

Each morning throughout that cold, grey winter of 1946, Arielle awoke with a start just before dawn, when the bells of the local church, L'Eglise St-Sevérain, and those of Notre Dame Cathedral on the Isle de la Cité started pealing for matins across the rooftops. As she awoke, the first lorries and buses were already rumbling along the Boulevard St Germain vibrating the windows of her narrow bedroom. Her first thought each and every day was for her father. He was sinking fast, and she was always terrified that when she went through to his room to check on him, he would have finally succumbed to his illness and slipped away.

There was little she could do to help him, other than to keep him as comfortable as possible, make sure he was well fed, and to try to keep his spirits up. But the circumstances of his captivity in the Citadel had weakened an elderly man who was no longer in the best of health, and having to leave his beloved Indochina, the country he'd devoted his whole adult life to, had sapped his morale still further.

It was difficult to care for him in this alien city, where food was expensive and the chill wind from the River Seine found its way inside through cracks in the window frames and under the front door of the apartment. The old-fashioned radiators were operated centrally by the concierge and were rarely switched on, and although there was a small fireplace in the living room, Arielle often had trouble finding fuel.

On one occasion, she'd gone to Papa's bedside at dawn and found him wheezing and gasping for breath. His face was pallid and grey. She rushed out to find a doctor, having seen several brass doctors' plaques on front doors along the boulevard and in neighbouring streets. She'd had to knock on four or five doors before someone answered. The white whiskered doctor looked at her sceptically when she told him her father was seriously ill, clearly wondering if she would be able to pay.

'My father is French,' she assured him, and he raised his eyebrows and quickly fetched his bag. They hurried together along the windswept boulevard and up the two flights of stairs in the apartment block. She watched anxiously as the doctor examined her father thoroughly. He listened to his chest with a stethoscope, took his temperature, removed his pyjama top and examined his chest and back. All the time the doctor's face was impassive, not giving anything away. When he'd finished, he turned to her and said in a matter-of-fact tone,

'Your father has pleurisy, I'm afraid. Inflammation of the lungs. He is in very poor health though, even for a man of his age. I can prescribe some drugs for him, and you must ensure that he takes them regularly. You will be able to buy them at any pharmacy in the district.'

He went over to the table, pulled out a pad and scribbled on it. He then presented Arielle with two pieces of paper: a prescription for drugs and a bill for his services. Arielle stared at him, open mouthed. The amount of his bill alone would take most of their savings. The doctor stood watching her, his head on one side, an expectant expression on his face. There was no choice, she went over to the pot on the sideboard where they kept their money, pulled out most of their remaining francs and paid the doctor what he was asking. As she saw him out through the front door, she knew that she wouldn't be able to afford to call him again. They were on their own.

It was that day that she realised she needed to look for work. When they'd first arrived in Paris, a few months before, she'd decided not to do that for as long as possible, in the hope that her father would soon be well enough to look after himself. But he wasn't showing any signs of improvement and now it had become a necessity. Perhaps she would be able to work in the evenings when he was asleep? He always went to sleep early, straight after they'd eaten supper, so if she could find an evening job, she would be able to look after him in the daytime as well as work.

So, once she'd been down to the local pharmacy to fetch the medicine for her father, made sure he'd taken it and was as comfortable as possible, she set off in search of a job.

At first, she tried the local bars and brasseries, including the one where she'd lingered to watch the GIs that rainy day a few weeks before. She'd been back many times since too, to stand under the shelter of its awning and look out for a glimpse of that flash of red hair, the sound of that old familiar laugh. She'd glanced into other bars too, searching for any sign of him. Just being near the GIs, knowing they were in the city and hearing their brash, confident voices made her feel a little happier. But there was no sign of the man she was looking for and she'd had to content herself with going home and looking longingly at the little charcoal sketch of the Tran Quoc pagoda and remembering his smile when he gave it to her.

Today was the first day she'd actually ventured inside any of the bars, and she felt awkward and self-conscious as she pushed the door open and wandered in. There were only a few early customers, sipping coffee and reading newspapers. She went up to the bar and asked for the manager.

'He's not around,' said the waiter. He was young, with slicked back dark hair and an arrogant tilt of the head. He carried on polishing glasses with a cloth. 'You could speak to me, perhaps?'

Arielle took a deep breath. 'I was wondering if you had any vacancies... for work, that is?'

The young man looked at her scornfully. 'Not at the moment. And if we did, you would need experience before you could be considered. Do you have that?'

'I am trained as a secretary,' she replied, and he laughed.

'That wouldn't be much good behind the bar,' he said. 'I would try elsewhere. You might get a position as a bottle washer, or kitchen porter somewhere. But for waiting or bar work, you will need experience. I don't know about where you come from, but it is a *profession* here in Paris.'

She left quickly, stunned by his rudeness. Realising she was getting nowhere, she trudged on through the Latin Quarter, stopping to ask in every bar and café she came to, only to be rebuffed at every one. From the way the managers and waiters looked her up and down, she knew that it was the colour of her skin that was stopping them from hiring her. Just as she had when she was out shopping, she felt humiliated and degraded by their treatment. She began to despair of ever finding a position.

Soon she'd left the Latin Quarter behind and was heading east. At one point she emerged from one of the side streets onto a cobbled quayside that ran beside the river. Opposite her was a metal footbridge. She crossed it aimlessly, wanting nothing more than to put some space between herself and the place where she'd suffered humiliation after humiliation. Halfway across she stopped and stared down at the murky waters of the Seine. How different this was from the steaming, earthy Red River at home that she knew and loved. How different this city was too, she thought, looking out over the creamy stone and grey roofs of the Ile St Louis and Ile de la Cité, from the exotic, colourful, noisy city in her heart. Tears flooded her eyes and she brushed them aside impatiently. She had to do this, whatever the indignities she had to suffer. For Papa's sake and for her own. There was no choice.

On the other side of the river a great train station loomed up ahead of her. With its arched windows, steep roofs and clocktower, the building looked like a grand chateau. It reminded Arielle a little of Hanoi station. She wandered inside the bustling concourse and saw a sign which said; *Gare de Lyon*. She stopped and watched the busy platforms. This was where she and Papa had arrived after their interminable journey by sea and boat train from Haiphong only a few months before. That day, she'd been so preoccupied with getting Papa and the luggage safely off the train and finding a taxi, that she'd hardly noticed her surroundings. Now, she wandered along the concourse at the end of the platforms, looking at the steam engines being readied for journeys. On the announcement boards she read the names of destinations; places she'd only heard about from books; Lyon, Nice, Montpellier, Perpignan, Dijon, Grenoble and finally Marseille. As she reached the last platform a train was coming in, belching out smoke and steam and announcing its arrival with an elaborate toot of its whistle. She stood and watched, curious as the great engine drew closer. With a creaking of rolling stock, hissing of steam and grinding of brakes, it finally came to a halt.

Immediately doors on the carriages flew open and people began to get down, hauling luggage and children with them. Uniformed porters with sack barrows flocked around the passengers, touting for trade. The first passengers began to walk up the platform towards her and as they got closer she noticed that some of them were dark-skinned like herself. From their colouring and features she realised that they were Annamese too. Her heart beat faster. She needed to speak to them. She approached a man carrying a heavy suitcase and spoke to him in her own language.

'Please sir,' she said. 'Have you come from Haiphong? Saigon?'

His face was etched with exhaustion. 'Yes. Saigon. Our ship docked yesterday, sister. This was the overnight boat train from Marseille. Things are not good at home, you must be aware of that. Many of us have lost everything and have come to seek a new life overseas.'

'Yes, I understand. Thank you, and good luck, sir,' she replied and watched the diminutive figure go on his way, struggling along with his heavy luggage.

With a shudder she recalled the final few days in Hanoi; the bloody violence, the rioting that had erupted between the Viet Minh and the French once the Japanese had surrendered. It wasn't widely covered in the French newspapers, but she'd occasionally seen a headline that had confirmed that the situation continued. Earlier in the year, things had looked hopeful when she'd read that negotiations were underway between the French colonial government and Ho Chi Minh and that the French had recognised communist rule in the north. But that month, she'd read with horror that French naval vessels had fired cannons on Haiphong, with thousands of civilian casualties. The uneasy peace was over, and Indochina was at war again, this time with its French rulers.

When would she ever be able to return to her beloved homeland?

But now she scanned the crowd of passengers carefully, straining her eyes for a glimpse of that flaming red hair. He could be on this very train. This would definitely be where he would come if and when he arrived in Paris. Why hadn't she thought of that before? But gradually, as she watched, the stream of weary travellers dried to a trickle, then the guards and ticket collectors walked up the platform, laughing and joking together, and the driver jumped down from the engine and joined them. She turned away, her hopes dashed.

She walked back up the platform, wondering why she hadn't thought to come here to the Gare de Lyon before. Why had she stood outside bars peering in through steamy windows, searching for any sign of him, when she could simply have come and checked the boat train for arrivals? She thought back to the letters she'd sent him, telling him of the trials and tribulations of the journey from Hanoi and her address in Paris. They had received no response, but she'd had to write to a poste restante address in Hanoi. She envisaged them gathering dust in the post office. But it was quite possible that he was stuck on some airbase in the north, or on some peacekeeping mission in the south, unable to get to Hanoi to collect them.

She was on the main concourse of the Gare de Lyon now, and the crowds had thinned out. Ahead of her was the station café-bar and her eyes were drawn to a sign in the window; *Waiting staff required. Apply within.* What a stroke of luck! She pushed the mahogany and glass door open and as she went inside, she was hit by a blast of stale, smoky air. Blinking against the fumes, she made her way between the tables towards the bar, noting that the surfaces were cluttered with dirty glasses and crockery and the place was full of men, smoking and drinking alone, even at this hour. Many of them looked like derelicts who'd managed to beg a few centimes on the street to buy a coffee and get warm inside. She already felt discouraged, but when she reached the bar, the harassed looking woman who greeted her was friendly and welcoming. She didn't stop scrubbing glasses in the sink whilst they spoke.

'Not many people have enquired and as you can see, we are very short staffed. When could you start?'

'I could start today,' Arielle replied, 'but I can only really work during the evenings.'

The woman's face fell. 'We would need you to work a morning and evening shift. That's when we get really busy.'

Arielle pondered for a few moments. Perhaps it would work? Papa usually rested after breakfast. And if she was here during the daytime, she would be able to keep an eye on when the boat trains came in from Marseille.

'Alright. I'll take it,' she said.

'Fantastic. That's such a relief. Come back at six o'clock this evening and I'll show you the ropes.'

So that very evening, Arielle began a new routine. She cooked Papa an early supper, got him settled and left the apartment to walk to the Gare de Lyon. She was given a uniform; a black cotton dress and white pinafore, and the proprietor of the station café, Violette, showed her how to wait at the table, how to mix drinks, wash up, and prepare snacks. Violette, with her big smile and ample bosom was kind and motherly. She took Arielle under her wing and Arielle was grateful for that and repaid her by working well. It was hard work and the customers were sometimes rude or difficult, but just going out into the world every day and having some social contact and a routine helped to lift her mood.

In the mornings, after giving Papa breakfast and clearing up the apartment, she would walk through the busy morning streets of the Latin Quarter and over the River Seine to the Gare de Lyon once again. The morning shift was easier than the evening one; there were fewer belligerent drunks, but it was always very busy, and the customers were demanding, often in a hurry to catch trains, but she got used to that too and was soon able to anticipate their needs. Many appreciative customers left her generous tips as a result, and she soon found she didn't have to scrimp and save to buy food.

After one morning shift, she joined the long queue for the ticket office and when she finally reached the front, asked about the boat trains from Marseille. The man behind the counter peered at her, frowning.

'But you are asking about arrivals. You don't want a ticket?'

'No, I just want to know how often those trains come in.'

'They come in every day,' he said grudgingly. 'At eleven o'clock.'

'And is it possible to find out which ships they connect with?' she asked.

'I don't know about that,' the man said testily. 'Now if that's all and you don't want a ticket, could you move on please, madame.'

She turned away reluctantly, wondering how she would find out how often the boat trains brought passengers from Indochina. She wandered around the station, peering at posters, timetables, anything that might give her a clue, but the information seemed impossible to find. In the end she decided that there was only one way to find out, and that was to meet each and every boat train, to watch the passengers come off it and see if there were any from Indochina.

So that's what she did. She explained her difficulties to Violette who allowed her a fifteen-minute break at eleven o'clock. She would rush along to the platform and wait for the Marseille train to come puffing in. Sometimes it was late, but often she was able to see it coming in. It wasn't until almost a week of doing that had passed that she saw Annamese and Tonkinese passengers alighting from the train again and she realised that there must only be one ship from Indochina each week. That made it easier in a way. She now knew that the Tuesday morning train was the one to wait for. This gave her hope. One day, in the not too distant future, he was bound to come and, when he did, she would be there on the platform waiting for him.

15

HANOI, 1945

A s she hurried to work in the Mairie the morning after she'd been approached by the man from the Viet Minh at the Tran Quoc pagoda, she couldn't stop thinking back over the unsettling encounter and reminding herself what it meant for her. It was already terrifying and shaming to have to work for the Japanese officers, but on top of that to be asked to spy on them sent chills down her spine. How would she be able to make copies of secret maps and papers and smuggle them out of the building right under the noses of her Japanese masters? What would happen if she was caught? She suspected that such a crime would warrant a more severe penalty, even than being locked up in the Citadel. The Japanese wouldn't treat such a betrayal lightly. They would surely torture her to give up the names of her contacts before killing her. Who would take food to Papa at the Citadel then? Who would look after him if he ever got out? It would break his heart to lose her. She couldn't bear to think about it.

But there was no way out. The Viet Minh had her backed into a corner. 'We know your secret, Madame Garnier. Your

dark secret, and we're quite sure you wouldn't want that information to go any further...' the man had hissed and the hair
on the back of her neck had stood on end. She knew exactly
what he meant. She'd barely been able to lift her eyes to his
when he'd said those words, aware that guilt and shame were
written all over her face.

For ten years she'd lived with the pain of what she'd done
that fateful evening back in 1935. Afterwards, she'd virtually
gone to ground, quietly moving in with her father, getting a
low-profile administrative job with the French Government.
She shook her head as she hurried along the pavement beside
the Hoan Kiem Lake towards the Mairie. There was no getting
out of this. She would have to do what the man had
demanded, and he'd made her promise to meet him again at
the pagoda that evening. That meant that she needed to
produce some papers straight away.

The Viet Minh agent had solved one problem that had
been troubling her, though. She'd told him about the difficulty
of having no identity papers, and he'd looked at her and said,
'We can take care of that for you. What name did you say you
were using? I will send you some documents this evening.'
Sure enough, after she and Trang had eaten supper, someone
pushed a large brown envelope through the letter box. She ran
to the door and looked out, but whoever it had been had
already melted back into the humid evening air.

It was a little after eight by the time she arrived at the
Mairie that morning. She hadn't slept well and had found it
difficult to get up. The soldier on the door examined the
papers she presented to him with a frown, but he handed
them back and waved her inside. The general looked up from
his desk when she walked into the big room.

'You're late, Miss Nguyen,' he boomed, a scowl on his face.
'Come here.'

She approached his desk, her knees quaking, her eyes cast down, thinking that her secret would be plain to see if she returned his gaze.

'No... Come round *here*. To my chair.'

'But sir,' she protested.

'No buts. Come, here Miss Nguyen.'

Slowly, reluctantly, she moved round the desk to where he sat. He reached out a hand and pinched her backside, then laughed uproariously as she jumped.

'Don't be afraid of me,' he said, still laughing at her discomfort. 'There is nothing to fear from me. It's just a bit of harmless fun. Now, get on with your work please. There is already a pile of papers waiting for you.'

She went over to her desk and settled herself as best she could while her heart was hammering as hard as it was. The humiliation of the encounter was still washing over her in waves as well as the fear of similar encounters yet to come. She picked up the first report and prepared to type it up, quickly inserting an extra piece of carbon copy paper and another sheet of paper into the typewriter roll. This was the most discreet and simple way she could think of to make copies of what she typed.

She began to type, and quickly realised that it was a report to the Japanese government stating that Japan intended to rule Indochina through the former emperor Bao Dai and that a ceremony was to take place the following day at which Bao Dai would be handed the reins of power. At the same ceremony he would rename his country Vietnam and declare that it was independent from the French. Arielle's hands began to shake as she typed the letter and as she quickly understood its significance. This was exactly the sort of document that the Viet Minh would be interested in. When she'd finished, she took it out of the typewriter, and discreetly removed the bottom copy. Making sure that the general and his colleagues were occupied, she slipped it into a gap between the leather and the lining of her bag that she'd cut and sewed for this purpose the night before.

All day she continued to type up documents. There was nothing as momentous as the first report although she wasn't quite sure exactly what information the Viet Minh were looking for. There were a couple of letters about troop movements and one that contained a list of ammunition dumps. She made copies of these three letters, but the others, which concerned routine orders for food and uniforms for Japanese soldiers, she typed without copying.

The hours dragged, but she kept her head down, not wanting to draw the general's attention to her and invite another lewd comment, a pinch on her bottom or even worse. At lunchtime she slipped out of the building and bought soup at a street market and then went straight back to work. She felt very alone. How she missed Camille. They used to take lunch together most days and Arielle would sit opposite her glamourous friend and listen, wide-eyed, to stories of Camille's roller-coaster existence; her trysts with married men which seemed to sit oddly with her role as a spy for the Allies.

Arielle had always admired how coolly Camille went about copying classified information and taking it out of the building. And now it was Arielle's turn to do the same, but she suspected that now the stakes were higher, that the consequences had Camille been discovered would not have been quite as catastrophic as they would be for her, if she was caught. She wondered how Camille was faring inside the Citadel. She sincerely hoped she wasn't suffering too much. But the thought of her there wasn't as hard to bear as the thought of Papa struggling in that forbidding place. Camille was clever, resourceful and strong, and if anyone was built to survive such an ordeal, it was her.

At six o'clock sharp the general and the other officers got up from their desks and left the building, just as they had on the previous day.

'Go home, Miss Nguyen,' the general barked as he walked past her desk. 'And don't be late to work tomorrow. You won't get a second chance.'

Wondering what he meant, she rose from the desk, her legs quaking beneath her, and glanced over at the armed guards who still stood beside the door. Now was the true test. She would have to walk past those soldiers just as she had the day before, as if there was nothing to arouse their suspicion. She felt sick to the stomach thinking about what might happen if they searched her bag, but she knew that there was no avoiding what she had to do.

She zipped her bag up and put it over her shoulder, just as she normally did, then she walked towards the door as casually as she could. As she drew abreast of the first guard, he cleared his throat. She forced herself to look up at him, hoping against hope that he wouldn't see the fear in her eyes or notice that every inch of her body was trembling.

'Goodnight, Miss Nguyen,' he said, without smiling, his eyes on her face.

'Goodnight,' she said and hurried on through the door and down the stairs.

Once outside, she walked quickly across the square and away from the building, until she was sure she was out of sight of the guards, then she hailed a cyclo and asked the rider to take her to the Tran Quoc Pagoda. She sat rigid in the seat, her bag on her lap, as the cyclo rider pedalled her through the busy, rush hour streets. She hardly took in her surroundings or anything about the journey, although she was vaguely aware that the sun was setting over the lake, staining the sky and the buildings a deep golden hue, shot through with crimson. All she could think of was ridding herself of the papers, that seemed to burn her lap through the leather of the bag.

The Viet Minh agent was already there, lounging beside the gate, smoking a cheroot, when she arrived, breathless.

'I thought you weren't coming,' he said, with a lazy smile. 'But that would have been very foolish of you.'

'Of course I was coming,' she said. 'It's just that I can't get away from the office until six o'clock.'

'I was admiring the sunset,' he said, motioning towards the reflection of the blood red sun shimmering on the dark waters of West Lake. 'It's particularly beautiful this evening.'

She swallowed, just wanting to get on with the transaction.

'Do you have something for me?' he asked.

She nodded.

'I thought as much. I can see it in your eyes. I can always see it in people's eyes when they bring me important information. It is like a special kind of fear. But fear mixed with pride, too.'

'I have the papers in my bag. Can I give them to you please?' she said, her voice hoarse with nerves.

He laughed. 'What? Out here by the temple gate? In full view of everyone? Any of these people passing by on their way to the pagoda could be a Japanese spy. You really need to be more careful, Madame Garnier.'

'Well, where then?' She was becoming impatient now. She wanted to be away from here; she had very little time left to get home and collect the food she wanted to take to the Citadel for Papa that evening.

'Come into the trees with me and you can give them to me there,' he said, taking a quick look around and stepping off the path into the little group of banyan trees that grew beside the gate. She followed him into the darkness, remembering, with a pang, how Xan used to wait under these very trees for her. It seemed like a lifetime ago.

'OK. What have you got?'

'There are a couple of reports about troop movements, and a letter about the Emperor Bao Dai and a ceremony to take place tomorrow,' she said, reaching in her bag and handing him the papers. She heard the man draw a sharp intake of breath.

'You have done well, Madame Garnier. Very well. These will be useful to us, but we will want more. I will be here this time tomorrow, and every day from now on, so please bring me what you have.'

'But please. Does it have to be every day? That is too much. I need to get home,' she protested.

'This is more important than getting home,' the man hissed angrily. 'Don't you realise? The future of your country is at stake. It is only through us in the Viet Minh and through the efforts of people like you that our people will be freed from the tyranny of the Japanese occupation. It is important, and you need to remember that.'

'But my father is in the Citadel and I need to take him food in the evenings.'

Suddenly she felt the man's fingers grabbing both her arms, squeezing them tight, his nails digging into her skin. He began to shake her. She did her best not to squeal.

'You are forgetting what we know about you and your past,' he said, his face so close to hers that she could smell the bitter cheroot on his breath. 'Your father can wait. He is a Frenchman, a colonial, and he doesn't deserve your pity. If you don't co-operate with me, your secret will no longer be your secret. I'm surprised that you've already forgotten that fact.'

'Of course. Of course, I'm sorry. I will do as you ask,' she

said, terrified that he would tell her secret, wanting him to
stop hurting her, wanting to be away from here. He let go of
her arms and she stepped away from him.

'Go now. And be back here tomorrow. At the same time, or
there will be serious consequences.'

She ran out of the trees and up the promontory towards
the road without a backward glance. Her breath was coming
in uneven gulps, and she was forcing back tears at every step.
But as she neared the road, she noticed with a start that there
were Japanese soldiers milling about near the stalls, so she
stopped running and tried to melt into the crowd of worshippers at the temple entrance.

THE NEXT MORNING, she set off early for the Mairie, remembering the general's words as she'd left the day before. What
did he mean, she wouldn't get a second chance? Would he
send her to the Citadel, with all the other people who'd
worked for the French regime? A shudder went through her as
she thought about her experience the evening before, when
she'd taken food for her father to the Citadel gates. On the
first two evenings, the same guards had been stationed at the
gate and the second day they appeared to have recognised her
and taken the cannister of soup from her without a word.
She'd tried to say her father's name to remind them who it was
meant for, but they just shooed her away. She'd hoped and
prayed that the food had found its way to her father, but she
had no way of knowing. On the third occasion, though, there
were different soldiers guarding the gate. These men seemed
older, rougher than the first ones. When she'd approached,
they started laughing at her and nudging each other. It was
clear to her that they were making lewd comments about her

in their own language. But she'd swallowed her fears and walked up to them boldly.

'Could you give this food to Monsieur Dupont please,' she'd said. 'He is a French prisoner inside the Citadel.'

One of the guards came up to her, took the cannister in one hand and made a lunge for her breasts with the other. She felt his rough hand squeeze her and she backed away to peals of laughter from both the guards.

'The food is for Monsieur Dupont,' she repeated with a catch in her voice. She turned and ran back down the street, but she was sure that the food wouldn't reach her father that evening.

When she got home, tearful and distressed, Trang had pressed her about what had happened, and when, hesitantly, Arielle had told her how the guards had insulted her, Trang had insisted that she could go and deliver the food instead.

'They won't try anything like that with an old woman like me,' she said with a wry laugh. 'And in any case, I can go along to the Citadel while you are still at work. There's no need for anyone to go there in the dark that way.'

Reluctantly, Arielle had agreed that it would probably be for the best, but she felt a little guilty about putting the old lady in direct contact with the Japanese army, when otherwise she would have no need to have anything to do with them. But Trang was very insistent, so the matter was settled.

Now, as she neared the Mairie and glanced at her watch, she saw that it was still only ten to eight. At least the general would have no cause to reprimand her or single her out for special treatment this morning. She went inside the building and up the stairs to the first floor to where the guards stood in front of the double doors.

'Papers,' barked one of them, clicking his fingers and holding out his hand, and she fished in her bag and handed them to him. He glanced at them then gave them back and nodded her through. The vast room was empty. None of the officers, not even the general was at their desk. Puzzled, Arielle went to her own desk and sat down. There was a pile of reports waiting for her to work on, so she picked up the first one and started to type. She carried on typing all morning. As on the previous day, whenever she came across anything that related to troop movements, positions of arms dumps or army camps, she copied the report discreetly and slid the copy into the lining of her bag. It was easier to do so that day, without the officers in the room.

At lunchtime she left her desk and went out to get some soup at the local street market as usual. She wondered whether to take her bag out with her, but decided not to risk it being searched, so she left it locked in her desk drawer. As she passed the guards, she asked them where the general and his colleagues were that day. They both carried on staring straight ahead, but one of them said, 'The general go to ceremony for Emperor today.'

'Oh, will he be back later, do you know?'

The man shrugged. 'I not know,' he replied and, thanking him, she went out to get her lunch.

During the afternoon, she came across more information about planned troop movements into Thailand and, sensing that this would be of great interest to the Viet Minh, after checking that the guards weren't looking, she made a copy as she typed and slipped it into her bag. At six o'clock she got up to leave her desk and, putting her bag over her shoulder as usual, strolled over towards the door as nonchalantly as she could. She kept her eyes lowered, but she could sense the twin beams of the guards' searchlight gazes panning round to scrutinise her as she walked across the room towards them. As she reached the door, one of them put his rifle out in front of her, barring her way. Her heart did a somersault and she looked up at him.

'We must search your bag,' he said, holding out his hand. 'Give it to me, please.'

This was it. This was the end for her. Trying to remain calm, she handed her bag to the guard, who started to unzip it, but the zip was stuck and he struggled with it, swearing under his breath. Arielle watched him, helplessly, her heart pounding.

16

HANOI, MARCH 1945

A rielle watched, paralysed with fear, as the guard struggled with clumsy fingers to open her bag. But suddenly there was a commotion down on the lower floor; the sound of the double doors being opened and flung aside, banging against the wall. Then came heavy footsteps on the stairs. The guard dropped Arielle's bag on the floor and both he and his comrade swung round and turned their eyes to the stairs, rifles trained on the stairwell. Arielle hastily picked her bag up and slid it onto her shoulder again. One of the guards shouted something down the stairs, and a familiar voice responded. It was the general. Soon his head and those of his officers appeared. His face fell when he saw the guards with their guns cocked, and he shouted at them in rapid Japanese, shaking his fist. They quickly withdrew their guns and stood to attention as the general and his officers strutted past them and into the room.

'Ah, Miss Nguyen,' the general said, seeing Arielle standing there beside the door. 'Come on, back inside! We are going to toast the health of Bao Dai, the Emperor. We have just come from his inauguration ceremony. A new era has begun for your country today. Indochina is now Vietnam, free from French rule, but protected by a benevolent and friendly force, the Imperial Japanese Army. I have whisky in my desk, please, stay and drink with us.'

Arielle swallowed hard and tried to force a smile. She had no choice but to accept the offer.

'Come. Let us drink, then.'

She followed reluctantly as the officers gathered around the general's desk. He produced two large bottles of Scotch and four glasses and poured a generous measure into each. Then, beaming, he held up his glass.

'Kanpai!' he said, and the other officers repeated, 'Kanpai! Kanpai!' enthusiastically, clinked their glasses together, then drained them in one gulp.

'Drink, Miss Nguyen, drink!' urged the general and Arielle took a tentative sip, not wanting to get drunk or even tipsy in this company.

The Scotch tasted a great deal smoother than Bà Ngoại's snake whisky, but felt just as potent, running like fire down her throat and flooding her whole body with a warm glow. The general immediately refilled his own glass and those of the officers and raised his glass in another toast. Arielle had no intention of matching the speed with which these Japanese men downed their spirits, so she hovered in the background, sipping her drink discreetly, nodding politely to their conversation. All the time she was worrying that she should be at the temple by now, picturing the Viet Minh agent pacing the walkway impatiently, wondering how long he would wait for her if she didn't arrive. But she gritted her teeth and smiled as the Japanese officers carried on drinking and became more and more drunk. It didn't take long before they were laughing uncontrollably and singing tunelessly at the tops of their voices. She began to fear for her safety, but quickly realised that none of these men would be able to control their limbs sufficiently to assault her. In any case, they seemed to have forgotten about her in their drunken show of patriotic cama-raderie.

In time, the general's energy subsided and soon he was collapsed on his desk, snoring loudly, the other two men slumped in their chairs, barely conscious either. Now was the time to act. Arielle snatched up her bag and marched straight to the door. To her surprise the guards were no longer there. Perhaps the general had dismissed them when he arrived. Relief washed over her as she rushed out into the hallway and hurried down the stairs. To her dismay, when she reached the bottom of the steps, there was another guard stationed at the door of the building. But after a couple of heart-stopping seconds when he turned towards her and unsmilingly watched her coming towards him, he pushed open the door for her, nodded goodnight and allowed her to go through.

She hailed the first cyclo that appeared and asked him to take her to the Tran Quoc Pagoda as quickly as he could. The traffic was busy, and even though the man did his best, progress was slower than usual. Passing the clocktower on St Joseph's Cathedral, Arielle noticed with dismay that it was already seven o'clock. Would the agent have waited? She prayed that he would, feeling sick to the stomach with the thought of what would happen if he had given up on her.

When the cyclo rider dropped her at the entrance to the pagoda, she ran down the promontory as fast as her legs would take her, elbowing her way through the evening crowds. When she reached the gate she stopped and looked around desperately. He wasn't leaning on the railings looking over the lake, smoking a cheroot as he had been the day before. The sun had set over half an hour before. She stood in one spot and turned full circle, straining her eyes for a glimpse of him but as she did so she felt a tap on her shoulder and she spun round.

'You are very late, Madame Garnier,' he said and this time there was no mocking amusement in his dark eyes.

'The general made me stay,' she stammered breathlessly. 'He wanted to toast the emperor. I had no choice.'

'Excuses, excuses. I was about to leave, but the information you brought me yesterday was very useful, so I felt you were worth another half hour of my time.'

'I have more information for you today,' she said. 'But I nearly got searched as I was leaving the building. It is very dangerous for me. One day they will discover me and then we will both be the losers.'

'Come, let us go into the shadows and you can pass me what you have. And let us have no more talk of discovery. You are a smart woman, Madame Garnier. I know that. And I also know I can rely on you to keep bringing me information. You are sitting on a gold mine in that office in the Mairie and you are our one and only source inside that building.'

She passed him the letters and reports she'd copied. 'Can I go now?' she asked.

'Of course. Thank you for the information. See you tomorrow. Do try not to be late.'

OVER THE NEXT FEW WEEKS, Arielle met the Viet Minh agent each and every evening beside the pagoda gate. They would go into the trees together and she would give him whatever she'd managed to copy that day. She never found out his name. That didn't bother her; she figured that the less she knew about him and his masters the better.

Every day was a waking nightmare for her, living as she

did with the fear of being caught spying by the Japanese. And that was on top of the constant and unpleasant attention she received from the general, and if his back was turned, from the other officers. Often, when she visited the bathroom along the corridor, the general would be waiting for her in the passageway on her return. He would bar her way, press her against the wall, squeeze her breasts and try to kiss her. Her cries of disgust and disapproval seemed to goad him on, and were either not heard, or completely ignored by the others working in the room. If she ever had to approach the general's desk he would try to slide his hand up her skirt or pinch her backside. She had a horror of being left alone in the room with him; without others around, these attacks would surely escalate.

But at least she managed to discover a way of getting out of the Mairie building without the guards having a chance to search her. She discovered that if she walked out at the same time as the general and his officers at six o'clock sharp, the guards didn't dare to stop her or ask to look inside her bag. That method held its own dangers though. If she didn't slip away across the square as soon as they were outside the building, the general would put his arm around her and ask her to go for a drink with him. He did that on a couple of occasions, but she told him that her father was ill and that she needed to go and check how he was. It was only half a lie and she hoped and prayed that the general would never have cause to look into her family background or ask to see her home.

The Viet Minh agent kept her informed of how the risks she was taking were helping the Viet Minh and Allied causes. A Japanese camp she had sent them details of had been surrounded by Allied soldiers and all the Japanese troops inside captured; a railway bridge had been blown up preventing the movement of Japanese troops, and a huge weapons dump had been raided, depriving a whole Japanese battalion of its arms and delaying their offensive for weeks.

'All this is helping the Allies win the war against the Japs,' he assured her. 'It won't be long now, they are on the retreat everywhere.'

'But if the Allies win, doesn't that mean the French will come back to govern Indochina? Surely that's not what you and your organisation want?'

He smiled knowingly. 'Ah, you are perceptive, Madame Garnier. But what I haven't told you is that we are working closely with the Americans. In fact, members of the US army are training our men in the hills to fight with modern weapons at this very moment. The Americans have no interest in re-establishing a colonial power in Indochina. The French won't be allowed back here. Once the Japanese enemy is defeated, our esteemed leader, Ho Chi Minh, will declare Vietnam an independent and free state.'

'You sound very certain...' she said, recognising the revolutionary fervour in his tone and suspecting that the truth was a lot less black and white.

'We *have* to be certain,' he replied, his fierce black eyes steady on hers. 'We have to be sure this will happen, and then it *will* happen.'

Sometimes, after the meeting with the agent, she would venture inside the temple to make offerings to the Buddha at the pagoda, but on other days she would feel so deflated she would just want to hurry home and see how Trang had got on at the Citadel that day.

But something else was happening in Hanoi and in the surrounding provinces that was impossible for Arielle to ignore. Since the Japanese coup, she noticed that there were more and more beggars on the streets of Hanoi, many of them pitifully thin. Most looked like peasant farmers, who'd deserted their fields to find food in the city. The Viet Minh agent told Arielle that a famine had taken hold in the villages of northern Indochina, caused first by the French, then by the Japanese. The French had stopped farmers growing rice and maize and forced them instead to grow cotton and jute for export. As well as that, the Imperial Japanese Army forcibly seized any food the farmers did manage to grow to feed their troops. There were around one hundred and forty thousand Japanese troops in Indochina and their needs were put before the needs of the locals. And on top of all that, the last harvest had been destroyed by pests and floods.

Arielle was aghast at the state of these pitiful people, squatting on the pavement alongside the lake, begging in the markets in the Old Quarter. She always gave them whatever she could spare. If she saw someone begging on the street outside her house, she would invite them inside the kitchen and Trang would make them some wholesome soup, or chicken and rice. Arielle couldn't believe that this was happening in her country. She'd always been taught that Indochina was blessed with boundless natural resources and fertile soil and that there was no need for anyone to go hungry. It brought home to her the impact of the Japanese occupation and each day, when she went to work, she looked upon the general and his officers with increasing fear and disdain.

The strain of what Arielle was doing was beginning to show in her face and her body. She had lost weight and her ribs and hipbones stuck out, her cheeks were hollow and her eyes were ringed with dark shadows. Each night she lay awake into the small hours imagining what would happen to her if and when she was discovered. It would surely happen soon; she could hardly believe how long she'd managed to go on doing what she was doing right under the noses of the Japanese officers. She also worried about Papa and about her colleagues, especially Camille, in the Citadel. Trang still went there every day with food which was always taken from her by the Japanese guards on the gate, but she didn't know if it had been passed to Papa, eaten by the guards themselves or simply thrown away. Arielle worried for her father, elderly as he was, prone to bouts of malaria and with a weak chest. How ever was he coping inside that austere and forbidding prison? Was he sick? Was he still even alive?

One day she could bear the anxiety no longer. She resolved to go to the Citadel and ask after him, perhaps even try pleading to see him. She knew it was risky, but she couldn't bear to sit back and do nothing any longer. So, she asked the general if she could take the next day off work.

'After all, sir, I have worked for several weeks without any time off,' she reminded him.

'Why? What do you need a day off for?' he asked suspiciously.

'It's my father. As I mentioned, he is elderly and very ill. I need to take him to see a doctor.'

The general's face clouded over and he huffed angrily.

'One day and one day only,' he said, banging the desk with his fist. 'We are very generous towards you, Miss Nguyen. Please do not abuse our generosity and our trust.'

She bowed her head and backed away from his desk, not wanting him to see the anxiety in her eyes at the mention of trust.

The general's reaction worried her, but she put it to the back of her mind; she needed to go to the prison and find out about Papa and this was the only way.

The next morning, she rose just after dawn and put on an old, inconspicuous ao dai and a dark headscarf. She left the house as the sun was coming up and took a cyclo to the Citadel gates. The two soldiers guarding them this morning weren't familiar and she approached one, bowed politely and said, 'My father is in the prison. He has been there for many weeks. He is getting old and in poor health. I would like to see him if I can.'

The soldier laughed. 'No visitor,' he said.

'But please. He is a sick man. I need to know if he needs medicines. Could I speak to your superior officer please?'

The soldier conferred with his colleague and then, to her astonishment, unbarred the gate and pushed it open. Behind the gate was a cobbled courtyard between the outer and inner walls of the Citadel.

'Go to office,' he nodded her through. 'Senior officer is there. You can speak to him.'

She crossed the cobbles towards a door in the inner wall. As she walked, she heard the slam of the gates behind her. It sent shivers down her spine. What must it have been like for Papa, Camille and the others when they heard those gates shut behind them on the day they'd been brought here, knowing that they were then captive, unable to leave?

Feeling apprehensive, she walked towards the door and knocked as firmly as she could.

'Hairu,' an imperious voice said from inside. She knew this meant 'Enter' so she pushed the door open and went inside. There, a large, squat officer sat behind a desk munching his way through a huge baguette. He looked at her enquiringly.

'Do you speak French, please sir?' she asked, bowing deeply, and he replied, 'Little.'

'I have come to enquire about my father, Monsieur Dupont,' she said. 'He is a member of the French government, and he was brought here on March 9th. He is elderly and I'm concerned that he may be sick.'

The man put his baguette down on the desk and regarded her contemptuously.

'No visitor here. Not for French prisoner,' he said sternly, then he picked the baguette up again and resumed his munching.

'I have been sending him food each day,' she said. 'Do you know if it got to him?'

A broad smile crossed the officer's face. 'Ah, food very good. Very good indeed. Pho soup, broth. Thank you. Thank you very much.'

Arielle's mouth dropped open. So, the food she and Trang had lovingly prepared for Papa, which Trang had risked her life to bring to the Citadel had been eaten by this gluttonous officer.

'If he didn't get the food, please could I see him? He could well be sick.'

Anger clouded the man's face. 'He *always* get the food!' he shouted. 'I taste only. Just to check. But there is no need for extra food. Prisoner are fed very well. Imperial Japanese Army very generous.' He picked up the baguette and started eating again.

She stood there helplessly, watching him munch away, wondering what she could do to convince him to let her see Papa. When he'd finished, he wiped his hands on his trousers and stood up.

'You want to see you father? Come.'

He motioned her over to a window, high in the back wall of his office. It had upright bars, and the glass was grubby, but the officer rubbed a patch clear with the back of his hand.

'Look!' he said, and she stood on tiptoe and peered out of the window. Behind the office was a patch of scrubby land surrounded on all sides by the buildings of the Citadel. There were a few people walking round it, emaciated and dressed in rags, clinging to each other. With shock, Arielle recognised several of her former colleagues. All were shadows of their former selves and walked slowly and with difficulty, wandering around the yard aimlessly in the heat of the morning sun. She stared, dumbstruck. If this was what a few months in the Citadel had done to these formerly fit and healthy people, what would it have done to Papa?

Within seconds she had her answer. Through a gate in one of the walls, more prisoners came to join the few already walking on the patch of land. When Papa emerged through the gate, she hardly recognised him. His hair had gone from grey to completely white and he now had a straggly beard. He was desperately thin and could barely stagger along. He was being supported by a woman, whom Arielle instantly recognised by her blue dress and dirty blonde hair as Camille. Camille too looked thin and gaunt, her ragged dress sagged from her shoulders.

'Papa,' Arielle breathed, with tears in her eyes.

The pair began to walk slowly around the yard. As they drew closer Arielle couldn't hold back; she hammered on the window with her fists.

'Papa! Camille!' she yelled. They turned slowly and looked in her direction, but at that moment she felt the chubby hands of the officer on her shoulders, yanking her away from the window.

'That is forbidden,' he shouted at her. 'You go now!'

And he hauled her across the room and pushed her out of the door into the outer courtyard where she fell sprawling on the ground.

'You not come back here,' the officer yelled before slamming his office door.

She lay there for a few seconds before hauling herself to her feet and heading, dazed and shaken, towards the gate. There, she had to bang on the panels and shout for several minutes before the guards opened the gate and let her onto the street. She staggered out of the courtyard, tears streaming down her face, not caring that the guards were laughing at her. She began to walk down the street towards home, and all she could think of were the tragic, emaciated figures of Papa and Camille, clinging to each other as they walked out into the daylight.

WHEN SHE RETURNED to work the next day, the general asked her how her father was. She blinked at him, confused for a few seconds, then she said, 'He is a little better thank you sir. I'm glad I could take him to see the doctor. The doctor was able to help him.'

'That is good news Miss Nguyen. I hope that means that you will have no further need of days away from the office in future. As you can see, there is a pile of work waiting for your return.'

She went over to her desk and sat down as if in a dream. She'd been unable to sleep the night before for thinking about poor Papa, remembering his pitiful figure clad in rags, holding onto Camille, as they'd walked out into the exercise yard together. She knew there was nothing she could do to help him but she couldn't stop tormenting herself with anxious thoughts. The only comforting things about her visit to the prison, were that Camille was there helping Papa and that, if the Japanese officer was to be believed, at least some of the food Trang was taking there was making its way to Papa.

The day passed relatively uneventfully and she took what she'd been able to copy to the pagoda after work and gave it to the agent. She'd been the previous evening to tell him she hadn't been at work that day. She'd asked him if there was any way he could help get her father released, or at least given better conditions, and he'd shaken his head.

'I've told you already. Your father was one of the French oppressors. We cannot be seen to be helping them.'

'He was not an oppressor! He was a professional who took pride in his work. He gave up his life to serve this country.'

The agent laughed and shrugged his shoulders. 'I think however you try to dress it up, you will find he was one of the oppressors.'

'But wouldn't you do it to help me? Think of what I've already done for you. What I've risked for your organisation.'

The agent's eyes narrowed and took on that flinty, deadly serious look that sent chills through her bones.

'You are in no position to ask favours of us. Remember what we know about the events of 1935 and your part in them. Just think about that when you are wavering.'

So, she carried on going through the motions, copying whatever she found that she judged the Viet Minh would find useful, running the gauntlet of the guards at the door every evening. If she ever had to walk out of the building alone, she was terrified that they would search her, but so far she had been lucky.

But a few days later her luck ran out. She had found some classified maps during the day which showed battle plans for the front in Thailand, and had surreptitiously copied them with tracing paper. She'd never done that before, but it was the only way she could think of to get an accurate copy for the Viet Minh. She folded them carefully and put them inside the lining of her bag alongside a couple of reports of troop movements that she'd copied earlier. As she got up to leave, she noticed some activity at the door. Someone was entering the building. She looked up to see who it was and when she saw the stout figure of the senior prison officer from the Citadel enter the room, shockwaves coursed through her. She sat back down at her desk, keeping her head bowed as the general strode forward to greet the officer, hand outstretched.

She knew she had to get out of the room. He would be sure to recognise her. So, as the general and the prison officer exchanged greetings, she put her bag on her shoulder and strode purposefully towards the door. She got level with the guards when the general's voice boomed out.

'Miss Nguyen, I would like you to take notes at an important meeting please. You are not free to go yet.'

She ignored him and kept walking. She could not risk the officer recognising her and telling the general that she'd visited the Citadel, that her father was French, that she'd been working here under false pretences all along.

She walked past the guards and was at the top of the staircase when she heard the general's voice again, this time apoplectic with rage.

'Guards! Don't let her go! Seize her! Search her bags! Bring her back here!'

17

HANOI, 1945

A rielle fled down the stairs as fast as her legs would carry her. The two guards were right behind her, hot on her heels. She could hear them panting and swearing under their breath, but they moved clumsily, encumbered by stiff uniforms and heavy weapons. She reached the front door, thanked Buddha that there was no guard stationed there this evening, wrenched it open and ran outside, slamming it in the faces of the guards who were a couple of steps behind her. Then she sprinted as fast as she could away from the building, across the square and into a side-street and out onto the pavement that ran along the side of the Hoan Kiem lake. There, she slowed down a little and caught her breath, allowing her heartbeat to settle as she tried to blend in with the early evening crowds, checking over her shoulder to see if the guards were still following her. When she was sure that no one was, she hailed a passing cyclo and asked him to take her as quickly as he could to the Lake Pagoda.

The Viet Minh agent was leaning on the railings near the temple gate, watching the sunset on the lake and smoking a cheroot, just as he often was when she arrived. She hurried up to him and when he saw the distress on her face, he motioned her to follow him into the trees.

'What's happened?' he asked.

'My cover is blown. I had to run away from the Mairie. An officer came who would have recognised me, so I tried to leave the building. The general gave the order to seize me and search my bags as I left so I had to run.'

The agent swore under his breath. He was silent for a moment, then he asked, 'But why would the officer have recognised you? No one knows what you do for us.'

'He works at the Citadel,' she said, dropping her gaze. 'He saw me when I tried to visit my father. He would definitely have told the general that I'm half French and that my father's a prisoner.'

'You visited your father?' the agent's voice was incredulous. 'Whyever did you do that? That's so risky.'

She shrugged wordlessly, and suddenly the horror and torment she'd been living under for months came to the surface and she took a great shuddering sob and let the tears fall. The agent just stood there watching her. He didn't soften his expression or try to comfort her in any way.

'You have been a useful informant to us these past few months, but that has run its course now,' he said.

Relief flooded through Arielle. This was it. The strain and fear of these past few months was over for her. She started planning where she might go. It might be dangerous to go home, there was a chance that the prison officer could have recognised her even across the room and the Japanese might look for her there. Perhaps she could hide in Bà Ngoại's apartment. Since her grandmother's death, just before the Japanese occupation, her father had kept the apartment, in memory of

Arielle's Annamese mother and grandmother. She might be safer there, but if she did that, she would need to get word to Trang who would be bound to worry otherwise.

'We will have to use you some other way,' the agent's voice cut into her thoughts. She stared at him.

'Some other way? Whatever do you mean?'

'We need help in our training camps in the hills. The Americans are training us in guerrilla warfare so we can help in the fight against the Japanese. More people are needed to be taught to use weapons, and others to run the camp. You have shown yourself to be brave and dedicated, Madame Garnier. You would be an asset up there. I will radio my comrades this evening and let them know you're coming. You can start out tomorrow morning.'

'But what if I don't want to do that?' she asked. 'I've done enough for you and your organisation. I just want to go away and live in peace.'

'No one can live in peace in this country while it is ruled by a foreign enemy,' he snapped. 'Your country needs you.'

'But you're forgetting; I'm half French. How do you know I would be loyal to your cause?'

'And you're forgetting why you agreed to help us in the first place,' he said, suddenly gripping her arms and shaking her. 'Nothing has changed in that regard. Never forget that we know all about what happened in 1935 and your part in it.'

She couldn't reply and she couldn't return his gaze. She sobbed again and looked down at the grass beneath her feet. She knew she was beaten. The Viet Minh would always have this over her and she wasn't going to risk the truth of what she'd done coming out.

'Alright,' she said finally, 'I will go. But I can't risk going home before I leave. The Japanese might look for me there. But I will need some clothes...'

'I can go there and get them for you. I will make sure there are no Japanese there before I do.'

'Could you give a note to our housekeeper for me too? She will worry about me if I don't let her know that I'm leaving.'

'Of course. Write a list of things you need and your note. I will take it to your home.'

She scribbled a hasty note to Trang with tears in her eyes.

My dearest Trang,

I don't know when I will be home, but it is no longer safe for me to be here. I have to go away for a time. It is better if you don't know where I'm going or why. I hope you don't mind me asking you to please take care of the place for me while I'm away. And I hope you can carry on taking food to my father each day too. I know some of it is getting to him and that might be keeping him alive. I will think of you while I'm away and will be in touch again as soon as I can.

Love, Arielle.

THE AIRCRAFT that took Arielle into the mountains close to the Chinese border was a Douglas C-47 transport plane with bench seats running along either side of the fuselage. The Viet Minh agent drove her to the remote airstrip hidden in the back of a van, together with four young men, two of whom already looked like guerrilla fighters and the other two looked like raw new recruits.

Arielle had never flown before and clambered up into the battered old plane with feelings of dread and trepidation. She wasn't prepared for the rush of adrenaline as the aircraft belted down the airstrip before take-off, or the lurching feeling in her belly as the plane climbed quickly in an attempt to get into the clouds before being spotted by Japanese aircraft.

She looked around at her fellow passengers, at their expressions of intense concentration, and guessed that they were feeling exactly as she was. But as she stared out of the window opposite, at the white fluffy clouds that enveloped the aircraft, her mind was full of regret that she'd had to leave Hanoi where Papa was still in prison and that her attempts at getting him released, or even of being able to visit him, had come to nothing.

She'd spent her last night in the city in Bà Ngoại's old apartment, thinking about happier times. She remembered how she'd always relied on the constant love of both Bà Ngoại and her father, neither of whom was here to guide her now. She knew she'd had no choice about joining the mission into the hills, but it still felt as though she was abandoning Papa by leaving Hanoi, even though there was little she could have done to help him there. She tried to comfort herself with the thought that Trang would still faithfully take food to the prison gates each day, but even so, the guilt still remained.

The flight into the northern mountains didn't take long; less than an hour, and Arielle was just getting used to the loud drone of the engines and the lurching and tipping of the plane in the turbulent wind currents, when it began its descent towards the remote jungle airstrip.

'We have to go down steeply to avoid detection,' the man next to her said. 'Hold on tight.'

She grabbed the bench with both hands as the plane banked and made a sudden dive towards the earth. Her stomach gave a sickening lurch, and her ears began to burn as the plane broke free of the clouds and plummeted downwards. After a few, nail-biting seconds, they bumped down on the rough airstrip and the plane quickly came to a shuddering halt, engines roaring.

As soon as the plane had come to a rest, the side door was opened from the outside, and a man dressed in combat gear put his head into the plane. 'Everybody out,' he said, and everyone scrambled from their seats and headed to the door.

The guerrilla held his hand up for Arielle to take. She grabbed her pack which she'd stowed under the bench and went to the edge of the aircraft. Standing there by the door and staring at the ground, it seemed a long way down, but she threw her pack out, took a deep breath and gripped the man's hand. When she landed, sprawling on the long grass, he helped her to her feet and said, 'The plane needs to take off again straight away, then my comrades will cover the airstrip with bamboo and palm leaves as camouflage. We all need to get away from here quickly without drawing attention to the place.'

The six of them stood under the trees on the edge of the jungle and watched the little plane take off, ascend sharply, and disappear into the clouds as it turned back towards Hanoi. Then, a swarm of guerrillas, dressed in ragged camouflage gear emerged from under the trees dragging branches and great canes of bamboo with them, and proceeded to cover the airstrip with the greenery until it was completely hidden from view.

'Come. We go now,' the lead guerrilla, who Arielle learned was called Long, snapped his fingers. She shouldered her pack and followed him along an earth path that led round the edge of a patch of jungle and emerged onto a bank between paddy fields. As they walked the length of the field, Arielle stared either side of her at the bare earth. No one was working the field and the rice plants were blackened and shrivelled in the ground.

'Famine here. Crop has failed,' Long commented simply.

'This is terrible,' Arielle murmured, thinking of those ragged, starving people on the streets of Hanoi and those with sunken cheeks she'd offered food to in her kitchen. She'd never seen fields like this before and this sight brought home to her just how serious the famine was. But after they'd passed the first field there were many others to follow. The whole district had suffered the same fate. Eventually they reached a village; just a circle of huts around a village pond. There were no animals rooting about under the houses, no dogs rushing out barking to meet them. It was eerily silent, with a deathly stillness that sent shivers down Arielle's spine.

'Where are the people?' Arielle asked. 'Perhaps we can help them?'

Long shook his head. 'All are dead. All died weeks ago. Men, women, children, all the same.'

On their long walk through the devastated fields, they came upon many villages just like the first one. In some, emaciated bodies lay on the ground, their flesh eaten away by rats and birds, ribs and skulls bleached by the relentless sun. Arielle could scarcely believe what she was seeing and remembered how the Viet Minh agent had told her that this had started with the French forcing farmers to grow industrial products instead of food and had carried on more aggressively with the Japanese doing the same.

'This is the fault of the French and the Japanese,' Long said, confirming her thoughts. 'The Japanese commandeered food for the army, leaving villagers to starve. They have no morals, no compassion. That is why we must fight against them.'

In some villages they found people barely alive; sitting on the ground amongst the dead bodies, the rats and the vultures waiting for them to die. They gave them what rations they had with them.

'It will not help them really,' Long said. 'What we have given them won't last. They will all be dead in a few days.'

'But isn't there anything else we can do?' Arielle asked, her heart full of pity and grief at what she'd witnessed.

'There is, but it involves drastic action. When we reach the camp in the hills you will learn more.'

At the edge of the plain where once rice had grown in abundance and villages had flourished, the ground began to rise. Here, the earth was covered in jungle and the path carried on under the great trees. Instantly the jungle closed around them, hot, steamy and dark. Long led them along a tiny path between the teak trees, climbing higher and higher, past enormous ferns that brushed their faces, massive clumps of towering bamboo, through curtains of creepers and bushes with prickles that dragged on their skin. The path itself was virtually invisible. Arielle kept close to Long and was aware that the man behind her was following her closely too. It would be all too easy to get lost here. It was tough going and the air was clammy and steamy and before long Arielle was soaked in sweat.

They trekked over the jungle covered hills for an hour or more, then came to a clearing, high up in the hills, near a rocky peak.

'Here is our camp,' said Long proudly, gesturing to a circle of a dozen or so simple bamboo and thatch huts that nestled beneath the rocks. A stream tumbled down the rocks and past the camp. In the centre of the clearing was a gently burning bonfire, but there seemed to be nobody around.

'All our comrades are in the hills being trained in guerrilla warfare,' Long explained. 'Only our leader, Mr Hoo, is here at the camp. He is in bed in the corner hut. He is very ill with malaria.'

'Now, I will show you where you will stay. Wait there,

comrade,' he said to Arielle as he led the three other men away to a hut at the other end of the clearing. She waited for him, her eyes scanning the camp. This looked to be a well-ordered place, tidy and neat. She wondered if there were any other women here, or if she was the only one. That didn't trouble her unduly. She could already tell that Long was a trustworthy, honourable man and that the camp was a disciplined place, but even so, it would be good to have some female company.

When Long returned, he showed her into one of the more central huts.

'This is for our female fighters,' he said, showing her inside. Arielle blinked, adjusting her eyes to the dark interior. There were four camp beds with mosquito netting suspended from the ceiling. So there *were* other women here, she thought with relief.

Long then showed them round the camp and explained the facilities – the stream for water which needed to be boiled, the latrine behind the rocks which had to be dug daily, the cooking utensils and stores of basic foodstuffs, kept in one of the huts, the firewood, stacked under some rocks. By the time the newcomers had settled in to the camp, it was mid-afternoon and Arielle's stomach was rumbling. She hadn't eaten since she'd grabbed some noodles from an early morning food stall in the Old Quarter in Hanoi. That seemed an age ago. Long distributed some flatbreads to everyone round the fire along with some tin mugs of green tea.

'The rest of the comrades will be back before sunset,' Long told them. 'So, we will prepare vegetables for the evening meal.'

He handed round knives and vegetables, and as they peeled and chopped, Long encouraged them to talk about their reasons for joining the Viet Minh. Two of them had had family members killed by the Japanese. 'My father was beaten to death on our farm for refusing to give up supplies for the Japanese Army,' one reported. 'My mother was raped and killed when the Japanese looted their village,' another said. Another said that his brother had been beaten and dragged off to the Citadel for refusing to bow to Japanese officers in the street.

'And what about you, comrade?' Long asked, turning to Arielle. 'What are your reasons for joining us and fighting for the cause?'

Arielle hesitated for a moment. She couldn't tell them the whole truth, so she told them an edited version.

'I was forced to work for the Japanese government at the Mairie in Hanoi. The Viet Minh asked me to pass secrets to them which I did. But one day I was almost discovered and had to run away. That's why I came here.'

The others looked at her with awed expressions and murmured their approval. She looked away in shame. If they'd known the real reason – that she'd been blackmailed into coming because the Viet Minh knew her dark secrets – they wouldn't have looked at her that way. She didn't deserve their respect, she knew that. And, as she looked up again, she met Long's eyes, and saw from his expression that he knew her secret too.

Her thoughts were interrupted by the drone of approaching aircraft and she looked up to see a dozen or so planes flying in formation, heading south.

'Those are US aircraft,' said Long. 'We often see them here. They are on their way to do a bombing raid on a Japanese base somewhere.'

They all shaded their eyes and stared up at the convoy, and a swarm of smaller aircraft appeared out of the clouds from all directions and started attacking the American planes. Even from where they sat on the ground, they could hear the ack-ack of machinegun fire and the buzz of aircraft engines. One Japanese plane peeled off and plummeted to earth, its engines screaming, smoke streaming from its fuselage. It disappeared into the jungle somewhere below them and a plume of smoke rose from where it hit the ground.

The dogfight in the sky went on for several minutes. Gradually the Japanese aircraft were all hit. They limped away, engines stuttering and the American convoy lumbered on.

'That happens a lot,' Long explained when the noise of the aircraft had faded away. 'Part of our mission here is to help locate and rescue downed US pilots. We've done that for a couple of men so far; nursed them back to health in the camp and sent them on their way. But I don't think there were any American casualties from that particular fight. They seemed to dispatch the Japs pretty swiftly.'

By now, the sun was beginning to dip behind the jungle-covered hills and other guerrillas started drifting back to the camp in twos and threes. They all looked dishevelled and weary from their day in the hills. They squatted round the fire and Long handed them tea in tin mugs and introduced them to the new arrivals. Around ten had arrived by the time a group of three young women appeared and joined the group. Like the others they were dressed in combat gear and camouflage helmets.

Long handed them mugs of tea and said, 'Let me introduce you to our three intrepid sisters, who are learning to handle weapons and fight in the jungle alongside us men. This is Chi, this is Mai, and this is Maki.'

Maki?

Arielle looked up, surprised, and peered closely at the third woman who had flopped down on a tree stump a few metres away from her. And as she stared into the young woman's eyes, she recognised that passionate young girl she'd met ten years before at the plantation in the south wearing a cocktail dress. It was she who had first alerted Arielle to the injustices and cruelty for which her husband was responsible and had set into motion that chain of unstoppable events that had brought her here.

18

TÂN TRÀO, TONKIN, 1945

A s the sun went down behind the jungle and the light gradually faded, the guerrillas began to drift back to their huts to rest, or to the stream to wash before the evening meal. When Maki rose alone to leave, Arielle went over to her and held out her hand.

'Maki? Do you remember me?'

Maki stared at her, puzzled, and then her face cleared.

'Arielle?' her voice was incredulous, but she took Arielle's hand. 'But they said your name was Tuyen.'

She smiled and Arielle recognised the distinctive gap between her two front teeth.

'Yes,' Arielle put her face close to Maki's and whispered. 'No one here but you and Long knows I'm half-French, and I'd like to keep it that way.'

'I understand. Come – sit down by the fire again,' said Maki warmly. 'Tell me why you're here.'

'Oh, it's a long story,' Arielle said, sitting back down on the logs. And while the two guerrillas assigned to cook the evening meal plucked two chickens, quartered them and began to roast them over the flames of the fire, she told Maki the basics of how she'd worked for the Japanese and had almost been discovered passing documents to the Viet Minh. She deliberately kept the details vague.

'But what about your husband, Monsieur Garnier? Etienne, wasn't it? What happened to him? He stopped coming to the plantation sometime in 1935, but no one knew why.'

'He died, Maki,' Arielle replied simply. 'A few months after we met you.'

'Oh!' Maki looked shocked momentarily, then her face relaxed and she said, 'But I can see from your eyes that you are not grieving him... He was a cruel man.'

'He was indeed,' Arielle said with a shudder trying to suppress the memories. 'But what about Bertrand? However did you get away from him and from the plantation?'

'Bertrand was killed at the beginning of the war, by an uprising on the plantation. People had had enough of the cruelty and the starvation, and seeing the French regime toppled gave them the inspiration to protest. But things got out of hand and Bertrand was mobbed and stabbed to death. The French sent another manager, but by that time most of the workers had escaped. The place has gone to rack and ruin since the Japanese invasion.'

'Are your parents still there?'

'My father died, but my mother still lives in the same hut. I haven't seen her for a long time, but I write when I can.'

'So, how did you come to join up with the Viet Minh?'

'I'd always been passionate about independence for our country and wanted to fight the injustices of the French. Towards the end, some Viet Minh members actually managed to infiltrate the tappers gangs on the plantation. It was them who started the uprising, and afterwards, they persuaded many of us to join them. I've been helping out at the Viet

Minh HQ in Saigon for a long time, but it's only recently that they asked me to train to fight for the cause.'

In the flickering firelight, Arielle could see the fervour in Maki's eyes. How different she was now from the young woman Arielle had met in 1935, who loved to read about film stars and royalty and looked forward to trips to the cinema and the dressmaker in Saigon. But even then, she'd demonstrated that instinct for justice and that bravery. After all, it was only through her that Arielle herself had discovered about the cruelty and deaths on the plantation. It was just that in the intervening years, Maki had clearly grown up and found a cause she believed in. Arielle's own feelings for the same cause were much more ambivalent.

Later, after they'd eaten a meal of chicken and vegetable curry by the light of the fire, everyone gradually retired to their huts. Maki introduced Arielle properly to the two other women, Chi and Mai, who were much less talkative and friendly than Maki herself, and both eyed Arielle with suspicion.

Arielle laid down on the camp bed under the mosquito net and listened to the night sounds of the surrounding jungle. The whooping of monkeys, the buzzing of insects. Her mind went back to the shocking sights she'd witnessed on the walk up to the camp; the starving people, the rats, the skeletons, the empty villages. Those things had shocked her to the core. She thought too about Papa and Camille in the damp, austere Citadel and of Trang alone in the house in the French Quarter of the city. Her heart yearned to help them. How long would she have to stay in these hills until the Viet Minh were prepared to release her? At least having Maki here meant she had a friend, and made the ordeal slightly less forbidding, but she would be counting the days until they let her go so that she could return to Hanoi and at least be close to Papa.

In the morning, Arielle was woken before dawn by someone banging a tin at the door of the hut. After a quick wash in the stream, breakfast of tea, eggs and noodles was served beside the fire. As they ate, Long divided them into groups for the day's training. Arielle was put with the four young men she'd travelled up with the day before.

'Today you will go to a nearby clearing and learn to handle a rifle,' Long told them. 'My comrade, Cong Son will take you there and you will be joined by two colleagues from the OSS who will teach you. Cong Son will translate for you. If you do well, they will start to teach you to shoot.'

'The OSS?' Arielle asked.

'That is the American Office of Strategic Services. This unit is called the Deer Team. They are here to train us to fight the Japanese.'

'American soldiers? But why?'

'Primarily they want us to sabotage Japanese transport links to prevent the Japanese from entering China. But the aims are wider than that. Together, we want to drive the Japanese from Indochina altogether.'

The four young men were clearly excited by the prospect of learning to shoot a gun, but Arielle shrunk inside. Handle and shoot a rifle? How ever could she do that? She wanted nothing to do with death or violence. She'd vowed long ago to lead a life of peace. The others started chattering excitedly amongst themselves, but Arielle remained silent, dreading the day ahead. Long came and sat beside her and said quietly, so that no one else could hear, 'This will be good for you, sister. I can see reluctance in your face. But remember why you are here. We need you to fight for us. You don't have a choice about this.'

She looked at him. His face was open and kind, but his eyes blazed with the same passionate determination she'd seen in the eyes of the Viet Minh agent at the Pagoda, and in Maki's eyes too. She had no doubt that what Long had just said was a veiled threat. She was here on sufferance, and she really did have no choice but to comply with their wishes.

The training ground was in a muddy clearing, deep in the jungle, half an hour's trek from the main camp. When the five newcomers arrived they were introduced to two American servicemen; Sergeants Redmond and Leigh. To Arielle, the two Americans were larger than life; tall and tanned, exuding health and fitness, they were a sharp contrast to the skinny and rather shabby Annamese guerrillas.

During the morning, they were taught how to load, handle and carry a rifle. Although Arielle shrunk from the task, when she gritted her teeth and got on with it, she actually found it fairly easy and received many compliments from the Americans as a result. After lunch of plain rice and green tea, they were taught to shoot at a target – a watermelon set on top of a tree stump. The three men went first and all had a reasonable attempt at hitting the watermelon, although their bullets ricocheted off into the trees behind. When it came to Arielle's turn, her sweaty hands were shaking so much that she thought she would drop the gun. She remembered all the times she'd visited the Lake Pagoda and meditated on peace and kindness, yet here she was about to fire a lethal weapon.

She walked tentatively up to the firing spot. Then, one of the Americans stood behind her and gently coached her through the motions of holding the gun to her shoulder as steadily as she could, standing sideways with her non-trigger side facing the target, making sure her elbows were tucked tightly into her body. He showed her how to support the rifle with one hand, pull the butt to her shoulder, then rest her cheek against the rifle and line up the sights with the target. She felt the cold, smooth wood of the gun. Then, he told her to breathe steadily and fire as she exhaled. She'd started sweaty and panicky, but the methodical steps the American made her practice several times, slowed her heartbeat, and by the time she actually came to firing, she was as calm and focused as she'd ever been.

When she fired, the gun kicked back, thumping into her shoulder, but her eyes were fixed on the target and although she started backwards and nearly toppled over, she hardly noticed the pain. She watched the bullet graze the top of the melon, making a shallow groove in its skin.

'Hey! Great shot!' Sergeant Redmond shouted thumping her on the back, and, caught up in the excitement of the moment, she forgot her initial abhorrence and lifted her arms triumphantly.

They practiced again and again, throughout that long afternoon, and everyone got gradually better with each shot, but Arielle was the first to hit the target square on. Everyone cheered and she looked around at their faces. For the first time, her misgivings about the Viet Minh were fading into the background. She felt part of something. It was a feeling she hadn't experienced for a very long time.

'You've got a real feel for firearms,' Cong Son said as they trekked back through the darkening jungle. 'Have you done anything like this before?' She shook her head.

'Never,' she said. 'I can't quite believe it.'

'Some people are just born with it,' he said with grudging admiration, 'Most of us have to work hard at it to achieve the same results.'

At supper that evening Maki sidled up and sat down beside Arielle, and the cooks handed round tin plates of river fish and rice.

'I hear you have quite a talent for shooting,' Maki said. 'One of the boys told me just now. You are lucky. When I first came, it took me days, weeks probably, to be able to shoot straight. You will be a real asset to our group.'

Arielle shrugged. 'I've no idea why. Perhaps it was a fluke. I've never even imagined shooting a gun before. I've always been a person of peace.'

Maki looked at her sharply. 'Peace is a luxury no one in this country can afford,' she said. 'Anyone who thinks they don't have a responsibility to act is a coward. It would be the easiest thing in the world to sit back and leave the dirty work to everyone else. But if we all do that, we will never throw off Japanese rule, or the French for that matter.'

Arielle was silent, staring into the flames. She thought of her father and Camille, suffering inside the Citadel. They were just as much victims of circumstance as everyone here was, only they were on the wrong side of justice now. She'd never really analysed whether French rule was a good or bad thing, she'd just accepted it as the normal state of affairs. Her father, with his high ideals and principles, represented the best side of colonialism, but her experience with Etienne had taught her about the other side; the exploitation and the cruelty. It was over, she realised. It had to come to an end sooner or later, she just fervently hoped that there was as little bloodshed as possible in the process.

Over the next few weeks, camp life fell into a regular routine. Each morning they were up before dawn and were given half an hour of physical education instruction before washing in the stream and taking breakfast by the camp fire. Then, they were split into their groups and went off into the jungle for different stages of their training. Some groups went to gather supplies, or to patrol the area monitoring Japanese troop movements, others stayed in camp to chop wood and prepare food.

Arielle and her little group perfected the art of shooting

the American M-1 rifles from every different position. They also learned how to convert and handle their rifles as bayonets. After that they were taught how to use mortars, grenades, bazookas and machine guns. They learned all about guerrilla warfare; about moving about silently in the jungle, so that even the jungle creatures wouldn't stir at their approach; they learned about surviving in the wild from berries, and how to trap, kill and cook fish and wild animals.

One evening, when they returned from their day's training, a diminutive old man with a lined face, white hair and a goatee beard was sitting in front of the fire with some of the guerrillas, helping them to peel vegetables.

'That is our leader, Mr Hoo,' Cong Son whispered to the group, and he went forward and greeted the old man with a bow.

'I'm so pleased to see you are recovered, Mr Hoo,' he said, and the old man chuckled.

'If it hadn't been for the Americans and the medicines they brought with them I wouldn't have done. But it's good to see so many new recruits to our little band,' he said, looking round with twinkling eyes at the small group of exhausted recruits.

'May I introduce them to you, sir?' and when the old man nodded, Cong Son went ahead and presented each of them to the leader. When it came to Arielle's turn, Mr Hoo took her hand and looked up at her with a broad, open smile. He said, 'I've heard a lot about you from our agent in Hanoi, comrade Tuyen. I know you put yourself at risk to bring us information from Japanese HQ and for that I thank you. We are indebted to you, and you are very welcome here in our humble camp.'

Arielle returned his handshake and looked into his eyes. She was expecting to see cynicism there, a hint that he knew her secret and that he wouldn't hesitate to remind her of that fact, but what she saw instead was deep, genuine kindness, an unusual strength of character and an unshakeable resolve. She saw instantly why everyone in the camp revered Mr Hoo. She bowed her head respectfully and thanked him for his kind words.

After Arielle had been in the camp for two weeks, one evening at supper, Long came and squatted beside her.

'I have had good reports of your progress from our American comrades, comrade Tuyen,' he said. 'Tomorrow, I would like you to join a mission I am leading.'

Arielle's nerves fizzed. She wasn't sure if she was excited or terrified. She nodded wordlessly, and waited for him to go on.

'It is a mission into the Japanese depot at Tân Trào,' he said. 'Our intelligence has found that there are plentiful supplies of food there, while all the villagers around are starving. Our mission will be to raid the foodbank, capture as much food as we can and distribute it to the poor of the surrounding villages.'

Arielle stared at him. 'That sounds dangerous, comrade.'

He laughed. 'All our missions are dangerous. That's why we're trained to shoot. That's why we have guns.'

He stood up and patted her shoulder. 'I'll call you first thing and you need to be ready right after breakfast. We must make an early start.'

Arielle hardly slept that night, racked with anxiety about what the next day would bring. In her mind she went over and over everything she'd learned since she'd been in the camp, but was plagued with the worry that when it came down to reality, she might not be able to put it into practice. Would she actually be able to fire at another human being? She broke out in a cold sweat at the thought and hoped fervently that she wouldn't be put in that position.

The next morning, the group was woken even earlier than usual, before the first rays of sun had started to creep over the horizon. Long put his head around the door of Arielle's hut and whispered to her to wake up, but she was already wide awake. She'd slept in her combat clothes and was up and out of the hut in no time, her nerves taut with anticipation of the day ahead. The four others in her group were already sitting on the tree stumps around the fire. They were each handed hard boiled eggs for breakfast, as well as a short length of hollowed out bamboo filled with fried rice which would be their rations for the day. Arielle sat down and bit into her egg, but her stomach quickly recoiled, and she was unable to take another bite. She was anxious to be off and getting on with the mission. She could hardly sit still.

As the sun came up, burning the dew off the undergrowth and steam rose up in clouds all around them, they left the camp and trekked through the jungle, Long leading the column. They walked in silence; everyone appeared as tense as Arielle felt. After an hour or so they reached the top of a small hill. Long led them out of the trees and came to a halt. He pointed down into the valley below. They stood in a line and shaded their eyes against the fierce sun. Long passed his binoculars to each in turn and they peered at what was below them. Down there in the valley, amongst the devastated rice fields and destroyed villages, a great army encampment had been built. Row upon row of white canvas tents were pitched around a group of more substantial wooden huts. At one end of the camp the sun glinted on rows of jeeps and armoured vehicles.

'That's the Japanese garrison here at Tân Trào,' Long explained. 'As you know, we're interested in the food store, which our intelligence informs us is in one of those huts bang in the middle of the camp. That means we will have to approach it from between the tents, as stealthily as we can to avoid detection. When we reach the food store, we need to take as many sacks of rice as we are able to haul out. I'd like to avoid bloodshed, but if we have to kill or injure to get it, so be it.'

'Why didn't we come in the dark?' Nerves made Arielle blurt her thoughts out loud, but then she stopped herself, realising this could be regarded as insubordination.

But Long smiled and responded thoughtfully, 'It's a good question, comrade Tuyen. And we did consider that. But the food store is shut up at night and heavily guarded. At least in the daytime there is no guard, and only unarmed cooks go in there from time to time to get supplies for the cookhouse. We debated the pros and cons of daylight or darkness and took a considered decision to do the raid in the daytime.'

Then he looked around at the party. 'Ready? OK, we go now.'

They moved back under cover of the trees and made their way down through the steep jungled hillside until they reached the valley floor. When they emerged from the shelter of the canopy, they were only a few metres from the white canvas wall of the first row of tents. They crouched behind some thorny bushes and peered into the camp. Chills went through Arielle at what she saw. Between the tents they could see into the clearing where soldiers were sitting around a campfire in vests and shorts. They were eating breakfast, chatting amongst themselves. They're just like us, she thought. Panic and regret flooded through her at the thought of what they were about to do.

'By the time we get round to the side nearest to the buildings, they will have finished their food and be washing up in the cookhouse,' Long whispered. 'So hopefully there will be no one at the food store when we arrive. Come, we will go round the perimeter.'

To keep within the shelter of the surrounding bushes, they

had to crawl around the edge of the camp on their hands and knees. They'd been trained to do this and had practised many times before. Arielle was first in line behind Long. He scurried along expertly, covering the dusty ground at speed. She struggled to keep up with him and quickly found herself out of breath. By the time they had skirted the entire camp and reached the other side, they could see the buildings of the cookhouse and food store only a few metres from where they crouched. Arielle's knees and the palms of her hands were red raw, but in the adrenaline rush of knowing that they were about to breach the perimeter and break into the enemy camp, she felt no pain at all. Her heart was hammering away against her ribs and she looked around at her comrades. All of them had that same look in their eyes; they shone with excitement and terror in equal measure.

'We will go two at a time,' Long said. 'We will use bayonets, if needed. They will be quieter than gunshots. Please ready your weapons. I will go first with comrade Duc here.'

Once they had fixed their bayonets, Long and Duc set off. Arielle watched, gripping her bayonet, and holding her breath, as they scurried down a narrow passageway between the tents, making for the huts in the middle. There was then a long pause while they were out of sight. Waiting for them to return was unbearable. Each second felt like an age. She sat there watching the gap between the tents, willing Long and the other boy to appear. Eventually they did, each hauling a sack of rice on his back, their faces triumphant. They reached the perimeter of the camp and dived into the shelter of the bushes.

'You go now,' Long said, nodding to the next two. 'You will be last, comrades,' he said to Arielle and Hoc, the remaining man.

The next two scurried off between the tents and once

again there was that agonising wait for them to return. Arielle's stomach churned with nerves at the knowledge that she was next. Within minutes the second pair were returning with their loads and threw themselves down on the ground.

'Now you go,' Long said, nodding to Arielle and Hoc.

As Arielle followed Hoc between the tents, she thought her heart would burst. All she could hear was blood rushing in her ears and the erratic surge of her heartbeat. Again, she struggled to breathe, her chest was so constricted with panic.

They emerged from the narrow strip between the tents and had to cross a patch of open ground to get to the food store. The door to the store stood wide open.

'Come!' urged Hoc. They ran across the open ground together and within seconds they were inside the hut. It took a moment for their eyes to adjust to the gloom. Then they saw the sacks of rice stashed against one wall.

'Quick, grab a sack,' Hoc said, lunging at one himself and lifting it up.

Arielle stepped forward to take a sack and it was then that she saw him. A terrified cook in a filthy apron, cowering at the end of the hut, his eyes bulging with terror. For a few seconds she was paralysed with fear and indecision, and as she dithered, the man started to scream. In an instant, Hoc stepped forward and plunged his bayonet into the man's chest, dragged it out covered in blood and stabbed it into him again, this time in his stomach. The man doubled up, dropped to the floor, and lay there twitching as blood spurted from his body, his mouth frothing blood and spit, silenced for ever.

Arielle was shaking all over now, horrified that she was part of this.

'Quick, take a sack comrade and let's go,' Hoc said and she did as she was told, the sack heavy and slipping between her sweating fingers. Hauling it behind her, she followed Hoc out of the hut and they dived back between the tents. They could hear shouts, and footsteps running from all corners of the camp towards the food store. The screams of the cook must have alerted others.

When they reached the perimeter and threw themselves onto the ground beside Long and the others Hoc told him what had happened.

'We need to get back into the jungle quickly,' Long said. 'We can't go back round the edge of the camp or they will find us. Follow me.'

Arielle hoisted the sack onto her back and followed the others up through the trees and into the cover of the jungle. The hills were steeper on this side of the camp and the sack of rice felt incredibly heavy. She struggled with every step. The others, stronger and taller than she was, were soon drawing ahead and she began to panic, imagining that the Japanese soldiers would soon be upon her. But before long she reached a clearing near the top of the hill and the others were waiting for her, sitting beside their sacks of rice.

Long's face was triumphant. 'Well done, comrades. That was a successful mission. It is a longer trek back to our camp from this side of the valley, but we are safe now. They will not come for us up here through the jungle.'

The others cheered, raising their hands in triumph and slapping each other on the back, but Arielle couldn't share their happiness. She stayed silent. All she could think of was the sight of the terrified cook squirming on the ground, blood spurting from his bayonet wounds. How could they celebrate when they'd just taken an innocent life?

19

TÂN TRÀO, TONKIN, 1945

I t was late afternoon by the time they got back to camp with their sacks of rice, and by then, Arielle's whole body was aching with the effort of humping her sack along jungle tracks and up steep gradients. They dumped their spoils in one of the huts and went to sit down in the clearing where they were given mugs of hot tea and a supper of rice and chicken. Long was ebullient at the success of the mission, and the others responded to his joy, singing war songs, sipping whisky from bamboo cups, gradually getting tipsy and raucous. But Arielle couldn't join in with the celebrations. She was haunted by the memory of the poor cook, cowering in the corner of the food store, the bayonet plunging into his chest, the sound of his ribs cracking. Had they forgotten about the life they had taken? It may have been a Japanese life, but it was a life all the same.

'Early tomorrow morning we will take the rice down to the villages, but now we must rest,' said Long after darkness had enveloped the camp.

Eventually everyone trailed back to their huts. Maki caught up with Arielle as she walked back to hers.

'You should be proud, comrade,' Maki said, putting her arm around Arielle's shoulders and hugging her. 'That rice will save many people from starvation. But you were so quiet tonight. You looked unhappy.'

'We killed a man,' Arielle muttered. 'I can't get it out of my mind.'

'That was only a Jap,' Maki said. 'There is no need to feel guilt over such a death. The Japanese have occupied and brutalised this country for five years. How many of our people have they killed? They are the aggressors here.'

'But that man was innocent. He was unarmed, just a simple cook.'

'You should not be so sensitive, comrade,' said Maki. 'When you've done a few raids like that, you will become hardened to it.'

A few raids? Arielle's spirits sank. How could she go on another raid and witness more deaths, even be expected to kill others herself? How could she be part of this when she didn't share the passion and singlemindedness that carried the others through and enabled them to square their actions with their consciences?

She laid down under the mosquito net on her camp bed and stared up into the soft darkness, listening to the sounds of the jungle; the cries of the night-time creatures, the whine of insects. She couldn't put the image of that poor man dying in agony out of her mind, and sleep eluded her for a long time. But eventually, the exhaustion of the day overcame her senses and she drifted off.

In the morning, she was still in a deep sleep when the camp was woken at dawn. She quickly dressed and made her way outside to where everyone else was doing their exercises in the clearing. She fell into line beside Maki and, as they bent and stretched and did press-ups on the bare earth, Maki said,

'You were so sound asleep you didn't hear the excitement before dawn this morning.'

'Excitement?'

'There was another dogfight in the sky and a couple of American planes were hit. One got away, but the other came down. Long led a group of comrades into the jungle to find the airman. They managed to locate him amongst the wreckage and brought him with them. He is in poor shape, but he is going to survive.'

'Where is he?'

'He's in one of the huts. Long has asked if one of us women will care for him. Mai and Chi aren't keen and I too would prefer to be out on missions. But what about you?'

Arielle stared at Maki, relief gradually washing over her as it dawned on her what this might mean. 'Of course. I'd love to do that,' she said quickly.

If she was back in camp nursing a wounded airman, she wouldn't have to go out on any more raids. She wouldn't have to witness killings or fire a gun into someone's beating heart herself. It would give her a chance to save a life rather than taking one.

After the exercises had finished, she went to Long's hut. To her surprise there were two skinny ponies tied up behind his hut and he was feeding them hay. Their eyes were dull and their ribs were visible beneath their matted coats.

'Comrade Tuyen?' he said, looking up. 'The nearby villagers lent us these ponies so we can deliver the rice more easily,' he said. 'I shall need your help with them later on.'

'Of course. But I have come to volunteer to look after the American airman,' she said. 'Maki said you needed someone to nurse him.'

To her surprise Long looked reluctant.

'I would prefer you to be available for active missions,' he said. 'You did well yesterday. You know, you are one of the best shots in the camp. We could use your skills better that way.'

Arielle hung her head and said nothing. She had the impression that Long was well aware of her misgivings about the raid and he was punishing her for her weakness.

'Come. Let us go to the stream to bathe,' he said, leaving the ponies to eat the hay. They began to walk across the camp together.

'Do you have any experience of nursing?' he asked as they neared the edge of the clearing.

'My father is often sick,' she answered. 'He has had malaria several times and he also has a chest complaint. I have often had to nurse him over the years.'

Long laughed. 'But that is very different from nursing an injured man.'

They had reached the stream now and were about to part – there were separate sections of the bank designated for men and women to wash in. As he prepared to walk upstream, Long turned back to her and said, 'I'll think about it if you come down to the villages to distribute the rice today. When you've finished bathing, come to my hut and we will load the rice sacks onto the ponies. If you come with me and help with that today, I will consider your request.'

Later, they trekked together down the mountainside, along the narrow jungle paths towards the valley. It was the way they had walked up from the airstrip several weeks before, and Arielle remembered parts of the trail and how apprehensive she'd been coming up to the camp. A lot had happened since then. She remembered too the villages devastated by famine, the skeletons and the rats. Would there be anyone left for them now to give their rice to? Long went in front with the bigger pony and she led the smaller one behind. She knew little about horses and when the pony sometimes stopped dead and refused to move or to pass something that spooked him, she had no idea what to do.

'Make a clicking sound with your tongue,' Long said, laughing. She soon got the hang of the pony's whims and, feeling more confident, began to relax into the task.

After an hour or so they emerged from the jungle and reached the first village in the wide valley. Arielle remembered it from when they'd been through before. It was just a few straggly huts around a stagnant pond, set amongst bare rice fields. They led the ponies between the huts and stood beside the pond looking around.

'There are still a couple of families living here. It was them who loaned us the ponies,' Long told her. 'They live in the two last huts.'

There were no bodies here anymore and Arielle suspected that the vultures might have picked them clean, but she wondered with a shudder what had happened to the skeletons. They neared the last two huts and found people sitting in front of them. Nobody came out to greet them. They were obviously too weak to move from where they sat. At the first hut there was a family; a father and mother and two small, naked children. The little ones stared at Arielle with huge, sad eyes that protruded from hollow cheeks. Their bellies were bloated but their arms and legs were as thin as sticks. The father managed to get to his feet and hobble out to greet Long and Arielle.

'We have brought you rice, brother,' Long said and the man's sunken face lit up in a toothless smile. Long emptied a quarter of a sack of rice into a cannister that the man held out and did the same at the next house where two elderly people sat outside their door, so weak they were barely able to acknowledge the gift.

'Thank you for the ponies, sir, we will return them later,' Long said to the old man.

'Come,' Long said to Arielle, picking up the reins of his pony. 'We have a lot to do today.'

They went from village to village, doling out rice to whoever they found alive. In some places the smell of rotting flesh hung on the air and corpses still lay where they'd fallen. These villagers had lost the will to do anything and had no energy to bury or burn the dead. Most of the people they gave rice to were grateful for the gift, smiling into Arielle's eyes as she scooped rice from the sacks into their containers. Some though, were so emaciated that they didn't have the strength to move from where they lay to receive the rice. On two or three occasions, Long and Arielle cooked up some rice for desperate villagers and spooned it into their mouths to make sure they at least had some nutrition that day. But it was clear that their lives were in the balance.

Although Arielle was horrified by what she saw, she at least felt she was doing something to help these desperate people, however small that effort might be. In a way, she was glad that they'd stolen the sacks of rice from the Japanese if it meant they could alleviate the suffering of these people, but she still regretted the death of the cook. If only they'd been able to take the rice without taking his life.

'I know what you're thinking,' Long said to her, watching her face while they drank from their canteens, and rested for a while beside the track. 'But, you know, this is wartime, comrade. Lives are lost. And the loss of one life has meant we are able to help many other people. It isn't fair I know, but we have to be pragmatic.'

'I'm beginning to understand that,' she said, then, after a pause, 'Have you thought about my request?'

'Yes. You have done well today, comrade Tuyen. You can

nurse the wounded airman for one week. That should see him through the worst. After that, I want you available for missions as before.'

'Thank you,' she breathed.

'Now come,' Long said, smiling, 'we still have two sacks of rice on that pony, and we need to get rid of those before the light begins to fade.'

When they got back to the camp, after having returned the ponies to the first village, darkness had already fallen over the jungle.

'I will take you to see the airman now,' Long said. 'Comrade Cong Son has been looking after him today, but I think his skills would be better used out in the field.'

The airman lay under a mosquito net in the corner of one of the huts where a paraffin lamp cast a flickering yellow light.

Cong Son was squatting beside him but got to his feet as Long and Arielle entered. He looked relieved to see them.

'He has a fever,' he said to Long.

'It could be malaria,' Long said. 'Tomorrow I will ask the Americans for quinine, but tonight he will have to sweat it out.'

'What happened to him?' Arielle asked, looking at the man. His hair was dark with perspiration, but it was instantly clear that it was an unusual colour; a beautiful tawny colour, almost red. She'd never seen hair like that before. And even through the mosquito net she could see the beads of sweat standing out on his brow. His head was moving around restlessly, as if he was in great pain.

'His leg is broken,' said Long, 'And he suffered many scratches and bruises when his plane crashed. He must have bailed out and fallen through the trees. We have bound his leg to a wooden splint and it will take time to heal. You will need to bathe his wounds in boiled water regularly to stop him getting blood poisoning. The cooks will give it to you if you ask them.'

'Should I stay in here at night?' she asked.

'Of course. He will need attention throughout the night. Cong Son will bring your bed and mosquito net. Now, let us go and eat, then you can return here straight afterwards.'

Throughout that long night and for three more successive nights, Arielle lay on her camp bed in the opposite corner of the hut listening to the American thrashing around in his bed, groaning to himself, sometimes crying out in pain. He was unconscious most of the time, although he had lucid moments, when he was able to relieve himself in a bucket. Arielle had to help him off the bed and at first found this aspect of the task deeply embarrassing, but she realised he was so ill that he probably wouldn't remember much about it. Four times a day she put a quinine tablet on his tongue and held a cup of water to his lips and tried to get him to drink, but that wasn't easy either.

Sometimes his periods of unconsciousness went on for so long Arielle became afraid that he might not wake up. She quickly realised she wouldn't be able to bear it if he died. She would have failed him, failed herself and failed Long, too. It became vital to her that this man should get better.

She spent her days inside the stuffy hut tending to him. She only went out of the hut at mealtimes, ate quickly and went straight back in. The routines of the camp went on around her, but she barely noticed them, so absorbed was she in the fight to save the American.

She bathed his wounds several times a day. There were deep gouges and cuts all over his arms, back and chest, and she had to turn him over to bathe the wounds on his back. At one point she thought she was losing the battle against the blood poisoning; a few of the wounds turned yellow and started to swell, but she kept on with her bathing routine and in a couple of days they were looking less swollen and livid. She spent long hours just sitting on her camp bed and watching him. He had a tanned, well-made face, thick, luscious red hair and, when he occasionally opened them, she saw that his eyes were a beautiful hazel colour, flecked with green, with long, dark lashes.

She wondered about him. All she knew was that he was an American airman, that he'd been flying a mission against the Japanese and that he'd been shot down in the jungle close to the camp. After a couple of days though, she realised that she would be able to discover his name if she simply looked on the metal tag around his neck. She'd seen it there many times, moved it each time she'd bathed him, but it hadn't occurred to her at first that it might contain vital information.

She picked it up and read: *Kenneth P Jamieson*, followed by a long army number, followed by *Blood type O; Contact: Mrs Carol Jamieson, Long Grass, Big Horn County, Montana* followed by the letter *P*.

Kenneth P Jamieson. She knew his name now, but not much more about him. Was Mrs Carol Jamieson his wife, she wondered, fleetingly? Perhaps, but he wasn't wearing a ring. At least she also now knew that he came from the state of Montana and she tried to remember from her geography lessons where that was. What did he do in civilian life? Did he have a family? The more she looked at his face, the more curious she became about the man inside this wounded body. She started willing him to wake up and tell her the answers to her questions, and whenever she spoke to him now, she called him by his first name.

The days wore on and she was aware that the rest of the camp had been out on various missions; blowing bridges, dismantling railway tracks, raiding Japanese depots. Mr Hoo was a frequent presence at mealtimes, congratulating those who had returned from raids, shaking their hands and toasting their success, but mostly he kept himself to himself in his hut. Arielle knew from what Long had told her, that Mr Hoo spent his time in there listening to newscasts, reading reports, plotting and planning for the eventual Japanese surrender.

Arielle worried that the American wouldn't have regained consciousness before her seven days were up. She would count that as a failure. She had set herself the task of ensuring he was well on the road to complete recovery before she had to leave him and go out on missions. She tried not to dwell on what those missions might entail. If she ever thought about the details, it made her break out into a cold sweat.

On the fifth day her patience was rewarded. She'd just given the American his quinine and was trying to get him to sip some water to wash it down, when his eyes snapped open and he sat up suddenly and looked around him with a bemused expression on his face. He rubbed his eyes.

'Where the hell am I?' were his first words. Arielle understood English, she had been tutored in it at school, but his western drawl took her by surprise.

'You are safe,' she told him. 'You are in a Viet Minh training camp. We are all friends here.'

'My comrades?' he asked, awareness dawning in his eyes. 'There were four planes on that mission, was anyone else shot down?'

'No, the others got away.'

'Thank God,' he breathed. He was silent for a moment, then he turned his hazel and green eyes towards her and scrutinised her face.

'And who are you?' he asked.

She hesitated, she'd been about to tell him her real name but stopped herself just in time.

'My name is Tuyen. Tuyen Nguyen. I am Annamese. Well, Vietnamese really, now that we are a united country.'

'Well, very nice to meet you, Miss Tuyen,' he said, holding out a hand to shake hers. 'Although I expect you probably know me pretty well already.'

She laughed. 'I don't know very much about you at all, really,' she said, taking his hand. 'But I'm looking forward to finding out.'

From that moment on Kenneth Jamieson became a real, living, breathing person to Arielle, not just a body she had to care for. Now he'd finally woken up she could see that he was determined to get better. He didn't want to spend another day lying on his camp bed in the corner of the hut. She recognised that and saw that they had an instant connection there.

'Will you help me outside?' he said within minutes of waking.

'Is that a good idea?' she asked laughing. 'It seems very soon.'

He shrugged and laughed too, displaying white teeth, his eyes crinkling up in amusement. 'Well, it damned well feels like a good idea. I'd like to take a breath of that fresh, mountain air.'

'It's almost as hot out there as it is in here, I'm afraid,' she replied. 'But I'll happily help you out if that's what you want to do.'

'Come on then.'

He braced himself on the bed frame and made an effort to swing his legs over the side of the bed but stopped with a sharp intake of breath.

'I guess I broke my left leg in the crash,' he said, examining the crude wooden splint bound to his leg with bandages.

'I believe it was quite badly broken. It will take a while to heal.'

'I can't remember much about what happened,' he said, rubbing his stubbled chin, his face suddenly serious. 'Everything has gone blank. I know that we were flying a pre-dawn mission, trying to get up and out there before the Japs, and that they surrounded us and tried to shoot us down. I guess they succeeded.'

'You were incredibly lucky,' Arielle said.

'I guess I was. Lucky not to die in the crash and lucky not to be captured by the Japs. If that had happened, I might as well have died there and then.'

His face was serious again and his breathing became laboured. She saw beads of sweat on his brow.

'Try not to think about it,' she said. 'You didn't get captured, and you need to focus on getting better now. I'll get you some more water.'

She left him sitting on the bed and went out to where a group of guerrillas was preparing the evening meal. Long was there helping with the cooking.

'How is our patient?' he asked, seeing her filling the cup from one of the tanks of boiled water, and she told him that the pilot had just woken up.

'Well done, comrade Tuyen. You are clearly a young woman of many talents. It's good news because I need you on a mission tomorrow.'

'Tomorrow? But that's only day six.'

Long laughed. 'You've been in that hut long enough. He's over the worst now. Tomorrow we are blowing a railway bridge on the Haiphong to Kunming line. And I need your help with that.'

'Alright,' she agreed reluctantly, but her consent was irrelevant. She knew she had no choice.

'Remember. It's in a good cause, comrade, to help the Allies stop Japanese troops being transported into China.'

She remained silent, not knowing how to respond.

'We can discuss this later on at supper,' he said, 'Take the water to your patient. I will be in to talk to him later.'

Kenneth Jamieson was still sitting upright on the bed when she went back into the hut. He looked up at her and smiled. It was a genuine, open smile that reached all the way to his eyes.

She handed him the water and sat down beside him on the bed with a heavy sigh.

'What was that all about?'

'Tomorrow I have to go out on a mission. They said I could nurse you for seven days. But they've changed their minds.'

'That's a great shame. I'll miss your company. But I would have thought most young revolutionaries would prefer to be out sabotaging Jap targets than sitting in a stuffy hut nursing an incapacitated airman.'

She shrugged and looked away.

'Now why do I get the feeling that you're not like most young revolutionaries?'

She smiled at him and put her finger up to her lips to hush him. The door was still open.

'OK. I get the message,' he said quietly. 'Let's talk about it another time.' He settled back onto the bed, his face suddenly pale with exhaustion. He closed his eyes and from the rhythm of his breathing, she guessed that he had gone straight to sleep.

20

TÂN TRÀO, TONKIN, 1945

The railway bridge they were going to blow was on a curved section of the Haiphong to Kunming railroad, just as the track emerged from the jungle and crossed a wide, lazy river that snaked across the plane. Long led the party of five guerrillas; Arielle, Hoc and Tan, and to Arielle's surprise, Maki had also been chosen for the mission. They trekked through the hot, steamy jungle for five hours from the camp to reach the river. They carried everything they needed in packs on their backs, from sticks of gelignite, to the switches and wires needed to ignite it, to the food and water they would need to sustain them through the long march and until they returned to the camp.

They were silent, just as their training had taught them, as they made their way through the jungle. While she walked, Arielle's mind returned again and again to her American airman, Kenneth Jamieson. In the space of a few short hours since he'd woken from his fever, they'd struck up a friendly rapport. He was keen to talk, and Arielle guessed it was because being in a hut in the hills above the jungle in deepest Indochina amongst guerrillas had unsettled him. This was despite the fact that he had said he felt incredibly lucky to be alive. She did everything she could to allay his fears and to make him feel welcome.

He was effusively grateful for everything she did for him that day, from bringing him food and water, to bathing his wounds.

'I guess you must have been doing this for days without me even knowing,' he said, when she brought boiled water to bathe his wounds.

She smiled. 'I was happy to.'

'You're very kind. I can't thank you enough. You've saved my life for sure.'

'Oh, that wasn't me. That was our leader, Long. He took a party to find you in the jungle when your plane was shot down.'

Kenneth told her that he came from a ranch in Montana. It was where he'd grown up, the second of three brothers. She hadn't imagined that he was a country boy – all she knew about America was the names of cities on a map, and she'd automatically assumed he came from one of them. She was keen to find out more about his home and family.

But that would have to wait. There was little time to sit and chat that first day. Long had wanted to talk to Kenneth about his mission, then the two American sergeants, Redmond and Leigh, came to see him in the afternoon. Arielle left the hut so they could have some privacy, but when they were leaving to return to their billet deeper in the hills, they sought her out to thank her for nursing Flight Officer Jamieson back to health.

'I didn't do much really, just gave him quinine and bathed his wounds.'

'Well, nevertheless, he is very grateful, and we are too. He's a fine pilot, and we wouldn't want to lose him.'

Then Long came and told her to get ready for the next

day's mission into the jungle and she'd had to prepare her pack, change into her camouflage clothes and be briefed around the campfire with the others. When night had fallen, she'd returned to Kenneth's hut and slid quietly through the folds of her mosquito net into her camp bed, thinking the airman was already asleep.

'Good night, Miss Tuyen. Sweet dreams,' he'd murmured sleepily. She smiled into the darkness, glad that she now had a warm, caring companion who seemed to understand her, in contrast to all the zealous fanatics who seemed to put their cause above everything else, including love and friendship.

When she was woken by Long in the morning, Kenneth had woken too and wished her luck for the mission.

'I'll be thinking of you,' he said. 'And you'd better look after yourself and come back in one piece. I'm counting on you.'

WHEN THE GROUP reached the bridge, they stood on the river-bank and stared at it for a long time. It was an ugly structure, constructed of black metal girders and slung between three separate pillars across the wide, slow flowing river. The span was long, but the bridge itself was quite narrow, allowing only a single railway track to pass over it.

Long consulted his watch and some papers.

'I have intelligence that a Japanese troop train will pass through here at noon on its way to the Chinese border. That gives us almost an hour to wire the bridge. Let us base ourselves under those trees out of sight.'

They dumped their packs under the shelter of the jungle canopy and for the next hour they set to work. Arielle and Maki were put on sentry duty with their rifles at the ready.

Their job was to alert Long and the others if anyone approached, but there were no roads nearby and here the track ran through wild jungle so it seemed unlikely. They stood guard while the men unpacked the explosives and wired them to the bridge, then ran the wire back into the trees where they connected up the switches. As Arielle watched them work, she had that familiar feeling of dread in her stomach, knowing that people were going to die because of what they were doing. And here, it wouldn't be just one man, it could be dozens who were killed or maimed. She knew they were at war and that these were enemy soldiers they were targeting, but still her skin crawled at the thought of the loss of life she was about to witness. *You're not cut out for this*, she told herself.

Suddenly a small fishing craft appeared on the river and the two fishermen pulled it up onto a little beach beside the pillars of the bridge. Long left what he was doing and came to speak to Arielle.

'Go and tell them to move,' he told her. 'And if they won't, shoot them. We have no time to lose and we don't want them talking.'

She clambered down the bank onto the beach, her heart pounding. She approached the two men, old and wizened, their skin leathery from the sun, dressed in sarongs and sandals.

'You need to move from here,' she said, waving her gun at them. 'Get back in your boat and get away quickly.'

They shaded their eyes and stared at her. One of them spat betel juice on the sand; a stream of red spittle that looked like blood, landed near her feet.

'Please,' she said, trying to tell them with her eyes how important it was that they did as they were told. 'You need to go now.'

'This is where we land, sister,' the taller man said in a slow, deliberate tone. 'We have been doing this every day for sixty years.'

'Well today you can't. Get back in your boat and go downstream. A long way. Please. Just do it,' she was yelling at them now, pointing her gun, walking towards them. Her heart hammered against her ribs and she knew deep down that she couldn't shoot them.

The shorter man took a cheroot out of his mouth and threw it on the ground. He was hesitating now, frowning.

'Leave us be, sister,' the other man said. 'Put your gun away. We aren't doing any harm.'

Suddenly, from behind Arielle a shot rang out and the taller man fell to the ground, his mouth and eyes wide open, his expression frozen as he fell, blood spreading from a wound on his chest.

'No!' Arielle screamed and turned. Maki was behind her, her rifle smoking.

'Now get in your boat and get away from here,' Maki screamed at the other man, who was by now trying desperately to push the boat back to the water.

'Don't shoot him,' Arielle yelled at Maki who was lifting her rifle again. Arielle leapt forward and helped the old man push the boat into the water, then he scrambled in himself and rowed furiously downstream and out of sight.

'Why did you do that?' Arielle stormed at Maki. 'They would have gone.'

Maki shrugged. 'That man was obstinate. They wouldn't have left without a long argument. We don't have time to bargain with fools.'

'She did the right thing, comrade Tuyen. Let her be.' Long swung down from the bridge onto the sand and checked a length of wiring. 'Comrade Maki was right. We have little time. The train will be here in ten minutes.'

Numb with shock, Arielle went back to her post, but by now the wiring was ready. From where she stood, she could see the sticks of gelignite tied to the underside of the bridge.

'Alright. Let's get back under the trees and wait for the train,' Long said. 'It should be along in a few minutes.'

They trooped away from the bridge and crouched on the edge of the jungle, beside the track, waiting tensely for the sound of the rails vibrating which would herald the approach of a train. They all had their packs on their backs, ready to run when the time was right. Long kept consulting his watch and the others were tense too, their foreheads screwed up in anxious frowns. Arielle looked at Maki, still stunned by the way she'd shot the old fisherman in cold blood. Her face showed no distress at the fact she'd just killed an innocent man. How she had hardened since the two of them had shared confidences ten years ago. Had she lost all that compassion she'd shown then for the workers, for the communists captured by Bertrand and held captive in the factory buildings?

'It's ten minutes late already,' Long said, getting up and pacing about. 'I wonder what the hold-up is.'

But within a few minutes came the tell-tale singing and shuddering of the tracks, and in the distance, through the jungle, the long, mournful hoot of an approaching train. The vibration of the rails intensified and in seconds they could hear the clickety-clack of the wheels on the track and the rhythmic puffing of the engine. It grew louder and louder, until the great train was upon them, and before long the engine drew parallel and burst into view in a cloud of steam. Arielle caught a glimpse of the great steel wheels and pistons, the glow of the fire and the coalman, bathed in sweat from head to toe furiously shovelling fuel. The engine was on the bridge then, with another great toot of the horn, and the wheels on the track made a hollow, metallic sound as it started to cross the river.

The carriages slid past filled with Japanese troops in full uniform, their forage caps visible through the open windows.

Long was poised over the plunger, waiting until the engine had almost crossed the bridge to inflict maximum damage and at a sign from Hoc, he shoved it down. There followed a series of almighty explosions, the crack of wood and metal splintering, a crashing sound as the bridge and the train collapsed into the water, followed by frantic screaming and yelling voices.

'Come. We must run now,' Long said, gathering the switches and starting back along the narrow path on which they'd arrived. Tan and Hoc followed, and Arielle set off behind them. Within seconds shots rang out and bullets whistled above their heads.

'Keep running,' Long shouted. 'We'll soon lose them.'

Arielle obeyed, but the shots kept coming and behind her she heard a thud and turned to see Maki struck down, sprawling on the jungle floor face down.

'It's Maki!' she yelled. 'She's shot.'

'Keep running,' came the order. 'We'll come back later.'

She wanted to stop but her instinct told her to keep running. Her mouth was dry with shock, her heart pounding, her breath coming in gasps. She kept glancing over her shoulder, hoping that by some miracle Maki would have got to her feet and be running behind her, but there was no sign of her. Within a few minutes the firing gradually died down and when they reached a clearing, they stopped to catch their breath.

'What about Maki?' she asked.

'We need to wait a few minutes, until we are sure the coast

is clear, then Hoc and I will go back and check on her,' Long said.

They sat down under the trees and drank some water. Long handed round some bread but Arielle shook her head. Her stomach was so churned up she couldn't think of eating. She thought of Maki, lying prone on the jungle path, and of all those soldiers, drowned or maimed in the explosion. She could barely take in what had happened. She just wanted it to be over.

After a time, Long and Hoc set off back down the path and Arielle sat there with Tan, hugging her knees, sobbing gently. Neither of them spoke. She listened to the jungle birds up in the canopy, the buzz and whirr of insects. The life of the jungle went on, oblivious to the tragedies that were playing out in its midst.

When Long and Hoc returned, Arielle saw instantly from the look on their faces that they had bad news. Long shook his head. 'I'm sorry, comrade. Maki is dead. She died outright. The bullet pierced her heart.'

Arielle hung her head, tears running down her cheeks, unable to speak. Whatever Maki had done, whatever she'd become, she didn't deserve to be cut down in the prime of her life like that. Arielle had a sudden image of Maki on the veranda of the plantation house, her head bent forward, totally engrossed in a glossy magazine. What had happened to that simple, joy-loving girl that she ended up dead on the jungle floor thousands of miles from her home? Arielle vowed to write to Maki's mother when all this was over.

The trek back to the camp was long and arduous and darkness had fallen by the time they reached it. The rest of the guerrillas were seated round the fire eating and a cheer went up as Long led the others back into camp.

'Come! Let us celebrate today's success,' Long said, beaming, but Arielle had no appetite for that. She left quietly and went to the hut where the American was lying alone. A paraffin lamp flickered in the corner.

He sat up when she entered. 'You're back, Miss Tuyen!' he said. 'Thank the good Lord for that. Come here. Sit down beside me and tell me all about it.'

Gladly, she went over to sit on his bed, and the warmth and relief in his voice brought fresh tears to her eyes.

21

TÂN TRÀO, TONKIN, 1945

The days in the camp wore on. Arielle's bed was moved back into the women's hut and she felt instantly lonely. Mai and Chi were efficient guerrillas but grudging companions and there was no chance of small talk with either of them. Her heart ached for Maki who, despite her transformation into a revolutionary, had retained a little of her human side. She missed sleeping in the American's hut too, but she was allowed to spend time nursing him during the daytime. Long still insisted that she join them for PE in the mornings and target practice with the rest of the camp. He also warned her that she would be expected to participate in future missions.

'Now we have lost comrade Maki you will be needed more than ever,' he said.

She dreaded the time when her services would be called upon, but in the days and weeks following the train mission, others were sent out and she was spared. So, she made the most of the opportunity to get to know her patient.

Gradually, his health improved. He no longer suffered from fevers and the wounds on his body healed, although deep scars were left in many places. With the help of Arielle and Cong Son, he began to get out of the hut and hobble around the clearing with a crutch made from bamboo, often taking his meals with the others. Within a few weeks, Long removed the splint from his leg and Kenneth began to walk with a stick instead. Arielle was happy to see the progress he was making. He grew stronger every day, but deep down she had a niggling fear that it could mean he might leave the camp imminently. How would she cope here without him?

Arielle was infinitely curious about the American's life. She had never travelled outside Indochina, and the west had always held a fascination for her. Kenneth was only too happy to talk about the sweeping green valleys, the forests, the lush hills of his homeland. He spoke about where he'd been raised – on his family's thirty-thousand-acre farm – where herds of cattle and horses roamed the vast tracts of land. He grew up running wild in the countryside with his two brothers, riding horses and climbing trees, hunting, fishing and shooting, and when he'd left school, he had started working on the farm. It was all he'd ever known until the war came and he was called up to fight. Then his life had changed dramatically. But he seemed to have embraced the experience of training to fly bombing missions with energy and enthusiasm. His curious nature and his thirst for new experiences had carried him through.

Arielle was spellbound, transported to that vast, beautiful landscape with its towering skies, so far away from everything she'd ever known.

In turn Kenneth asked her about her own life; he was as curious about her world as she was about his. She told him about her life in Hanoi, all about Bà Ngoại, Trang, her father. She even told him of Bà Ngoại's opium habit and about her sadness at her grandmother's passing. She also mentioned her anguish that her father was imprisoned in the Citadel. Kenneth clenched his fists when she told him about her attempt to visit him.

'This terrible war,' he said shaking his head.

One afternoon, Arielle was returning from the clearing, having just finished washing some clothes in the stream. Kenneth was sitting on one of the tree stumps round the fire. Walking up behind him, she noticed that his head was bent forward and that he was concentrating intently on something. Moving closer, she saw that he was drawing with a piece of charcoal from the fire on a section of sawn-off tree trunk.

'I didn't know you were an artist,' she said, touching his shoulder. He looked up, smiling into her eyes.

'Oh, it's just a hobby. Pa likes me to do portraits of his favourite horses and Ma frames them and hangs them up around the house.'

She came closer and looked at the drawing. It was a detailed sketch of the camp, with several people bent over tasks near a fire. He had brought them to life in a way that was so skilful and realistic, she was able to recognise each of the figures he had sketched and even point them out by name.

'I'll draw you if you like,' he said. 'You'd make a great subject.'

She shook her head hastily. 'I don't think I could sit still for that long.'

But from then on, Kenneth was frequently to be seen with a stump of charcoal, sketching away on a piece of bare wood. The guerrillas were fascinated by the images he conjured, pictures of the jungle and the surrounding hills, the camp. He even drew portraits of each one of them. From memory he sketched the aircraft he'd flown and almost died in just a few kilometres away. Drawing seemed to give him deep pleasure, and Arielle was impressed by his skills and pleased that he'd found something to absorb him through the long hours of recovery.

One day, when she'd been sitting beside him in the hut, talking to him about her fears for Papa, Kenneth said slowly, 'So, you still live at home with your father. Did you never think about marriage?'

She dropped her gaze. Was she ready to tell him about Etienne? She looked into his face, his honest, friendly eyes.

'Yes. I was married when I was very young,' she admitted. 'Too young. Only eighteen years old. To a Frenchman.'

'And?'

'My husband died,' she said quietly.

'Oh, I'm so, so, sorry,' he said, genuine sympathy in his hazel eyes.

'Please don't be,' she said simply. 'He wasn't a good man.'

'So, what happened?' he asked, a surprised look in his eyes. She hesitated. She knew she could trust him, but still...

She opened her mouth to tell him, but she couldn't quite bring herself to. Something was stopping her describing the details of that fateful night, and deep down she knew why. She was afraid of him thinking less of her when he knew the truth.

Long came to her rescue then, knocking on the door and entering the hut.

'I need you tomorrow, comrade Tuyen,' he said, and her heart sank.

'We've found a Japanese arms dump down in the plain, close to the railway. We're planning on taking what weapons we can and setting the rest on fire.'

'I'll come too,' Kenneth chipped in and Long snorted with laughter.

'You're not well enough, comrade. When your leg is better, perhaps...'

When Long had gone, Kenneth put his hand on Arielle's.

'Don't worry, Miss Tuyen,' he said. 'This mission could pass off without a hitch and when you're asked on the next one, I should be well enough to come with you.'

This cheered her a little and she turned and looked into his eyes. 'Is that why you want to come?' she asked. 'To help me?'

'Partly, yes. I know you find the missions difficult. Perhaps if I came along, I could do something to make it less so. But it's also partly that I just want to get out there and do something useful again. Sitting inside this hut isn't doing me or anyone else any good.'

It turned out that Kenneth was right. The mission to the arms dump was relatively straightforward. There were four of them who crept down silently through the jungle in the early evening, made their way between the devastated paddy fields to the railway and waited there out of sight for nightfall. The arms dump was housed in an old engine shed near the railway station in a small town. They crept through the dark, deserted streets and crouched behind the back wall of the building while Long gave them their instructions. Then they approached the big, wooden doors on the other side of the building, having made sure the only Japanese soldiers around were those guarding it.

They approached soundlessly and as they got close two shots rang out. One from Long's rifle and the other from Hoc's and the two guards crumpled to the ground. Long leapt forward and searched their bodies. He held up the keys to the building, then ran to the doors and flung them open.

Gritting her teeth and trying not to look, Arielle stepped over the blood-soaked bodies and followed the others into the engine shed. Long flashed a torch around. There were boxes of guns, bullets, and drums of explosives. Following their orders, each filled their packs with as many bullets, grenades, rifles and handguns as they could carry. Then, Long doused petrol all over the remaining crates and boxes and as they left the building, threw a match at it.

'Run!' he said, starting down the road the way they had come. They all followed him, running hard until they reached the paddies, then along the banks between rice fields and down rough, country tracks by the light of the moon until they reached the edge of the jungle. Arielle struggled to keep up with the others. Her backpack was heavy, dragging on her shoulders, but she was desperate not to be left behind. She was breathing quickly, and her blood was pumping in her ears, but in the background she could hear bangs and explosions as the rest of the ammunition went up in flames. Under the trees, they stopped to catch their breath and to look back at their work. The whole town was lit up by the burning building, from which rained showers of sparks from the explosions.

'We did it!' Long's face was triumphant. 'Well done indeed, comrades!'

Then they began the long, hard march up through the jungle to the camp deep in the hills. It was after midnight by the time they reached the base, but when they arrived in the clearing, Kenneth was sitting by the dying embers of the fire, waiting for them.

'I'm so pleased you all got back safely,' he said, standing up to greet them, relief in his tone.

'Thank you, comrade, but there was no need to wait up for us,' said Long.

Arielle felt blood rush into her cheeks and was glad of the cover of darkness. She was quite sure that Kenneth did care about everyone on the mission, but she suspected the truth was that he had waited up to make sure she got back safely.

A week later, Kenneth's leg had visibly improved. He was able to walk normally without a stick, and when Long came and asked Arielle to help him on a raid to blow a road bridge, Kenneth asked again if he could be part of it.

Long hesitated, rubbing his chin. 'We will be targeting some high-ranking Japanese officers. There will probably be shooting.'

'I can shoot straight,' Kenneth said. 'I'm used to combat, and I can walk pretty normally now.'

'You might need to run,' Long said. 'Look, you could jeopardise everyone's safety if you aren't fit.'

'I *can* run, look,' Kenneth assured him and attempted a limping jog, in a circle round the fire, to demonstrate.

'Alright,' Long agreed at last, reluctance in his tone. 'But I'll try to keep you away from the front line, and it's your risk that if we have to run you might get left behind.'

In the morning, five of them trooped down through the jungle towards the narrow road that led from the valley where the Japanese garrison was camped at Tân Trào, towards the Hanoi road. It zig-zagged over the hills, with many hairpin bends, and passed over high bridges across rocky ravines. It took the group several hours' trek through the jungle to reach the bridge they'd targeted. They marched in silence as usual. Arielle walked behind Kenneth and kept her eyes on his flaming red hair. She was filled with a warm feeling, just knowing that he was there with her, and she didn't have that usual feeling of dread that normally accompanied her on missions.

It was late morning when they reached the bridge. Like many others on that road, it was constructed of wood. It crossed a ravine where a river tumbled down the valley over rocks, a dizzying drop below. As soon as they arrived, Long, Hoc and Cong Son scrambled down the rocks and began setting the explosives to the underside of the bridge. Then they ran wires back into the bushes where they set up the switches, while Arielle and Kenneth were stationed on the road, checking in each direction for anyone approaching. Arielle stood with her rifle at her shoulder, looking uphill, her eyes glued to the bend in the road. She willed Long and the others to be quick, trying not to think of the innocent fisherman that Maki had shot, or the bulging eyes of the cook in the food store on her first raid. She just held her breath and hoped against hope that no one would appear on the road in front of her, so she didn't have to face an impossible choice.

The three guerrillas were efficient and quick, and in minutes she heard Long's voice, telling her to return to the bridge.

'My sources tell me that the jeep carrying the two officers will leave the camp at thirteen hundred hours. They will take about half an hour to get from the garrison at Tân Trào to this point. Comrade Tuyen, go back to your bend in the road, and when the jeep comes, fire two shots in the air, then get out of its way quickly. Comrade Kenneth, you and comrade Hoc can cover the bridge with your rifles in case anything goes wrong and the bridge doesn't collapse. If any of the Japs get out of the jeep, you'll need to deal with them. Cong Son and I will work the switches. Afterwards, we need to get back on the path as quickly as we can and make our way back to the camp.'

Everyone was listening to him intently, their minds on the task ahead.

'Understood?' he looked round at their faces. 'OK, let's get to it then.'

As Arielle turned to walk back up the road, Kenneth touched her arm; 'Good luck, Miss Tuyen,' he said, his earnest eyes on hers. 'It will all be fine, and soon we can go home.'

She stood on the bend looking up the hill, waiting for the sound of a vehicle. Her nerves were taut with anticipation. Every noise seemed to be like an engine, and a couple of times she almost mistook the rasping of cicadas for the sound of an approaching jeep.

It was ten minutes or so before she actually heard it approaching and then a few more seconds before it burst into view around a bend in the road above. She let it come a little closer to be sure it was an army vehicle, before raising her rifle and firing her two shots into the air, which echoed in the rocky ravine. Then she leapt into the bushes and watched the vehicle speed past her. It was an open-topped jeep with three men on board. A driver, two portly officers sitting in the back seat and two guards with rifles standing on the running boards. She stared at the passengers. With a shock she recognised one of the officers. It was General Nishihara, she was sure of it. Shuddering, she recalled the feel of his hands on her thighs, his hot breath on her face. She'd hated and feared him then, but did he actually deserve to die?

When she was sure the jeep had passed, she crawled back out of the bushes and stood on the road, watching it speed down the hill towards the bridge. From where she stood, she saw it slow down and drive onto the wooden bridge. Then there was the roar of an explosion and the sound of splintering wood and tearing metal as the bridge tore apart, boards and struts flew everywhere, and the jeep plunged into the ravine in a cloud of smoke. She started to run down the road to join the others. Flames were leaping from the ravine now and she could hear the shouts and screams of the dying soldiers. She didn't want to get too close or see what was happening down there, but she needed to go a little further down the road before she reached the jungle path.

Her heart was hammering and her mouth dry. Only a few more steps to reach the path. Out of the smoke one of the Japanese guards suddenly appeared on the road in front of her. He must have survived the blast and somehow managed to clamber out of the ravine. His face was blackened, his eyes blazing with anger, and he was brandishing a rifle. She stopped, stock still on the road, frozen with fear. This was it. This was the end for her, she knew it.

She raised her rifle to her shoulder. Then a shot rang out and the Japanese guard staggered and fell, sprawling face down on the road. She turned, stunned. Kenneth stood at the end of the path between the trees, holding his rifle. Blinded by tears, she ran to him and he took her hand.

'Thank you,' she muttered. 'Thank God you were here.'

'Quickly, we need to get away from here,' he said, his voice quite calm. 'We'll have to run to catch up with the others.'

On the long trek through the jungle back to the camp, Arielle was plagued by images of the Japanese guard; the hatred in his eyes, the rifle on his shoulder, its twin black barrels pointing directly at her. She knew that if Kenneth hadn't been there, she would have died there and then on that road. She would never have got to see Papa again, to laugh with Camille, to feel the warmth of Trang's arms around her. She shuddered again and again, thinking what might have been, and despite the steamy heat of the jungle, her skin was covered in goosebumps and she felt chilled to the bone. She walked as if in a dream, barely noticing the forest they were passing through, the cries of the jungle creatures, the prickly ferns brushing her skin. And when they finally reached the camp, shortly after sunset, she had no desire to celebrate with the others. She just wanted to sit by the fire and let the heat of the flames warm her frozen heart.

Kenneth sat beside her and although he was drinking whisky and trying to sing along with the victory songs, she was aware that he kept glancing her way, checking on her. At last though, she had had enough. She got up and walked away from the group, making for her hut. She just wanted to forget what had happened that day. The celebrations were only prolonging her pain.

Before she reached the hut though, she heard footsteps behind her. She turned. It was Kenneth.

'Are you alright? You must have had a hell of a shock.'

'I just need to get to bed. I don't want to think about it.'

'Come here.'

He took her in his arms and she yielded to his embrace and let his warmth envelop her. At his touch, the tears she'd been holding back for hours started to fall. She didn't even try to stop them, just stood there, sobbing in his arms. Then he was kissing the tears away, his lips on her eyelids and on her cheeks, and then his lips moved to her mouth, and he was kissing her and she was kissing him back hungrily. She didn't even think about what she was doing. It felt so natural, and she realised then that this was what she'd wanted since the moment Kenneth had woken from his fever.

22

TÂN TRÀO, TONKIN, 1945

From that moment on, life at the camp became bearable for Arielle. Kenneth was the first thing she thought about when she woke up in the mornings and the last thing she thought about before going to sleep at night. During the daytime, throughout the tough regime of exercises, target practice and camp chores, just knowing he was there with her made all the difference to her state of mind. She would catch his gaze lingering on her face as she sat by the campfire eating, or peeling vegetables for supper, and she would smile back at him longingly. When they trekked through the jungle on exercises or reconnaissance missions, just the knowledge that he was close by, that he cared for her and was looking out for her became essential to her wellbeing. She longed for the moments when they could slip away from the group and feel each other's warmth as they embraced.

That didn't happen often, though; they were very careful not to let any of the Viet Minh know how they felt about one another. They both sensed that loving relationships were frowned upon and viewed as frivolous by the others, and that if they were discovered, it could only spell difficulties for them both. For the next few days there were no more missions into the surrounding countryside. Long spent endless hours shut up in Mr Hoo's hut, conferring with him. It was becoming clear to everyone that Japan was losing the war, and that it was only a matter of time before they surrendered.

'Those two are planning their best move when that finally happens,' Kenneth said quietly to her one day as Arielle and he peeled vegetables for the evening meal together. 'The Viet Minh aren't just going to stand aside and let the French come back in and take over without a fight.'

'I know,' she said, biting her lip, thinking of all the years of insurgency she'd lived through, of those she'd known who'd died for the cause of independence. Perhaps they hadn't died in vain after all. But then she thought of Papa and Camille and all the others locked away in the Citadel. What would happen to them if the Viet Minh took over? Would they ever be released?

She and Kenneth had very little time alone together but volunteering to prepare the evening meal gave them a chance to sit side by side and talk. He often spoke about his home, about his brothers, both of whom were in the US military like him. 'My older brother, Jed, was in France. He went in on D-Day. He will be home by now. The younger one, Will, is in the Pacific somewhere, on a little island called Iwo Jima, fighting the Japs. No idea where that might be. But at least Ma and Pa will have one of their sons home by now.'

'Do they know you are here?' she asked, and he shrugged.

'The others in the Deer Team said they would try to get word to them that I am safe, but it's not easy from up here. I hope so, though. I don't want my folks to worry.'

'My father has no idea what has happened to me,' she said

quietly. 'Like I told you, I wasn't able to see him at all since he was taken there. He will be worried sick.'

'When the Japs surrender, you will be able to go back to Hanoi and he will be released,' Kenneth replied.

'Will he? I'm not so sure.'

There was a silence during which Arielle thought again about Papa. It was early evening; the sun was just starting to dip behind the jungle. Now was the time Trang would be making her way through the streets of Hanoi to the Citadel with her food cannister for Papa. Was she still doing that after all these weeks? Was the food still reaching Papa?

'Hey,' Kenneth said, squeezing her hand, looking into her eyes. 'It'll be OK. You'll see.'

'I feel so bad about Papa,' she said, almost to herself. 'He has always been there for me. He's helped me though some terrible times.'

'Terrible times?' Kenneth asked gently. 'Was that when your husband died?'

She nodded. She had stopped peeling the potato she'd started. It sat in her lap, smeared with mud.

'Do you want to talk about it? It might help.'

Again, she hesitated, but she wanted to be honest with Kenneth. She didn't want to have any secrets from him. She took a deep breath. Telling him the truth was surely worth the risk.

'Alright,' she said. 'But you can't speak about this to anyone. Not anyone. Do you promise?'

'Of course,' he said, looking a little wounded that she might doubt his loyalty.

'As I told you, when I married Etienne, I was very young and very naïve. He seemed a perfect match and my father encouraged it. Etienne was rich, educated, charming and he seemed to think the world of me. But it quickly became clear to me that he was a deeply dishonest man and that he was engaged in an evil business. He only married me to get to Papa because Papa worked in the government. He wanted to be sure that Papa would issue him with the transport permits he needed for his business. Etienne was nothing more than a slave trader...'

Kenneth listened in silence as she told him the story of her marriage. She told him about their trip to the plantation and how Maki had helped her discover the cruelty and exploitation that took place there. She told him about the lies that were told to tempt poor labourers from Tonkin to leave their homes and families and go south. She described her trip to Haiphong and how she'd seen the conditions on the boats, how workers were beaten and degraded. Then she told him about Xan, about how she met him at the Lake Pagoda, and how she'd fallen under his spell.

'Were you in love with him?' Kenneth asked.

'A little,' she admitted, looking down at the potato she'd started peeling again. 'I admired him. He seemed to be a good man. A man of principle. I sort of knew he was using me for information about Etienne, but I didn't really care. I began to look forward to seeing Xan and the more I found out, the more I was sure that Etienne didn't deserve my loyalty.'

She swallowed, put the peeled potato in a saucepan and picked up another one.

'Xan kept saying that he wanted to meet Etienne and that I should introduce them. I knew that wasn't a good idea, but after a while he changed his mind. He said that he would meet him and speak to him alone, if I told him Etienne's whereabouts.'

'So did you do that?'

She nodded miserably. 'I had my doubts. I wondered what would happen. I was going to refuse, but when Xan told me that Etienne had a mistress, I was so angry that I followed him when he left the house one evening and saw it with my own eyes. It was then that I wrote a note to Xan telling him where Etienne was.'

'Carry on,' he said, curiosity in his tone.

She was back there then, that fateful night in 1935, standing at the window in Bà Ngoại's apartment, watching the messenger boy wend his way through the crowd in Rue de la Soie carrying her note to Xan telling him where Etienne had gone for the evening. Her soul still burned with indignation at Xan's revelation. She'd kept it deep inside, gnawing at her throughout the day, until she was ready to burst with fury. But still, she kept quiet, demure on the outside, as her upbringing had taught her.

'Well done, Ari. You have done the right thing, for sure,' Bà Ngoại said as Arielle turned back into the room.

Have I? she bit her nail, besieged with doubts.

Later, Arielle left Bà Ngoại's apartment and took a cyclo back to the house on Boulevard Carreau. The whisky Bà Ngoại had given her had numbed her senses, but she knew she didn't want to think too hard about what she'd done. She had another drink from the decanter in the dining room when she got home, and when she got up to go to bed, the room pitched and swayed as she walked. She went upstairs alone and slept heavily, but despite that she was awoken early, just before dawn. Someone was banging on the front door, ringing the bell that was clanging in the hallway. No servants were up yet. She turned over, thinking she would ask Etienne to go, but he wasn't there beside her. His side of the bed hadn't been slept in.

She pulled on a silk dressing gown and ran down the stairs, her heart pumping. Hastily pulling back the bolts on the door, she threw it open. A gendarme in uniform stood on the step, holding his cap in his hands.

'Madame Garnier? May I come in?'

She moved aside and he stepped into the marble hallway.

'I have some bad news for you, I'm afraid. It's your husband. He was found dead in the early hours of the morning in the Rue Bourret.'

'What?' she stared at him, unable to process what he was telling her, and as she stared at his impassive face, nausea suddenly engulfed her, darks spots entered her vision and soon everything went black, and she was falling to the marble floor.

It was Papa who came to her rescue that day. Once the gendarme had called him, he arrived at the house in minutes. He took her upstairs and waited while she splashed water on her face and dressed in a white ao dai. Then Papa took her in his car to the Gendarmerie.

'I will identify Etienne's body,' he said.

'No, Papa. I must do it.'

'It's not a pretty sight,' the Head of Police said. 'I'm afraid he was beaten to death. I've never seen such savagery...'

'I will do it,' Arielle insisted quietly. She knew it was her duty and she wasn't going to shrink from this task. After all, she was responsible for this. It was her fault that Etienne had died.

Ten years later she still shivered at the memory of Etienne's bloody body lying on that slab in the Gendarmerie mortuary. She'd let out a cry of anguish when she saw him. His face had been beaten to a pulp and was virtually unrecognisable. His eyes were two red footballs, his nose broken, his lips split. Many of his teeth had been shattered too. His clothes were ripped and bloodied, and through the tears in his shirt and trousers, she could see that his body was covered in bruises and wheals. Even his hair was matted with blood. She turned away, trembling, and nodded to the waiting gendarme.

'That's my husband,' she said.

'Thank you, madame.'

As the gendarme ushered them out of the mortuary, Papa asked the Head of Police, in a shocked voice, 'Do you have any idea who did this?'

'We have a very good idea, Mr Dupont,' the man said, leaning back on his heels, his hands behind his back. He was running to fat and had a smug expression on his chubby face.

'How is that?'

'Well,' the chief looked sideways at Arielle, hesitating.

'Go on please. My daughter needs to know this too.'

'This won't be pleasant to hear I'm afraid, but a piece of paper was stuffed into his mouth. It was a signed confession from him that he'd exploited the poor, that he sold them to plantations knowing they would be badly treated and underpaid, that he'd swindled and cheated to get business, and that he'd had men killed who had tried to expose what he was doing. He must have been tortured and beaten to have signed something like that.'

They had reached the entrance to the Gendarmerie now. Papa sank down on a chair, shaking his head. 'So, do you have any idea...'

'Oh yes. We already have them in custody. Four of them. They are all communists. Troublemakers, of course. They are the reason this country is going to the dogs. They weren't hard to track down to their headquarters. We had a witness who'd seen them approach your son-in-law in the red light district. I can assure you they will soon feel the full force of the law upon them.'

'Do you have their names?' Arielle asked, alarmed.

'Yes, we do in fact. They are Tek Leng, Nguyen Uyen, Dung

Ut, and Xan Hoang. Hoang was the leader and we have been after him for a long time. He's responsible for many of the uprisings on plantations in the south, organising communists to infiltrate the workers. We have a lot we can charge him with.'

Arielle couldn't reply. She was trembling all over. She wanted to ask if she could go to the cells and speak to Xan but she knew that was impossible. She felt her father's arm around her shoulders, and she allowed him to usher her from the building and help her into the back of the car.

'Why don't you come and stay with me for a while?' he asked. 'Trang and I will look after you.'

Back at the townhouse she could barely walk upstairs, her legs felt so heavy, but eventually she managed to get up to her old bedroom, shut the shutters and lie down on the bed. Later, her father's doctor came and gave her some sedatives and she fell into a deep, dreamless sleep. She slept for days. Each time she awoke either the doctor or Trang was by the bedside and offered her another sedative. But on the third day she pushed the pills away.

'I want to get up now,' she said. 'I can't stay in bed any longer.'

Trang helped her out of bed and into the bath. Her body looked white and thin. It was shaky like an invalid's too. The guilt that engulfed her was all-consuming. Guilt at Etienne's death, guilt at Xan's arrest and imprisonment. She wondered if he would mention her under questioning. Though she hardly cared if he did. In those moments of deep despair it felt as though her life was over. Whatever life was left to her wasn't worth living anyway.

But Xan never did name her. She was stunned to read in the newspaper, *l'Avenir du Tonkin*, a week or so after Etienne's death, that all four of those arrested for Etienne's murder had been executed by guillotine. Dozens of other members of their movement had been arrested too and sentenced to long prison terms for insurgency.

She dropped the newspaper and crumpled to the floor in a heap, sobbing inconsolably. She thought of Xan, of his intelligent face, of his kindness towards her, of the touch of his cheek against hers, and she felt deeply responsible for his death. She felt terrible guilt for Etienne's death too, and for the brutal way he'd died. She pictured him surrounded by men, pushed to the floor, beaten with sticks, kicked and punched. What a dreadful weight of guilt she would have to bear now.

Over the next few weeks, Papa took care of everything. He sold Etienne's house, his warehouse, dissolved his business and paid off his workers. Arielle wouldn't touch any of Etienne's money, and instead, donated it to an orphanage where children of destitute workers from Tonkin were cared for. As far as she was concerned, the money was blood money and she wanted nothing further to do with it.

She bore the guilt and horror of that day for years and had never completely shrugged it off. It struck her down at low moments and made her vulnerable to anxiety. At those times the only thing that kept her going was visiting the Lake Pagoda regularly. There, in that beautiful, timeless spot she could forget her troubles, forget who she was, and make offerings to the Buddha and meditate just like everyone else.

Her father never asked any questions about Etienne's death. Perhaps he knew deep down that she had played some part in the events of that evening. After a few months, he helped her to get a job as a secretary with the colonial government. It was a good job, and she settled down into the routine of her new life with gratitude. She made new friends, Camille amongst them, and things seemed to be looking up for her, until the Japanese stormed the Mairie on March 9th 1945.

She'd been watching Kenneth's face as she'd been talking. He'd registered surprise at her words, but not disgust. Now she stopped and looked him in the eye. It was done now. She'd told him everything. Would he reject her now?

'That's why you're here, isn't it?' he asked, gently. 'The Viet Minh have this over you. They know what happened and they've been playing on your conscience.'

She nodded. 'They used it to get me to supply information to them about the Japanese when I was working for the general at the Mairie. I took dreadful risks to get it to them, and when I was almost discovered, they forced me to come up here to train with the guerrillas.'

'Look, you don't have anything to worry about. You did nothing wrong,' Kenneth said, leaning forward, looking into her eyes.

'It doesn't feel like that, though,' she said. 'I still feel as though I killed Etienne. The deaths of Xan and his comrades are on my conscience too.'

'All you did was to tell them where he was. You had no idea they were planning on killing him. And it's not surprising you told them after what you'd found out about him. Not only the exploitation he was involved in, but his Romanian mistress too. No one would blame you, Tuyen. You need to stop blaming yourself.'

She smiled at him, relieved. He wasn't going to blame her after all, and she wasn't going to lose his love.

'I've been meaning to tell you. It's not actually Tuyen,' she said quietly glancing around to check that no one was within earshot. 'It's Arielle. No one else here but Long knows that I'm half French.'

'That's a beautiful name,' he said. 'And it suits you so well.'

It was dark now and the guerrilla in charge of that evening's meal shouted over to them to bring the vegetables.

'What have you been doing, comrades? I need to start cooking.'

'Sorry.' Arielle stood up and heaved the saucepan of peeled potatoes across the clearing. When she turned round to return to her seat, she was surprised to see the two American sergeants were there, talking to Kenneth. She drew close.

'We have orders from Hanoi that we must pack up camp and get back down to the provincial capital, Thai Nguyen,' Redmond was saying. 'Our orders are to wait there for the Japs to surrender. After that we will be able to return to Hanoi. You need to come too, Jamieson. The Deer Team is being disbanded now. We've deliberately left you here with the Viet Minh because Mr Hoo reported you were doing good work, but all US officers have to report back to base in the next couple of days and that means you too. Get your kit together and be ready by six tomorrow morning. We'll pick you up on our way through.'

A lump rose in Arielle's throat. The only person she'd ever truly loved was going to leave her in the next few hours. Perhaps he would have to go straight back to the States from Hanoi. Would she ever see him again?

When the two sergeants had left, Arielle sank down beside Kenneth again.

'I'm sorry,' he said. 'I don't want to leave you here. But when the war is over, the Viet Minh will return to Hanoi and take you with them. US Command think it will be only a matter of days now, those guys told me. So, we won't be apart long.'

'I can't bear to lose you now, Kenneth,' Arielle said, tears flooding her eyes. She brushed them away, mindful of the watching eyes of the guerrillas.

'Don't cry, Arielle. Tell me where to find you in Hanoi and I will come there. I won't fail you. I promise.'

Later, after the evening meal, she went to Kenneth's hut with the address of the townhouse written on a scrap of paper. She couldn't prevent the tears falling as he took her in his arms and kissed her tenderly. Despite the sadness, and the lump in her throat, she tingled with pleasure at his touch. She slid her arms around his neck and returned the kiss, and before long they were kissing passionately. Then they sank down on the bed and lay there together, running their hands over each other's bodies, unbuttoning their clothes, pulling them off desperately and throwing them aside, feeling the warmth of each other's bare skin. Kenneth moved on top of her and she pulled him close and soon they were moving together, as if they were one.

23

HANOI, AUGUST 19TH 1945

I t had taken the band of ragged guerrillas almost three days to march from their camp in the hills near Tân Trào down to Hanoi. They walked through thick jungle, over hilly terrain, skirting around the bare rice fields in the valleys, wading across shallow rivers. Sometimes they followed narrow jungle paths, sometimes unmade tracks and sometimes metalled roads. At night they unrolled the bedding they carried on their backs and slept under the trees. They were never far from a village where many had died of starvation and those left were still suffering. They handed out nearly all their rations and left little to sustain themselves on the march.

There were only ten of them left. Most of their comrades, led by Long, had gone separately to the provincial capital, Thai Nguyen, with the Americans, where they were preparing for a final battle with the Japanese. The rest of the camp, led by Cong Son was making its way down to Hanoi. Mr Hoo had already gone on ahead by vehicle. They'd watched him leave on foot, together with a guide and a couple of companions, carrying his own pack. He was bound for the nearest road, a four-to-five-hour trek from the camp. There, he would be picked up and taken down to Hanoi by road. Before he'd gone, he'd shaken hands with them all and thanked them sincerely for their help in the fight against the Japanese.

'The next few days will be critical for us, comrades,' he said as he left with a cheery wave.

As they finally neared the capital, Arielle's spirits rose. She began to pick out landmarks she knew; villages she'd passed through on train journeys, familiar rivers and stretches of countryside. Her heart soared as they neared Hanoi. They would soon be back in her hometown, and when Kenneth made his way down there from Thai Nguyen, she would see him again. And now the war was over there was a chance that Papa would finally be released from the Citadel.

The Japanese had surrendered the day before they set out. Long had received a crackly message on his radio transmitter that the Americans had dropped two devastating bombs on Japanese cities Hiroshima and Nagasaki, resulting in tens of thousands of casualties and that the Japanese Emperor had finally given up the fight. When Long relayed the news to the camp there were uproarious celebrations; the guerrillas showed emotions that Arielle had never seen them reveal before, and they stayed up into the night drinking and dancing round the campfire. Arielle had watched them, relieved that this phase of her life was almost over, but still apprehensive about what the coming days would bring. She sat by the fire thinking with horror about the loss of life that had brought them to this point; of all the innocent Japanese civilians caught up in the bombings. To her, it didn't seem to be the cause for celebrations.

They reached the outskirts of Hanoi early on the evening of the third day and entered a run-down area beside the Red River, full of wooden and corrugated iron huts, where open drains ran the edge of the road and naked children played in the dirt. Cong Son showed them to a covered barn with some rough wooden bunks built against the walls.

'We will stay here,' he said, looking around at the others, 'In this suburb. We have friends here who will shelter us and keep us safe. We need to wait for word from Mr Hoo to march into the city. We are not quite ready for our victory parade yet.'

'Victory parade?' Arielle asked.

'Yes. Didn't you know? Mr Hoo is going to declare Vietnam a free country and set up a government. He is waiting for the official surrender of the Japanese. He will send word when we can march in.'

She looked into his eyes that brimmed with fervent pride. 'But comrade Cong Son, could you release me now please? My home is in this city. I would like to go there as soon as I can and see my family.'

The look on Cong Son's face changed instantly. He narrowed his eyes. 'Comrade Tuyen. This is no time for weakness and sentiment. *We* are your brothers and sisters now. We have fought side by side for many months. Don't you want to share in our final triumph?'

'Of course... but...'

He came up close to her then, held his rifle across her chest and put his face up to hers. He growled, 'Comrade Long said you might be difficult and that if you were, I was to remind you of why you are here.'

She stared back at him, defiant. She thought of Kenneth's words. *You don't have anything to worry about. You did nothing wrong.* But still the guilt nagged at the back of her mind. She dropped her gaze and stepped back. Would it matter so much if she stayed a few more days here? She was longing to go home and see Trang, to find out if Papa had been released, and if Kenneth had been to the house yet, but if she defied

Cong Son now, things could quickly get dangerous for her. She'd lasted this long, better to wait it out.

So, they stayed there in the uncomfortable barn for several days and the local people were so happy to have the Viet Minh in their midst that they brought them food every day and even cooked meals for them. Within a couple of days, though, reports of fierce fighting and many casualties at Thai Nguyen filtered through to them. Arielle immediately thought of Kenneth. Was he still there with the guerrillas? Was he fighting too? She pressed Cong Son for information about the casualties, but he had only heard very basic details over the crackly portable radio he'd brought down from the camp. Not knowing whether Kenneth was safe made Arielle anxious and jumpy. But it cemented in her mind how much he meant to her. She thought of him constantly, of his hazel eyes, his beautiful smile and the feel of his warm arms around her. She willed him to come back to her, willed him not to have been injured in the battle.

After a few nail-biting days, Cong Son heard the news that the battle was over and that the Americans, Long and the rest of their group were on their way down to Hanoi.

'The official Japanese surrender is set for September 2nd. That's tomorrow. In the afternoon we will march into Hanoi, to Ba Dinh Square and watch Mr Hoo give his speech,' he said. 'That will be a historic moment for our whole country.'

'Do you know if they are *all* coming back to Hanoi? The Americans too?' Arielle asked and Cong Son stared at her, frowning.

'As many as survived the battle. But we do know that we were victorious at Thai Nguyen, and that the French capitulated. That's all that matters here, surely comrade?'

Later that day, they began their march through the streets of the city to the centre of Hanoi. The route was filled with joyous people singing and shouting, cheering the Viet Minh as they passed through. Many people marched alongside them, waving the flag of the Viet Minh – a blood red background with a five-pointed yellow star in the centre. Arielle marched shoulder to shoulder with Cong Son and Mai. She was swept up with the mood of the crowd. It was indeed a momentous day for her country, but still, she worried about Papa and the others. Had they been released and if they had would they be safe? The anti-French sentiment in the crowd was palpable.

It took an hour or more to reach Ba Dinh Square which was already packed with chanting people, celebrating their release from Japanese domination and French rule. Cong Son pushed through the crowd, leading the little band of guerrillas to the centre of the square where a garlanded podium had been set up with microphones. They joined other Viet Minh ranged in lines in front of the podium, brandishing their rifles. Arielle stood beside Mai and looked around her for Kenneth. Although she recognised some of the comrades who had gone down to Thai Nguyen in the massed lines around her, there were no American faces to be seen anywhere in the crowd. Anxiety stirred in the back of her mind, but it was impossible to be anxious for long in this rousing atmosphere.

Mr Hoo, or Ho Chi Minh as he was known to everyone except those closest to him, arrived in a black limousine and mounted slowly to the podium. Thrills went through Arielle as she watched this diminutive figure with his goatee beard, dressed in a white uniform, mount the steps to give the biggest speech of his life. Lined up behind him on the podium were several dignitaries, including one she knew to be the Major in command of the OSS Deer Team. The crowd fell silent and Ho Chi Minh began to speak.

'All men are created equal. They are endowed by their

Creator with certain inalienable rights, among them are Life, Liberty, and the pursuit of Happiness.

'This immortal statement was made in the Declaration of Independence of the United States of America in 1776. In a broader sense, this means: All the peoples on the earth are equal from birth, all the peoples have a right to live, to be happy and free...'

The crowd was spellbound. He spoke for several minutes, listing the injustices heaped on the Vietnamese people by the French and Japanese rulers. He commanded complete attention and as Arielle watched, she thought of the kindly figure who'd pottered around the camp in the mountains, encouraging the guerrillas in their training and on their missions, keeping up morale. She'd admired his courage and conviction then, but now she saw how he could command the attention of a huge audience with his vision and sense of purpose. He was a true leader.

He ended his speech with a proclamation of the independence of Vietnam and a promise that its people would mobilise all their strength, and sacrifice lives and property to safeguard that independence and liberty. As he finished, the crowd erupted, cheering and shouting, jumping in the air, embracing one another. The sound was deafening. It reverberated around the square. Arielle looked around her at faces brimming over with happiness and hope. Just at that moment, an aeroplane flew over the square and everyone looked up. It was a silver propeller plane, clearly marked with the stars and stripes of the American flag.

When the cheering had died down there were more speeches. Ho Chi Minh introduced other Viet Minh leaders to the crowd as members of the new government he was forming that day. As the proceedings drew to a close, people began to drift away. The guerrillas in Arielle's group were chatting amongst themselves and Cong Son and Long were deep in conversation. Nerves prickled her stomach. Perhaps now was the time to make her escape? She could just melt into the crowd and disappear.

When a group of people passed, waving flags, she allowed herself to get swept along with them, leaving the guerrillas behind. Soon they were out of sight and she was on the opposite side of the square. She carried on walking without looking back. She still held her rifle and carried her pack on her back. People stepped aside for her respectfully and, wishing she wasn't quite so conspicuous, she slung her rifle over her shoulder.

Ba Dinh Square was near the West Lake and the Tran Quoc Pagoda. She hadn't seen it for a long time and part of her longed to go back there, but she knew she must go home, even though it was a long walk. She yearned to see her old home, to hug Trang and find out about her father. Perhaps he was even there already?

It took her over an hour to walk from Ba Dinh Square to the French Quarter. The streets were crowded with people making their way home from the ceremony, and there were no cyclos to be found anywhere. The sun was high in the sky. The air was hot and sticky and soon she was bathed in sweat, her combat clothes sticking to her body. Entering the French Quarter, although she was exhausted, she quickened her pace. She couldn't wait to get home. She even dared to hope that Kenneth might already have been there to look for her.

As she turned into the end of her road, she noticed that the streets were far quieter here in the French Quarter than in the rest of the city. Many of the villas and townhouses had been boarded up. Had citizens already left the town for France, fearing the Viet Minh? Some of them must have been held in the Citadel like Papa for several months now.

Rounding a bend in the road, her father's house came into view, but she paused when she saw it. It looked different. She shaded her eyes, wondering what it was and started walking again, this time faster than before. As she got closer she realised why it looked different. The primrose-yellow walls were blackened with soot, the window and door frames charred, some of the windows were broken. She stood on the pavement staring at it, shockwaves going through her. How had this happened? When had it happened?

Opening the front gate, she crossed the overgrown drive to the front door. Her heart in her mouth, she peered through the letter box. She gasped. The front hall was black with soot, the staircase had collapsed in on itself. There was no furniture except for the blackened skeletons of a couple of chairs. She sat down on the front step, put her head in her hands and started to sob.

24

HANOI, SEPTEMBER 1945

W hen she'd cried herself out, Arielle got up slowly from the front step and, picking her way through the debris and looking out for intruders, went round the side of the house to the kitchen door. It was where Trang used to take the shopping into the house, where she would receive deliveries and stand gossiping with the gardener. The glass in the window was broken and one look through into the devastated, blackened kitchen told her that Trang wasn't here and that no one could possibly live or work in this house as it was now.

She thought for a minute and remembered where Trang lived; it was in the Old Quarter, a few streets away from Bà Ngoại's old apartment. Although exhausted, Arielle knew that she had to go there. She had to make sure that Trang was alright, and she had to find out what had happened here. But there was something that niggled at the back of her mind. What if Kenneth were to come here looking for her? It was the only address she had given him. He would worry for her safety if he saw the house like this, and how would he know where to find her? She thought of leaving a note pinned to the door, then realised there was a chance that the Viet Minh might find it and discover their relationship. That seemed unwise, perhaps even dangerous. She would have to keep coming back to the house in the hope of meeting Kenneth here. There was nothing else for it.

Arielle shouldered her rifle and backpack and set off with a heavy heart towards the Old Quarter. By now her legs were aching and her feet were developing blisters from the crude rubber Viet Minh sandals she wore, and all the kilometres she'd walked in them that day. As she made her way back through the wide boulevards of the French Quarter, she saw again how the whole area had suffered under Japanese rule. Many once proud villas were deserted, their windows broken or boarded up, their gardens full of weeds. So many French occupiers must have fled the capital or had been locked up in the Citadel like Papa and Camille.

She passed along Boulevard Carreau. With a quickening heart she noticed her old home. The once brash, opulent villa that Etienne had bought with his blood money. That too looked run down and shabby. Its paint was peeling and walls dirty, but the building hadn't suffered as much as some of the other houses in the quarter. She recalled that she'd heard a rumour that the house had been commandeered by the Japanese to house officers. Perhaps Nishihara had lived here? It was just a few streets away from her own home. She shuddered, remembering the shock of the explosion, the acrid smell of smoke rising from the ravine as the jeep plunged down it in a ball of flames.

Within a few minutes she'd reached the Hoan Kiem lake and started to walk north along beside the water. This was her old route to work. She remembered how she used to enjoy looking out over the lake, watching fishing boats and pleasure craft bobbing on the surface, mingling with people at leisure strolling along beside the water. But today there were no boats, and few people walking along the lakeside. She soon drew level with the Mairie and couldn't prevent that familiar anxiety from mounting inside her. It was a reflex action; mirroring how she'd felt each time she'd approached the building while the Japanese were in charge. Now, automatically, she checked for Japanese guards on the front steps, but of course, there were none there now. Instead, two stony-faced Viet Minh guerrilla soldiers stood in their place. She hurried on, her head down, praying they wouldn't notice her. After all, she had deserted her unit and they could well be looking for her.

She entered the Old Quarter and to her relief the streets here seemed little changed. There was the same buzz and throng about the place that there had always been, although stocks of food and other goods on the stalls looked depleted. She pushed her way through the crowds until she reached Rue du Papier. She'd only visited Trang at her home once or twice and that was years ago, but she was sure this was the right place. Trang lived above a paper shop. Her apartment was a little like Bà Ngoại's, only smaller. Arielle found the familiar blue door and mounted the concrete steps to the apartment. It took several minutes for Trang to answer after Arielle's knock and when she did, Arielle was shocked at what she saw. In the space of a few months, Trang had aged visibly. She now walked with a stoop and her skin was sallow and lined. But when she saw Arielle, she gasped in astonishment. Then her eyes filled with tears and she held out her arms. Arielle fell into them, and they both sobbed together and held each other tight.

'Come. Sit down my child,' said Trang, drying her eyes. 'I thought I would never see you again. Let me make you some tea.'

'I went to the house. Whatever happened there, Trang?'

Trang shook her head and was silent for a moment, tears still oozing from her eyes. Then she turned away and placed a kettle on a small hob in the corner.

'It was Japanese soldiers, I'm sure of it,' she muttered. 'I was in the kitchen when I heard something shoved through the letter box in the hall. I ran through and the room stank of petrol and was already alight. Through the window I saw a Japanese army lorry speeding off down the street. I tried to put the fire out, but it had already taken hold and no matter what I did, the flames kept spreading around me. The stairs collapsed so I couldn't get up there. I had to go back into the kitchen. I tried to hold the fire off but the door burned down and that was it. I had to leave.'

'The order would have come from General Nishihara, I'm positive,' Arielle murmured.

'That beast of a man you worked for? But why?'

'I was passing information to the Viet Minh.'

Trang's mouth fell open in surprise.

'I was forced to, Trang. But I was almost caught and had to run away. The Japanese must have guessed what I'd been doing and come here to punish me.'

'So that's why you're dressed like a ruffian, and toting a gun?' Trang asked, her old twinkle returning.

Arielle nodded, smiling. 'They made me join them up in the hills. I've been living with the guerrillas since I left, training to fight.'

'The guerrillas!' The kettle started whistling and Trang went over to it and poured boiling water into a teapot.

To Arielle's relief, Trang didn't ask her how the Viet Minh had been able to force her to spy for them and get her to join them. She probably had a shrewd idea about what they had over her. After all, Trang had been there when Papa brought

Arielle home that fateful night in 1935 after they'd identified Etienne's body.

'Do you have any news of Papa?' Arielle asked and Trang shook her head. She poured out two cups of tea and handed one to Arielle. Arielle took a sip of the delicate jasmine infusion. She'd missed this in the camp where the tea was rough and strong.

'I still go there every day with food,' said Trang, 'although things have got difficult lately. There are no longer Japanese guards on the gates, but there are Viet Minh ones instead. They always take the food from me and I still don't know if it gets to him.'

'I was hoping he would have been released by now.'

Trang shook her head. 'The Viet Minh aren't going to let the French go, just like that. There's been no news of his release, or of any of the other prisoners who used to work for the French administration.'

'I need to go there and plead for them to let him go... Except I'm meant to be with the guerrillas now and they might be looking for me. If I go to the Citadel and they recognise me, they might lock me up too for desertion.'

'Well, you don't need to go there in those clothes, surely? If you wore a pretty ao dai and cleaned yourself up a bit, they surely wouldn't recognise you.'

'All my clothes have been destroyed in the fire. All I have in this pack is a pair of combat trousers and a camouflage jacket.'

Trang stood up. 'I have some old clothes you could wear. I used to love dressing up and I've kept all my pretty ao dais even though I haven't worn any of them for years. Come through to my bedroom and choose one. I used to be petite like you so they should fit.'

Within a few minutes, Arielle was transformed. She'd chosen a simple pale-yellow cotton ao dai, had washed her face and put her hair up. Trang was right. It was unlikely that anyone would recognise her as the tough-looking female guerrilla who had walked into the flat half an hour before. She left her pack, her clothes and her rifle in the care of Trang.

'Come back later on. I need to know you are safe,' the old woman said, squeezing her hand. 'Why don't you stay here tonight? There is plenty of space.'

'Of course. Thank you. And thank you too for all you have done for Papa, Trang.'

Arielle left the apartment and headed towards the Citadel. She was carrying a cannister of noodle soup Trang had handed her to leave for Papa. It felt liberating to be wearing the ao dai. It floated around her body and cooled her skin rather than the constraining combat clothes she'd been forced to wear in the camp. And now she was able to meld into the crowd, just a normal girl from the Old Quarter going about her business. No one stared at her or stood aside deferentially as they had done when she'd been a Viet Minh solder walking through with her rifle.

But as she approached the Citadel, she began to feel her nerves tightening. Just as Trang had said, there were two Viet Minh soldiers on the gate. They looked around warily and pointed their rifles at Arielle as she approached.

'Stop right there. What is your business?'

'I bring food for one of the prisoners. Monsieur Dupont.'

'Normally it is an old woman who comes with food.'

'She cannot come today. So, I have brought it. Please could you ensure Monsieur Dupont gets this?' she held out the cannister and one of the guerrillas stepped forward and took it from her. He was still looking at her suspiciously.

'I would also like to speak to your superior officer,' she said. The two guerrillas exchanged looks.

'That is not possible,' said the one who'd taken the food.

'But please. It is imperative that I talk to him. Monsieur Dupont is weak and unwell. I would like to ensure he is being cared for properly. I beg you, comrades. I know the Viet Minh cares deeply for the people. Well, he is a sick old man... he may be French but he is still a human being.'

'Our superior officer is not here at the moment. He will be back soon though. If you wait here, you can try speaking to him when he arrives.'

'Alright.'

She squatted down by the wall and watched as one of the soldiers went in through the gate with the cannister. There must be a chance that it was getting to Papa. The Viet Minh had to be more compassionate than the Japanese, surely?

There was nothing to do, sitting there outside the Citadel, but she was determined to wait, and in half an hour or so her patience was rewarded. There was the sound of a jeep entering the road at the far end. It accelerated towards the gate and screeched to a halt. Arielle got to her feet, about to step forward and speak to the Viet Minh officer as he crossed the pavement but as he got down from the jeep she caught a glimpse of his face. It was none other than the agent whom she'd met many times at the Lake Pagoda. She would recognise that face anywhere, the distinctive jagged scar on the forehead. She remembered his narrowed eyes as he threatened her, his ruthless fanaticism. He would recognise her instantly and take her back to join the other guerrillas. He would probably ensure she was punished too for running away from the group.

In a split second she realised that it was impossible for her to speak to this man. It certainly wouldn't result in the release of her father and it could well have severe repercussions for her. Before the soldiers even looked her way she turned away and began to walk quickly towards the end of the road, praying that they wouldn't call her back. As soon as she was a safe distance away, she started to run. When she reached the end of the road and emerged onto Boulevard Carnot, she was out of breath and Trang's ao dai was clinging to her sweating body. She stopped to recover for a few moments, angry and frustrated that her plans had been thwarted. As her heart slowed, she realised that it wasn't far to West Lake and the promontory to the Lake Pagoda. And even though she was exhausted, the pagoda was drawing her back. Almost unconsciously she started to walk towards it.

The sun was setting over West Lake when she reached the water's edge and marvelled at the beauty of the shimmering reds and golds dancing on the water as she had many times before. It occurred to her that the sun was setting on a different Hanoi to the one it had risen over. Something momentous had happened in the city that day and even though she had mixed feelings about the Viet Minh, she was happy that her country had at last gained its independence.

The old, familiar stalls were still stationed at the temple entrance, and, just as she'd always done, Arielle stopped to buy lotus flowers and incense, but when the woman handed them to her, she realised she had no money on her.

'I'm sorry,' she said to the woman. 'But I didn't bring any coins with me.'

The woman smiled broadly. 'No matter, sister. I remember you. And today is a great day for our country. Take the flowers and incense and make your devotions with a glad heart.'

Thanking the woman profusely, she joined the others thronging to make offerings to the Buddha and moved on down the walkway towards the pagoda gate. The monk nodded her through with a bow and a smile. She stopped to take her sandals off, then carried on towards the temple. She paused in the courtyard where the bodhi tree grew, looking up at the pagoda with its many roofs, her heart full of gratitude to be back here at last. Then she noticed someone sitting under the bodhi tree sketching, his head down, absorbed in his task. She looked again. There was no mistaking the colour of that hair. Just like the red-gold of the setting sun, it filled her heart with joy.

'Kenneth!' she cried, running towards him and he looked up and smiled at her, his eyes lit up with love.

25

HANOI, SEPTEMBER 1945

After they'd embraced, Arielle asked Kenneth what he was doing at the pagoda.

'I was waiting for you, of course,' he replied, smiling. 'We got back to Hanoi from Thai Nguyen a couple of days ago. I've been to your house several times. I couldn't believe what I saw! I was terrified that you'd been hurt in the blaze, but then realised that you must have still been in the hills when it happened. I didn't know how to find you, so I just kept on going back there.'

'The Japanese Army did it,' she told him. 'It was them who burned the house down. They must have guessed I was passing information to the Viet Minh. They did it to punish me.'

Kenneth shook his head. 'That's terrible for you. You must be devastated to lose your home,' he said quietly.

'Yes, it was a dreadful shock. But at least no one was hurt. Our old housekeeper, Trang, is safe. I went to see her earlier. But I was worried sick about you too.' Arielle sat down beside him on the low wall under the bodhi tree. 'People said there was fierce fighting at Thai Nguyen.'

'There was no need for you to worry,' Kenneth said. 'None of us Americans were allowed to fight. They kept us in a safe house away from the action. I'm sorry to have caused you anxiety, Arielle.'

'But you're here now. I'm so glad you thought of coming to the temple,' she said, and he smiled.

'I knew you would come here as soon as you were able, once you were back in Hanoi. You talked about it so much, I was sure you wouldn't be able to keep away.'

Arielle returned his smile and looked up into his eyes. 'You already know me very well.'

'By the way, you look beautiful in those clothes,' he said. 'You took my breath away when you came towards me just now.'

She laughed, realising he had only ever seen her in shapeless combat gear before. Then her eyes strayed to the sketch he was doing. It was the first time she'd seen him draw on any surface other than wood. He was sketching with a charcoal pencil on a piece of thick paper. It was a faithful representation of the pagoda, surrounded by palms and exotic foliage. He'd captured the pagoda's soaring roofs and its imposing presence perfectly.

'I did this for you,' he said, seeing her eyes on the drawing. 'I've finished it now. I'd like you to keep it.'

'Thank you. I shall treasure it. It's so wonderful to see you, Kenneth. I can't quite believe my luck.'

They looked into each other's eyes and didn't speak for a while. The gongs of the temple, the chanting of monks and the gentle voices of the worshippers making their way to the pagoda, floated to them on the evening air.

'I can see that you've come with offerings for the Buddha,' Kenneth said, breaking into their silence. 'Do you want to go and do that while I wait here for you?'

'Why don't you come with me?' she asked instantly, suddenly anxious. 'I don't want to lose you again. I would be afraid you wouldn't be here when I got back.'

'Alright. If you're quite sure. I wouldn't want to intrude, though. This is your place of worship, after all.'

'Everyone is welcome here,' she said. 'Come with me.'

They left the bodhi tree and began to wander side by side towards the pagoda. As they walked, Arielle told Kenneth about how her father was still locked up in the Citadel and how she'd almost run into the ruthless Viet Minh agent when she'd gone there to plead for his release.

'I'm so worried for Papa, Kenneth. He was already frail before he was taken to that terrible prison. I dread to think what six months of deprivation in that place will have done to him. I can't believe the Viet Minh won't release all the prisoners now they have taken over.'

Kenneth shook his head. 'Resentment of the French runs deep in the Viet Minh. Perhaps they're afraid of a French backlash against their rule.'

'Perhaps,' she murmured.

'Maybe I could help you? I could come with you and try to plead for your father's release? I could speak to the Viet Minh in charge. He doesn't know me. And US military stock is high with the Viet Minh at the moment. Stories have spread amongst them about how we helped train the guerrillas in the mountains and helped them out on their raids.'

'Would you do that for me? You don't even know my father.'

'Of course I would. I don't know him, but I'd do anything for you, Arielle. You know that. Your father is an innocent civilian and should be set free now the Japanese have surrendered. I'd be only too happy to try for you.'

'Let us go there together in the morning. I don't think it

would be a good idea to go back there tonight. The same guards would be on duty and they would be suspicious of me because of what happened earlier.'

'I'll come with you whenever you're ready to go back there.'

They had reached the temple now. People were crowding forward towards the altar to place their offerings and light candles. Kenneth hung back. 'You go. I'll just wait back here.'

She flashed a smile over her shoulder and made her way slowly towards the altar with her lotus flowers and incense. When she reached it, she placed the flowers there, amongst the other offerings, lit her incense from a candle and planted it in a copper bowl already full of sticks giving out their heady scent.

Then she knelt and paid her respects to the Buddha, her thanks for Kenneth having survived and for being there that day. Afterwards, although she sat cross-legged amongst the other worshippers, she couldn't settle to meditate. Her mind was so restless, processing the events of the day, it was impossible to quiet it. Also, she had the continual urge to turn round and check that Kenneth was still there. So, after a few minutes, she gave up the struggle and went to join him where he stood on the edge of the courtyard.

'Shall we leave now?' she asked. 'Where are you staying?'

'In a house not far from here, with the other OSS officers who were at Thai Nguyen. What about you?'

'I should go back to Trang's apartment. She lent me these clothes. She wanted me to stay with her tonight.'

They walked together to the temple gate where they both found their sandals.

'I would love to be with you tonight, Arielle,' Kenneth said longingly, taking her hand as they went out through the gate and walked towards the road. 'Can I at least walk you home?'

'Of course you may. I would love to spend the night with you too, but I don't want Trang to worry about me. She's been through so much already and I promised I would stay with her tonight.'

'I understand,' he said. 'We will have time enough to be together.'

He put his arm round her shoulders and as they reached the road, she moved in closer to him, and they walked through the dark streets to the Old Quarter with their arms entwined. She told him all about the long march down to Hanoi from the hills and in turn, he told her about what he'd seen of the fighting in Thai Nguyen. Arielle felt enveloped in his love. She began to feel safe for the first time in months, although she couldn't let herself feel the joy she knew she deserved whilst Papa was still locked up in the Citadel. All around them were jubilant people, celebrating the events of the day. The atmosphere on the warm evening air was one of hope and festivity.

When they reached Trang's apartment, they slipped inside the doorway of the shop below and kissed goodbye, a long, passionate kiss full of love and longing. They arranged to meet the next morning at nine o'clock at the entrance to the Lake Pagoda. She thought about asking him to come to Bà Ngoại's old apartment but realised he would probably get lost in the maze of streets in the Old Quarter. He handed her his sketch before he left.

'Don't forget this,' he said.

'I will keep it with me always,' she replied, taking it from him.

Trang was waiting anxiously for Arielle and when she entered, came straight to her, put her arms around her and held her tight. 'I'm so pleased you came back, Ari. I was worried something had happened.'

'I'm sorry, Trang. I met a friend. An American I got to know in the hills. We walked home together.'

'So, there's no news about your father?' Trang looked at her anxiously.

Arielle shook her head. She told Trang that the man in charge of the Citadel knew who she was and that she couldn't approach him.

'He would have reported me to my unit and made me go back there. I ran away from them today and they would punish me for that.'

'Oh Ari, what a terrible situation,' Trang said, wringing her hands.

'Don't worry. I'm going to go back in the morning. My friend is going with me and he has more of a chance of convincing the Viet Minh to release Papa than I do.'

'You look exhausted. Go to sleep my child. You must have had a tough day, although you have more colour in your cheeks and your eyes are brighter now than when you left two hours ago.'

There was mischief in Trang's tone but Arielle was too tired to respond to her words. She sank down onto some cushions Trang had spread out on the floor and, lying back, she closed her eyes. As she drifted off to sleep, listening to the sounds of the Old Quarter through the open window, she felt Trang lay a sheet gently over her body.

IN THE MORNING she awoke early, as the stallholders in the street below were setting up their stalls for the day. As soon as she opened her eyes she remembered that she'd met Kenneth and that he was going with her to the Citadel that morning, and her heart filled with hope and happiness. She lay there and watched the sky change from grey to bright blue through the open window.

Later, after she and Trang had breakfasted on noodle soup, she set off for the temple again with a spring in her step. She'd changed into another of Trang's ao dais, this one pale blue. It felt good to be free and walking through the Old Quarter again, but until her father was released, his plight would continue to play on her mind. Her legs ached from the exertions of the previous day, but she walked quickly. She couldn't wait to see Kenneth. Her heart ached to be with him again.

Hanoi was settling down after the events of the previous day; sweepers were clearing the streets of rubbish, people were making their way to work, traffic crawled along the roads between the mule carts and bicycles. She virtually ran the last hundred metres to the temple entrance, but when she reached the stalls selling incense and flowers she stopped and looked around her. Kenneth wasn't there. Her heart sank. They'd arranged to meet at nine o'clock sharp. She hadn't imagined that he might not be there.

She sat down on a bench near the entrance to the walkway and waited, her eyes trained on the pavement, willing him to appear. Her eyes grew tired and dry as she sat there watching the path. The minutes ticked by.

'Arielle!' There was a shout from the direction of the road, and she turned and shaded her eyes to see. Kenneth was getting out of a taxi and coming towards her. Relief flooded through her. She ran to him and he took her into his arms and held her.

'I thought something had happened to you and that you weren't coming,' she breathed.

'I'm so sorry. I had something to do before I came. Come, there is someone in the taxi who wants to see you.'

He led her forward and she bent down to peer inside the

car, expecting one of the American sergeants who'd trained her to shoot in the hills to be sitting there on the back seat. Perhaps Kenneth had brought someone else along to help him negotiate with the Viet Minh. Instead, sitting on the back seat of the taxi, a familiar, well-loved face looked back at her. She couldn't believe what she saw. He was a lot frailer and thinner than when she'd last seen him, his face was pale but wreathed in smiles.

'Papa!' She jumped into the back seat of the taxi and hugged him tight, tears streaming down her face and, as she kissed him, she realised that he was crying too.

26
HANOI, SEPTEMBER 1945

The taxi driver drove them back to the Old Quarter, crawling through the clogged rush-hour streets, manoeuvring around street stalls, horse drawn vehicles and men with sack barrows loaded with produce. Kenneth sat in the front with the driver, and Arielle sat next to her father in the back, holding his bony hand on the seat. Everyone was too overwhelmed to speak, and Arielle was content just to sit there next to Papa, basking in the warm glow of happiness she felt knowing that he was no longer suffering in the Citadel, and that he was there with her at last.

Every time she glanced over at her father, she was shocked at the state he was in. His body was frail and thin and seemed to sag against the car seat; his skin was sallow and he still wore the clothes he had put on to go into the office on that fateful morning of 9th March. The clothes were torn and filthy and stank of sweat and worse. Poor Papa. He'd always taken such pride in his appearance and had loved to look smart when he went to work. She wondered if there had been any opportunity to wash either his body or his clothes while he'd been locked up in the Citadel.

With great skill, the driver managed to navigate his way down the Rue de Paniers. He turned right into the Rue de la Soie and at last drew up opposite Diep's silk shop beneath Bà Ngoại's old apartment.

'Why have we come here Ari? Shouldn't we go home?' Papa asked, his voice tremulous and confused.

'It's safer here, Papa,' she replied, not wanting to tell him about the house yet. It was far too soon and she needed to find the right moment.

'Safer? But isn't the war over?'

'Yes... but there is still unrest. The French are very unpopular. Come, let's go upstairs. You can rest there.'

Diep's face registered first astonishment and then pleasure when Arielle knocked at her door to ask for the key to Bà Ngoại's apartment.

'I thought I would never see you again, or your papa.' Diep smiled and handed Arielle the key.

'I thought that sometimes too. It's been a very difficult few months.'

'I've looked after your grandmother's place for you, all the same. Welcome back,' Diep said.

Papa needed help to get up the stairs. He leaned heavily on Kenneth, who had to virtually lift him bodily up each step. Arielle went ahead and unlocked the door. The apartment was clean and tidy, but smelled musty. Arielle went to the windows and threw them open, letting the cries of street sellers and the hubbub of the street float into the room. Kenneth helped Papa to Bà Ngoại's old armchair in the corner of the room and he slumped down into the cushions, breathing heavily, sweat standing out on his brow. As soon as he sat down he started coughing. A racking, wheezing cough that Arielle recognised from when he'd been ill before the war.

'I will make you some tea, Papa.' Arielle hastily filled the kettle at the sink and found a jar of tea and some cups.

'Why don't I go out and get some food?' Kenneth asked, hovering in the doorway. 'Give you a little time alone together.'

'Oh, Kenneth. I can't thank you enough for what you've done.'

She went over to him, put her arms around him and kissed him on the lips.

'No need to thank me.'

'But what a surprise. I didn't expect you to turn up at the pagoda with Papa.'

'I thought it was simpler for me to go to the Citadel alone, first thing in the morning. And it was. The guards showed me in to see the man in charge straight away. I told him how I'd worked in the hills with the Viet Minh guerrillas in Mr Hoo's camp, and after a bit of persuasion, he agreed to release your father into my care. It probably wouldn't have gone so smoothly if you'd been there, knowing your history with that man.'

'I still can't quite believe that Papa's free.' Then she frowned. 'He doesn't look well, though. And his cough sounds terrible.'

'He needs food and rest. He's obviously been through a dreadful ordeal.'

When Kenneth had gone, Arielle went back into the room and made jasmine tea for the two of them. Her father took the cup with shaking hands. He held it to his mouth and took tiny sips as if he didn't want to drink it too quickly. Now and again he had to put the cup down on the little table so he could cough. Arielle watched him with mounting alarm.

'It's so good to have you home, Papa. I will look after you and help you get better. When we've had something to eat, I will make up Bà Ngoại's bed for you. I'll help you along to the bathroom so you can have a shower too.'

'You're a good girl, Ari,' Papa said, reaching for her hand. 'Just like your friend.'

'Camille?' Arielle recalled how she'd seen the two of them helping each other around the exercise yard at the Citadel. 'How is she coping?'

Papa's eyes filled with tears and he put the cup down on the table, spilling some of the contents. He shook his head.

'She died, Arielle.'

Arielle felt the blood drain from her face.

'Camille? Dead?' she could scarcely believe it. This was one thing she hadn't even contemplated. Out of everyone taken from the Mairie by the Japanese that day, Camille had been the one Arielle was sure would survive. She thought of Camille's lovely face, her dancing eyes, her bravery. 'Oh Papa,' she said, holding his hand again. 'But why? What did she die of?'

'Typhus I believe. There was an outbreak amongst the prisoners...'

'That's truly terrible news.'

'She was a lovely girl,' Papa muttered. 'So generous and kind.'

His eyes wandered around the apartment. 'Where's Bà Ngoại?'

Arielle's mouth fell open. She hadn't expected this and she wondered how to deal with it. In the end she decided to be frank with her father.

'Bà Ngoại died, Papa. Peacefully, in her sleep, in 1939. Don't you remember?'

He stared at her, his eyes vague.

'So much has happened my child. It is difficult to remember everything.'

'It doesn't matter, Papa. You don't need to worry about anything. Just drink your tea and relax.'

They sat in silence until Kenneth returned. He'd brought cartons of street food: fried rice and noodles. He also had a parcel under one arm.

'I bought some new cotton pyjamas for your father,' he explained. 'When we've eaten, I'll help him get out of those old clothes.'

'Thank you, Kenneth,' she said, smiling into his eyes yet again.

'It's nothing, Arielle. Remember, you saved my life up in the hills.'

When Papa had finished his tea and eaten some noodles, Kenneth helped him along the passage to the basic washroom at the back of the building. Arielle tidied the room and made up Bà Ngoại's bed. All the time she worked, she was thinking about her father. It was wonderful that he was no longer in prison, but she couldn't help worrying at how vague and confused he was. She bit her nail, frowning to herself. Would that get better with time, or would the old, laughing, practical Papa never return to her?

'You'll need to be patient, Ari,' Kenneth was standing in the doorway. 'He's had a hell of an ordeal.' She looked up at him and couldn't hold back the tears. He came and held her, and she let them fall.

Later, leaving Papa with Kenneth, she walked through the Old Quarter to Rue de Papier. Trang jumped up when she entered her apartment and came over to embrace her.

'Is he free?' Trang asked and Arielle nodded. 'I knew it! I could tell by the look on your face as soon as you came in.'

Trang came back with her to Bà Ngoại's apartment and on the way, Arielle tried to warn her that Papa wasn't his old self, but she found it hard to put it into words. She need not have worried; when Trang entered the apartment, Papa's eyes lit up and he went over to Trang and put his arms around the old lady. 'I missed you, Trang,' he said. 'Thank you for looking after my house while I was away.'

Trang looked over at Arielle, mystified, and Arielle gently shook her head. 'Not yet,' she mouthed.

Over the course of the next few days, Arielle cared for her father night and day. She fetched food from the market, cooked meals for him, helped him to the bathroom and made sure he was comfortable. Trang often came to help care for him or just to keep him company. At night Papa slept in Bà Ngoại's bed and Arielle slept on the cushions in the living room. When Papa had gone off to sleep, Kenneth would lie down beside her and they would hold each other close and steal kisses, but although they yearned for more, it felt wrong with her father coughing away in the next room, knowing that he might get up to visit the bathroom at any time. But just being together was somehow enough; feeling the warmth of his skin next to hers made the anxiety of all those days of being apart melt away.

Late at night, Kenneth would get up and creep out of the apartment. He wasn't allowed to spend the night away from his billet. In the daytime he came and went. He was still living in the OSS house and although he had few duties, he was expected to report in daily. Whenever he could, he helped Arielle care for her father. He went to the tailors and bought some drawstring trousers and collarless shirts for Papa to wear. But each day he came with news of more unrest on the streets and on the fourth day he came to tell her that he had to report for duty the next day.

'There's to be a demonstration in the city centre tomorrow and the government is expecting trouble.'

'Trouble? What do you mean?' she asked, alarmed.

'Violence maybe. Things could get out of control.'

'But why? Isn't the Viet Minh in charge here now?'

'Nominally, yes. But the Japs left a vacuum here when they surrendered. Although the Viet Minh are meant to be in charge, they can't control all the different political factions that have sprung up everywhere. There's a lot of anti-French feeling and if I were you, I wouldn't let your father go onto the streets tomorrow.'

Arielle looked at him, worried. 'I'll make sure Papa stays inside, although he hasn't been out yet so that won't be difficult. How long do you think this will go on?'

Kenneth shrugged. 'Who knows? Vietnam is descending into chaos at the moment. Our officers are saying that Saigon is even worse than Hanoi. It's rife with demos and violence down south. French citizens have been killed. They've even had to enlist Japanese soldiers to help protect them. How ironic is that, hey?'

'That's absolutely terrible.' Arielle shuddered.

'Part of the problem is that no one has officially accepted the surrender of the Japanese here in Vietnam yet. I heard that Chinese troops are on their way to Hanoi to do that and to try to keep the peace and that the Brits are due in the South to do the same. I can't see the Brits co-operating with the Viet Minh though. Things could get very tricky.'

Arielle shook her head in dismay and disbelief. 'I thought everything would be alright once the war was over,' she said blankly.

'It doesn't look that way,' Kenneth replied. 'I'm so sorry, Ari. I wish this wasn't happening. I so want you to be safe. Look, I've been thinking... why don't you take your father and go to France. I've got this sneaking feeling that Vietnam isn't going to be safe for a long time.'

Her mouth dropped open in surprise. 'What? Leave my home? Leave you?'

'I could join you as soon as I'm released from duty. And you could return here as soon as things are safe again.'

She thought about his words. With his contacts in the OSS, he must know more than he'd been telling her, but the thought of leaving the city she loved filled her with sadness.

'I don't know, Kenneth. That feels like a huge step...'

'Let's talk about it again tomorrow. I'll come and see you in the evening as soon as I'm able. Please take care tomorrow, my love.'

After he'd kissed her tenderly and left, Arielle went back into the living room and sat down beside her father. He was sitting in his usual place, Bà Ngoại's armchair, looking blankly into space as he often did for long periods. She took his hand but didn't say anything, knowing that conversation was difficult for him and that it was better just to let him know she was here for him. Once, she'd been able to tell him everything. He'd been her rock throughout all the difficult times. But now she knew that it was she who needed to be the strong one. To her surprise though, this time he had a question for her.

'When can we go back to the house?' he asked, breaking the silence.

'Oh, Papa,' she said awkwardly, 'I've been meaning to tell you... I'm afraid it won't be possible to go back there at the moment.'

'Why is that, Ari? It's our home.' His voice was full of confusion.

She cleared her throat. 'I didn't want to worry you, Papa, but I'm afraid the house has been damaged. It was in a fire. When things have settled down here, I will look into getting it repaired.'

He started and sat bolt upright in the chair.

'Fire? Was it the Japs?'

Arielle nodded.

'Those bastards...' He didn't say any more but she noticed he sat clenching and unclenching his fists and in time his eyes grew misty with tears.

The next morning when Papa awoke he seemed restless. He started pacing the apartment, going over to the window repeatedly and leaning on the sill, staring out into the street.

'Who are all those people, Ari?'

She went to join him. There were no stalls set up today and shutters had been drawn over the shop windows. The street was thronging with people, dressed in the dark tunics and cloth turbans or conical hats of manual workers. They were all walking purposefully in one direction, towards the Hoan Kiem lake. Some held placards and some were chanting, 'French go home, French go home.'

There was a restless, ugly atmosphere in the crowd.

'Don't listen to them, Papa,' Arielle said gently. 'And come away from the window, please.'

'What has happened to this country?' he asked, bewildered. 'There used not to be such hatred here.'

'It is the war, Papa,' she said putting her arm around his waist. 'It has opened up so many wounds and everything is in turmoil. People need to blame somebody.'

He watched the crowd for a few more minutes, then left the window and went back to his armchair.

'Will Trang come today?' he asked, and Arielle shook her head. 'I expect she'll want to stay at home. It's not really safe on the streets.'

'What about Kenneth?'

'He's on duty, policing the demonstration.'

'He's a good man, Arielle. This time you've chosen well.'

She smiled and turned away to make tea, glowing inwardly. 'Thank you, Papa.'

Throughout the morning, Papa became more and more agitated. He got up repeatedly and crossed to the window, leaning out to watch what was happening in the street.

'What's the matter, Papa?' she asked, trying to get him to come away from the window.

'I need to go to the house,' he said. 'I've been thinking about it since you told me about the fire. I need to see it.'

'I don't think that's a good idea, Papa. It would only upset you.'

He frowned then and anger clouded his brow for the first time since he'd been released. For the first time in years in fact.

'Don't try to protect me, Arielle. I might look weak but I'm strong inside. I survived the Citadel, don't you forget that.'

'I'm sorry. I didn't mean any harm. We can go there if you insist. But we can't go today. It's not safe outside.'

He didn't reply. He just sat back in his chair and after a few minutes she was relieved to see that he'd closed his eyes and appeared to have drifted off. She pottered around the flat, tidying away the breakfast things, sweeping the floor, preparing vegetables for lunch. Then she went through to the bedroom to tidy up and make Papa's bed. He must have had a restless night because the sheets were tangled and the pillows strewn about on the floor. The task took her longer than it normally did. When she'd finished making the bed, she picked up Papa's discarded pyjamas to wash.

'Do you want more tea, Papa?' she asked going through to the living room, but the words froze on her lips as a bolt of shock shot through her. The armchair was empty, and it was clear from a quick glance around the tiny apartment that her father was no longer there. She dropped the washing and ran to the door, her mind racing. Had someone seen him at the window and come inside to take him away? She shivered, thinking of the anger and hatred of the crowd. Had he gone by himself? She thought of his words; *I need to go to the house.* Perhaps he'd decided to go there by himself on a whim, knowing that she would try to stop him if she'd seen him.

She dashed down the steps into the street. The crowd had thinned out a little now, but still groups of people were marching through the Old Quarter to join the demonstration, holding placards, chanting anti-French slogans. Luckily, they were marching in the direction of the French Quarter so she fell into step with them. She wanted to go more quickly, but it was impossible. All the time she was walking, she was straining to look ahead of her, above the heads of the marchers. Papa was a little taller than most of the local people, so she should see his head above the crowd if he hadn't gone too far. But there was no sign of him, and she really began to panic then. She was terrified that he'd been abducted. She knew he wasn't safe amongst this hostile crowd, whipping each other up with their hatred of the French.

The tide of moving bodies swept her along. She couldn't have stopped or turned around if she'd wanted to, but her focus was on the sea of heads surging through the narrow streets in front of her. He must be somewhere in this crowd, surely?

Gradually, the roads widened and opened up in front of the Hoan Kiem lake. Here, on a wide stretch of road on the corner of the Avenue Beauchamp, the demonstrators were gathering. The people in front of her spread out along the side of the lake and the chanting grew louder and louder. *French Out, French Out...* Arielle wanted to put her hands over her ears to drown out the words but didn't dare. Still she was straining her eyes, trying to see Papa in the crowd.

Up ahead came the sudden sound of frantic voices scream-ing. People started struggling to turn round and run away. As they dispersed, the crowd parted in front of her and through the bodies a few metres ahead of her she saw a terrible sight. A man was sprawled on the ground being kicked and punched by a group of demonstrators. They were attacking him ferociously, beating his prone body with all the savagery and pent-up venom of years of colonial rule. She pushed her way towards him and as she got closer she saw the terrible truth. It was Papa. Her mouth was open and she was screaming too, but she couldn't hear her own voice above the noise of the crowd.

'Papa! Papa!' she could barely see through the tears, but she knew she had to get to him. As she pressed closer she caught sight of the venom and hatred in the eyes of his attackers.

'Stop!' she screamed. 'Stop!'

She sprang forward and pummelled one of the men with her fists but he didn't stop or even pause in his brutal attack. But the next second came the sound of shots and a gasp went up. Guns were being fired in the air and three soldiers elbowed their way through the bodies. There was no mistaking the tall man who led them. No one else had that flaming red hair. She sank to her knees beside Papa's prone body sobbing, while Kenneth and his comrades pulled the attackers off and dragged them away, back through the crowd.

'Papa, can you hear me?' she knelt beside him. More soldiers appeared with a stretcher, lifted Papa onto it and carried him along the side of the lake to a waiting ambulance. Arielle followed and climbed into the vehicle beside him. As the ambulance set off, demonstrators were banging on the side shouting 'French out.'

An American soldier travelled with them.

'Take no notice. We'll be out of here soon.' But as they sped away, Arielle's eyes were glued to Papa's face. It was deathly pale, blood oozed from his swollen mouth and bruises were already forming on his cheeks and forehead. She shivered, remembering Etienne's body growing cold in the mortuary.

'Please don't leave me, Papa,' she pleaded, but his eyes remained closed.

A MONTH later Arielle stood on the deck of the liner Ile de France as it chugged out of Haiphong Harbour. She waved frantically to the red-headed man in the crowd and he waved back. But as the ship gathered steam and moved out into the river, heading towards the South China Sea, the crowd closed around him, and she could no longer pick him out from the others. Papa was not well enough to come on deck to wave goodbye. He'd been able to walk, with the help of a steward, to their cabin on the second-class deck, but the effort had so exhausted him, he'd lain down on the bottom bunk, his face pale. 'You go, Arielle. Wave goodbye to Kenneth for me too. I'm sorry. I just don't have the strength.'

She and Papa had said goodbye to Trang that morning. The old lady was leaving the dangers of the city behind, to stay with her sister in a remote fishing village on the coast. As Arielle hugged her for the last time, she'd wondered if they would ever meet again. Then, on the dockside, she and Kenneth had held each other tight until the very last moment, when the ship's sirens were announcing its imminent departure.

'Write to me at the Post Office in Hanoi and let me know where you are when you get to Paris,' he'd said and she saw tears welling in those hazel and green eyes for the very first time. 'I will come and join you as soon as I can. I'll be thinking of you every minute of every day, Ari. I love you.'

He'd been posted down south to Saigon on a peace keeping mission to help quell the rioting there and although he'd pleaded with his commanding officer, it was clear there was no chance of him being released early. But even though he couldn't accompany her, he'd insisted that Arielle and her father should leave the country as soon as they could. After the attack in Avenue Beauchamp, she knew he was right, and as soon as Papa was well enough to leave hospital, she booked a passage on the very next ship.

Now, she carried on waving, long after she'd lost sight of Kenneth, already missing his touch and his ready smile, wondering when she would see him again. The ship moved on, out to sea, heading into the mist that hung above the blue-green water. She looked back at the country she loved and, as it melted into the heat haze and gradually became a grey-blue smudge on the horizon, she wondered if she would ever see it again.

27

PARIS, 1947

A rielle didn't recognise the writing on the thin blue airmail envelope. When she'd first caught sight of it in the pigeonhole in the lobby of the apartment block when she came downstairs, her heart had quickened. The stamps were American; they were red, with a stern face of George Washington in the centre, and the post mark Montana, but the handwriting on the envelope wasn't Kenneth's. It was neat and flowing and unmistakeably feminine. She was on her way out to her shift at the station café at the Gare de Lyon but she knew she had to read the letter before taking another step. The concierge was standing in the doorway watching brazenly, but Arielle ignored her. She ripped the envelope open and drew out the letter.

My dear Arielle,

My son, Kenneth, asked me to write to you if I had any news of his whereabouts. I know you must hold a special place in his heart, so when I received a telegram from the OSS in Hanoi, Vietnam this morning, I knew I needed to get in touch and let you know what it said.

He may have written to let you know that he was being sent on a mission into the hills in northern Vietnam where some members of the OSS had gone missing during the last months of 1945. His commanding officer told me that it was very difficult to mail letters abroad from Hanoi, with the war between the Viet Minh and the French going on, so I don't know if that letter would have reached you. Today, I received a telegram to say that Kenneth has not returned from that trip and that a further search party is being sent into the mountains to look for them. I'm sorry to be the bearer of bad news, but there is still hope that he will be found. I am praying for his safety and will write to you again when I hear further.'

Yours,

Carol Jamieson

Arielle stared at the letter and the words seemed to become blurred and jumbled and to dance off the page towards her. They seemed to be mocking her.

'Bad news, mademoiselle?' The concierge's voice barely registered with her and she didn't reply. Instead, she shoved the letter in her bag, left the apartment block and set off down the Boulevard St Germain, feeling numb with shock. As she made her way through the busy streets towards the river and the Gare de Lyon, she hardly noticed her surroundings; the elegant buildings that lined the left bank, the cobbled streets along the water's edge, the beautiful silver birch trees with their grey-green foliage stirred by the breeze from the river.

She mounted the steps to the pedestrian bridge, walked to the middle of it and stopped there. Then, with her palms on the rail, she leaned out, looking down into the swirling dark water. All she could think of was Kenneth and the news she'd just read. Wherever was he? She'd longed to hear from him every moment of every day since she'd received his one and only letter two months before. And now she'd actually had some news about him and she wished she hadn't. He was lost somewhere deep in the hills in northern Vietnam.

She knew there were dangerous caves in the region where he'd gone. Perhaps their search had taken them into that treacherous area, and they had fallen or got trapped? Or maybe they'd been attacked and killed by guerrillas from some splinter group up there. She closed her eyes to hold back the tears. How would she get through today without knowing what had happened to him? How would she cope through all the long and difficult days to come? By rights he should be here with her now, by her side each day, they should be living and loving together. Instead, he was lost on some mountainside thousands of miles away. Taking a deep breath, she drew herself up. She must stop thinking like that or she would go mad. She must concentrate on getting through the day. If she let her thoughts run away with her, she would never be able to carry on, and Papa needed her to.

She walked on slowly towards the station and when she reached it went on along the concourse towards the café. The place was already busy with morning travellers, eating pastries and sipping coffee while they read their newspapers. There was a lively hubbub in the echoing room.

'Good morning. And how's my favourite waitress today?' Violette asked brightly as Arielle reached the counter.

'I'm fine thank you.' Arielle forced a smile but she knew it hadn't reached her eyes.

'Your papa is alright, isn't he?' Violette asked, frowning, her eyes suddenly full of concern.

'He's fine today, thank you. He coughed quite a bit during the night, but it was no worse than usual.'

'That's good. But is there something else? You look troubled, my child.'

Arielle shook her head. She wasn't ready to tell Violette about the news of Kenneth. She didn't trust herself not to cry. Violette knew that she was waiting for someone to come in from the boat train from Marseille, but she didn't know all the details.

The older woman slid her hand over Arielle's. 'Don't look so worried, my pet. Things will get better for you, you'll see.'

'Thank you for being so kind,' Arielle replied swallowing the lump in her throat. 'Now I'd better clear some of those tables. It looks really busy out there this morning.'

She went through the motions of her usual tasks like a sleepwalker that day. She cleared dirty cups and plates, wiped down tables and took orders as if on autopilot. When eleven o'clock came around, Violette bustled up to her.

'Isn't it time for your break?' she asked meaningfully with a nod towards the platform where the boat trains came in.

'It's alright. It's busy at the moment. I'll go later on when things have quietened down.'

Violette frowned and raised her eyebrows but didn't ask any awkward questions. The day dragged on but finally three o'clock came around and it was time to go home until the evening shift.

'See you later on,' Violette said, looking up from wiping the bar down to watch her go.

As soon as Arielle had left the thronging café her spirits deserted her. She'd managed to keep going while she was busy but now she was alone she felt the weight of her anxiety about Kenneth pressing down on her. She sat on one of the station benches for a while to calm herself before she could find the strength to walk home.

She was relieved to see that Papa looked a little brighter than usual when she entered the apartment, and she went over and kissed him on the forehead. He seemed to have turned the corner lately and Arielle had even dared to hope that he would soon be his old self again.

'How was the café?'

'Busy,' she replied.

'You're a good girl, Arielle,' he said patting her hand. 'Any news of young Kenneth?'

He asked every day and every day her response was the same; there had been no news, and no news was good news. Today she hesitated. Should she tell Papa about the letter? She decided not to. Partly because to give voice to the news that he was missing would reinforce the truth of it, and partly because she didn't want to cause Papa any distress. Instead of going through to the kitchen as she normally did, she went to her room and flopped down on the bed. The nervous tension was exhausting her. She took out Carol Jamieson's letter and read it again, then she reached in her bedside drawer and found the one and only letter she'd ever received from Kenneth. She read the words over and over again as she had many times before.

I think of you all the time Arielle and can't wait until we're together again. It's that thought that's keeping me going. I love you and I miss you, and I want to hold you in my arms so badly that it hurts to be away from you.

And once again, as she always did, she picked up Kenneth's drawing of the Lake Pagoda and stared at it, letting the image on the page transport her back to Hanoi. The sketch was so realistic, it always had the power to make her feel as if she was actually there, standing in front of the magical pagoda. She could almost smell the incense, hear the chanting of the monks, the chimes of the temple bells. Just looking at it gave her some comfort and the strength to get up from her bed and go through to the kitchen to prepare Papa's early evening meal.

After Papa had eaten and before setting off again for the Gare de Lyon, she sat down to write to Kenneth's mother. Written English didn't come easily to her, and she was so full of emotion, it was a difficult letter to write, so she kept it short.

Dear Mrs Jamieson,

Thank you for your letter and for sending me news of Kenneth. I am praying constantly for his survival and hope that he will be back with us very soon. I had one letter from him before he went into the hills and that was several weeks ago now.

It is good of you to think of me, and I thank you for your kindness in writing. I will let you know if I hear from Kenneth, and will be waiting anxiously for further news myself and praying for his safe return.

Yours sincerely,

Arielle Garnier

There was a post office near the Gare de Lyon, so she stopped off and mailed the letter on her way to work that afternoon. She imagined it arriving at the white clapperboard farmhouse nestled amongst the hills on the ranch that Kenneth had described, and Carol Jamieson sitting in her rocking chair on the wide porch to read it. She pictured a handsome woman in late middle age with kind, hazel eyes, tucking a lock of red-gold hair behind her ear as she ripped open the envelope.

The days wore on. At first Arielle had no idea how she would keep going. Paris was alien to her still. She felt homesick and adrift without any friends around her apart from Violette. Would life be like this for ever? Would she always have to spend all her time working in an exhausting, poorly paid, menial job just to make ends meet? There seemed no let up, no escape. She tried to focus on Papa and the fact she had to get up and go out every day for his sake. Without that, she would have stayed in bed, and descended further into despair.

But one morning another letter came with the same postmark, the same handwriting as before. And once again she snatched it out of the pigeonhole and ignored the inquisitive stares of the concierge. Her heart was beating fit to burst as she tore the envelope open. Was this the news she'd been dreading? Had Kenneth been found? Had he died out there in those unforgiving mountains?

My dear Arielle,

Thank you for your letter which arrived last week. I am writing again to let you know that I have had news of Kenneth today, although I haven't had word from him myself. He and some men from his OSS unit were found yesterday. They had been trapped by a rockfall in a cave deep in the mountains. One had died and the others were near starvation, but they are being taken back to Hanoi now. I believe Kenneth will be going to hospital there, but I cannot be sure.

If I hear from him or from his superior officer again, I will be sure to write.

Yours,

Carol Jamieson

Arielle read the words over and over. Was this good news? She hoped fervently that it was, but it didn't give her the comfort she was yearning. Kenneth might not have survived the journey down to Hanoi, he might have died in hospital. She glanced at the post mark on the envelope. The letter had taken over three weeks to reach her. What had happened to Kenneth in those intervening weeks?

'Are you alright my dear?' It was the concierge again. Arielle wiped away an anxious tear before turning round to look at her.

'I'm fine thank you madame. No need to worry. I need to get off to work now.'

As she went about her duties that day, her mind ran over and over the different possibilities. Kenneth could still be in hospital fighting for his life, or he could have recovered and be on his way home. If that was the case, why had he not written to her? Surely, he wouldn't have boarded a ship without sending word that he was on his way? But as his mother had said in the first letter, the post was notoriously poor between Vietnam and France, with the hostilities that were still going on between the Viet Minh and the French. At the best of times, letters could take several weeks to arrive; as long as the sea passage itself.

The next Tuesday she resumed her eleven o'clock breaks and her vigil on the platform where the boat train from Marseille arrived. It gave her a little thrill each week to watch the passengers climb down from the train and walk up the platform, knowing they had come from her beloved homeland.

Three further weeks passed with no sign of Kenneth, no further letters from Mrs Jamieson, and despair was threatening to overcome Arielle once again. That Tuesday morning she went to the platform as usual at eleven o'clock but the train wasn't there.

'It's going to be late today, mademoiselle,' the ticket inspector told her. 'Some hold up in Lyon I'm told. It will be at least an hour late. Come back later if you can.'

He was used to Arielle waiting there for the boat train and happy to give her information.

'Thank you, monsieur.'

She wandered back to the café. Violette was taking a food delivery and had asked her to work behind the bar over lunchtime, so there was no chance of going back to wait for the train at twelve. It was a busy time with people coming in for lunchtime beers and aperitifs and Arielle was less used to working the bar than serving on the tables, so she had to give her full attention to the task.

She was just opening the brass cash register to give a

customer some change when she looked up and glimpsed the great clock above the door. It was five past twelve. The train would probably be in now. With a sigh she handed the change to the man and was about to turn to serve the next customer when she happened to glance at the glass doors again. This time she couldn't tear her eyes away. Someone was coming through them. Someone with flaming red hair and dressed in dark green fatigues carrying a rucksack. He looked thinner than before, but he was unmistakeable.

'Kenneth!'

She left the bar and the bemused customers and ran across the café, pushing her way between the tables, knocking over a chair as she went. At the sound of her voice, Kenneth looked her way and when he saw her dashing towards him his whole face lit up with joy and love. She ran into his arms and he closed them around her, lifted her off her feet and held her tight. And as he held her there she felt enfolded in his love and suddenly all her cares and fears evaporated. The café and the customers and the hubbub of the concourse outside faded into the background. Then there was just the two of them, clinging to each other, and as she looked up into his eyes, happiness flooded through her and she wanted to hold onto that moment forever.

THANK you for reading *The Lake Pagoda*. I hope you've enjoyed reading it as much as I enjoyed writing it!

I'd love to hear your feedback either through my Facebook Page or my website (www.annbennettauthor.com) where you can sign up for news and updates about my books.

If you've enjoyed this book, you might also like to read *The Lake Palace* (an enchanting story of love and loss set in British India during the Burma Campaign in the Second World War). This book is a follow-up to *The Lake Pavilion*, but can also be read as a standalone story. Please turn over to read an extract.

EXTRACT FROM THE LAKE PALACE

CHAPTER 1

Uttar Pradesh, India, 1985

As the train swayed and bumped through the night across the great plain towards Ranipur, Iris leaned out of her bunk, lifted the frayed curtain and peered through the open window. It seemed as though the whole country was blanketed in darkness and it was difficult to see anything, other than twinkling pinpricks of light marking distant villages.

Occasionally, with much clattering and clanging of bells, the train rumbled over a level crossing. Iris would catch a glimpse of a dimly lit village street, lorries and motor-rickshaws lined up waiting for the train to pass, pedestrians waiting by the gate, their patient faces lit up by lamplight.

Iris returned to lying on her back, staring at the light flickering on the ceiling, unable to sleep, despite the soporific swaying of the train; there was far too much to think about.

It was magical to be back in India after almost forty years. Just lying there, imagining the vast plain they were travelling across, smelling the woodsmoke from village fires on the warm night air, brought the memories flooding back. She felt so at home here, how could she have been away for so long? And now she *was* back, it was almost as if she'd never left. She sighed. It was difficult to enthuse about India too much with Elspeth as her travelling companion. Iris hated to admit it to herself, but she knew now that it would have been far easier and far more congenial if she'd had the courage to make the journey alone. Even now, above the rattle of the wheels on the track, the sound of loud, persistent snoring floated up from the lower bunk, a constant reminder of her companion. Iris smiled to herself. Elspeth was so proper, so convinced of her own superiority, Iris hadn't dared mention the snoring, but it secretly amused her nonetheless.

Iris shuddered, as the numerous embarrassments Elspeth had caused on their trip came back to her. There had been several toe-curling moments already, even though they'd only been in India ten days or so. Iris realised that she should have known how Elspeth would react to her surroundings; after all, why would she have changed dramatically from how she'd been as a young woman? But the truth was, the passage of time had softened Iris' memories and removed some of the rough edges and troublesome traits from people she'd known back then.

It was clear from the moment they stepped off the plane at Indira Gandhi Airport in Delhi that Elspeth wasn't going to find India to her liking. Firstly, there was the waiter at the hotel, whom Elspeth had chided for not addressing her as madam.

'Let me tell you, young man,' she'd said, peering at him over her pince-nez as he poured her breakfast tea, 'In my father's day, you would have known to mind your Ps and Qs.

My father would not tolerate rudeness or insubordination. Not from anyone.'

'Elspeth, really!' Iris had hissed, her eyes fixed on the table, shrivelling inside with humiliation. Elspeth ignored her protests, but as Iris looked up she caught the waiter's eye. He smiled conspiratorially at her and raised an eyebrow. She'd looked away quickly, hoping that Elspeth hadn't noticed the exchange.

'This generation. Honestly!' Elspeth had muttered as the waiter walked away.

'I don't think it's a good idea to mention British rule, Elspeth,' Iris had whispered, leaning forward. 'They have left it behind and they don't want to be reminded. Especially the young people.'

Elspeth had fixed her with a cold, hard stare. 'Things were much better in this country back then. Surely even you can see that, Iris? Standards have slipped dreadfully.'

But Iris didn't agree. She'd been more than happy with her simple room in the hotel off Connaught Place in Delhi, and had not found anything to complain about. She'd been delighted with the feel of the cool marble tiles under her bare feet, the crisp linen sheets on the bed, lying awake watching the spindly ceiling fan whirring on its axis, listening to the horns of the motor rickshaws. In contrast, Elspeth had complained about everything; her toilet didn't flush properly, there was a lizard on the bathroom wall, there was no air-conditioning and the room was noisy.

Anyone would think she'd never been to India before, Iris had thought to herself as she stood twisting her hands helplessly while Elspeth berated the bemused man on the reception desk about the shortcomings of the hotel. *She grew up here. Surely, she can remember that lizards on the bathroom wall are a fact of life?*

'And I'll need a room on the ground floor,' Elspeth finished her diatribe. 'I can't possibly be expected to get up and down that awkward staircase with my poorly leg.' She waved her walking stick at the man, who bowed his head.

'I'm very sorry, madam,' he said. 'Not to worry. We will provide you with ground floor room without delay.'

Iris secretly wondered what was actually wrong with Elspeth's leg. She'd never dared ask. She and Elspeth were both in their early sixties, but where Iris was lithe and active, only a few grey hairs and lines on her face belying her years, Elspeth had already embraced old age with gusto. She was running to fat and the years showed in her face and in the way she moved. She leaned heavily on her stick when she walked. Her stick and her bad leg were two immutable facts and something told Iris it would have been unthinkable to enquire about them.

Then there had been the old rickshaw-wallah in Agra, who had generously offered Elspeth a blanket to keep her warm in the chilly morning air as he'd pedalled them through the wakening streets to watch the sun rise over the Taj Mahal. Elspeth had flinched and pushed the blanket away, shaking her head vehemently. 'No, thank you. I don't want to start itching,' she'd said, frowning.

'Oh, Elspeth,' Iris had said, seeing the man's crestfallen expression. Elspeth had harumphed noisily in the seat next to her. Iris had hoped desperately that the man hadn't understood.

Everywhere they went, Elspeth seemed to relish the fuss and attention that her leg and her stick afforded her. Bearers hovered round her in hotels, anxious to take her bags, to find her somewhere to sit; rickshaw wallahs would climb down from their cycles and help her up into the seat; the best tables were offered at restaurants, guards on trains helped her into carriages. But still she wasn't happy. Mopping her brow constantly, batting away insects and holding a handkerchief over her nose against the street smells, it seemed to Iris that Elspeth must have completely forgotten about India during her years in England.

'Dear Lord, the noise, Iris. However can you stand it?' Elspeth had shouted when they were halfway down Chandni Chowk in the Old Town in Delhi. Iris had managed to persuade her to visit the street market one evening and was revelling in the sights and sounds, the vibrant colours and the clamour of the street vendors, the smell of cooking spices on the evening air. At that point she was bargaining with a tenacious salesman over a length of aquamarine silk. She had no particular use for it, but she loved the colour so much she just had to have it. She turned to look at Elspeth, surprised at her words. Elspeth's grey curls were plastered to her forehead, her blouse was sticking to her skin and she held a handkerchief over her mouth. Iris had a vision then of how Elspeth had been in her youth in the 1940s, one of the club set, in a floral dress and bright red lipstick, sipping stengahs at the bar, laughing and joking with the other club bores. She realised then that the India Elspeth had inhabited as a young woman wasn't the one Iris herself had known. Elspeth had confined herself to the club, to her father's spacious bungalow with its large garden and deep veranda, to tea parties, and to watching polo matches on the maiden from the shade of a tent. Unlike Iris, she must never have explored the bazaars and markets of the old town, travelled into the countryside to seek out overgrown temples or deserted palaces. In that moment, Iris realised what a mistake it had been to decide to travel back here with Elspeth.

It had happened quite by chance. Doreen Mulligan, a mutual friend, who'd also lived in India in the forties, had brought them together. Iris had been sitting alone in her kitchen one gloomy afternoon, staring out at the frost-covered garden. She was grieving for her husband, Andrew, who'd died suddenly that January. Iris had found it difficult to accept. After thirty-five years of marriage, it was like losing part of herself and she felt at sea. Doreen had brought her flowers that day and had sat down at the table opposite her, peering at her with concern.

'You need something to cheer you up, Iris,' Doreen had pronounced. 'You're not yourself. A holiday, maybe?'

'Oh, I wouldn't know where to go. I've not been away by myself since I got married,' she'd murmured listlessly. It was true. There was nowhere that appealed to her.

'Why don't you go and stay with Caroline or Pete?'

Iris shook her head. Her son and daughter were both occupied with their own young families, with their busy careers. Although she loved them both dearly and they would have welcomed her, somehow it wouldn't have felt like a holiday.

'Well...is there anywhere you've dreamed about visiting? Always wanted to go but never got round to it?'

There was only one place she ever dreamed of and that was somewhere she would never, ever have suggested visiting to Andrew. It belonged to her alone, existed only in *her* memory, and over the years had taken on an almost mystical quality in her mind; the lake at Nagabhari and its palace built on an island, but seeming to float on the surface, with its domes and cupolas, shimmering white in the morning mist. The little town on the edge of the lake with its bustling market place and small British quarter where she'd lived in that tight-knit community with her parents. That's the place she'd dreamed about for forty years. She'd tried to put it all behind her; it held too many painful memories and associations, and until that moment she'd never contemplated actually returning.

'What about India?' Doreen had said suddenly.

Iris blinked. Could Doreen actually see it in her eyes? That sad, lonely longing of hers?

'What on earth made you think of India?' she asked.

'Well, I was going to mention this before. You remember Elspeth James? We exchange Christmas cards and vaguely keep in touch. Sadly, her husband also died last year and she happened to mention to me that she was thinking of taking a trip back there, only she didn't want to go alone. She asked me if I'd like to go.'

'And would you?'

Doreen shook her head. 'I'm far too busy, with my volunteering and the grandchildren. And besides, George would never go and he'd never want me to go away for long without him.'

Iris swallowed.

'Oh, I'm sorry, darling,' Doreen slid her hand over hers on the table. 'That was very tactless of me. But... well, why don't you give it some thought. I've got Elspeth's number. It might be good for both of you to catch up anyway.'

Iris tried to picture Elspeth and all she could conjure was the image of her in the club, the one that kept returning to her on the trip. They had never been close back in the forties, but perhaps they would have more in common now. Elspeth's father had been the commanding officer at Army HQ in Nagabhari, and Iris' own father was the British Resident of Ranipur, the British government's representative in the princely state. Their mothers were best friends though, Josie and Delphine, virtually inseparable. Always visiting each other in the afternoons for bridge or tiffin, sitting together on the club veranda with their cigarette holders and gin and tonics in the afternoon, their elegant heads bent together in endless gossip.

Iris had met Elspeth for an afternoon in London and despite some niggling misgivings, allowed herself to be persuaded into booking the trip. They would do the tourist sights of Delhi, Agra, Jaipur and Benares, before taking the sleeper train east to Ranipur, which lay on the border with Burma. Now, lying on the bunk, trying to sleep, Iris wondered what Elspeth's motivation for the trip was. It was clear that she wasn't enjoying the country and only occasionally, when they'd been exploring the Pink City of Jaipur, or wandering through the marbled halls of the Taj Mahal had she seen Elspeth relax enough to smile at the beauty of their surroundings. She concluded it must have been boredom and nostalgia for her youth and for the good old days of the Raj that had brought Elspeth back.

Perhaps it was a hankering for a time when she and her family had been in a position of wealth and power, but judging by what Elspeth had told Iris about her husband's wealth and success and her privileged life in England, there would seem to be no need for that. Elspeth clearly thought she was a cut above Iris – her husband had been the managing director of an engineering firm and she'd never worked in her life. She had made a couple of disparaging remarks about the fact that Iris had had her own career as a teacher when she'd returned to England after the war.

Iris wondered fleetingly whether Elspeth had a reason as compelling as her own to return to the place where they'd spent their early twenties. For many years, Iris had put those memories behind her. She'd settled down in England and lived happily with Andrew and their children. It was almost as if it was a different life and as if those momentous, magical but also painful events had never happened to her. She'd kept them shut away in a vault in the deepest recesses of her mind, but now the vault was open and those memories were flooding back, threatening to overwhelm her with their impact and their potency.

She sat up suddenly, switched on the reading light and reached for the knapsack she'd wedged at the bottom of the bunk. She'd been putting it off, but now the time was right. Rummaging amongst the detritus of travel; the pens and tissues, mosquito repellent and sunglasses, she pulled out the little hardback, mottled-blue exercise book that she'd written in religiously throughout that tumultuous time that had changed her life for ever. It had not been opened for forty years and the pages were stiff, some stuck together. She held it in her hands, staring at the cover, afraid to open up that Pandora's box of the past. And even as she did so, the lights in the carriage flickered and went out. She sighed and slipped the book back into her knapsack and snuggled down under the blanket. She could have found her torch, but perhaps the power failure was telling her something. Perhaps it would be better to wait until they reached Nagabhari after all. She closed her eyes and finally the gentle swaying of the train sent her off to sleep.

ACKNOWLEDGMENTS

Special thanks go to my friend and writing buddy Siobhan Daiko for her constant support and encouragement over the past ten years. To Rafa and Xavier at Cover Kitchen for their wonderful cover design; to Johnny Hudspith and Trenda Lundin for their inspirational editing, to my friend Mandy Lyon-Brown for her eagle-eyed proofreading, to my sisters, for reading and commenting on early drafts, and to everyone who's supported me down the years by reading my books.

ABOUT THE AUTHOR

Ann Bennett was born in Pury End, a small village in Northamptonshire and now lives in Surrey. *The Lake Pagoda* is her twelfth novel.

Her first book, *Bamboo Heart: A Daughter's Quest*, was inspired by researching her father's experience as a prisoner of war on the Thai-Burma Railway. *Bamboo Island: The Planter's Wife*, *A Daughter's Promise*, *Bamboo Road*: *The Home-coming*, *The Tea Planter's Club* and *The Amulet* are also about WWII in South East Asia. Together they form the Echoes of Empire collection.

She has also written *The Lake Pavilion,* set in British India in the 1930s, *The Lake Palace*, set in India during the Burma Campaign of WWII and *The Lake Villa*, set in Cambodia during WW2. Together with this book they make up the Oriental Lake Collection. Ann's other books, *The Runaway Sisters*, bestselling *The Orphan House*, *The Child Without a Home,* and *The Forgotten Children*, are published by Bookouture.

Ann is married with three grown up sons and a grand-daughter and works as a lawyer.

For more details please visit www.annbennettauthor.com

ALSO BY ANN BENNETT

Bamboo Heart: A Daughter's Quest

Bamboo Island: The Planter's Wife

Bamboo Road:The Homecoming

A Daughter's Promise

The Tea Planter's Club

The Amulet

The Lake Pavilion

The Lake Palace

The Lake Villa

The Orphan House

The Runaway Sisters

The Child Without a Home

The Forgotten Children

Printed in Great Britain
by Amazon

42169067R00182